A SAFFRON SUN

Cover Art by Ebook Launch

Printed in the United States of America

ISBN: 978-1-64456-582-7 [Hardback]
ISBN: 978-1-64456-583-4 [Paperback]
ISBN: 978-1-64456-584-1 [Mobi]
ISBN: 978-1-64456-585-8 [ePub]
ISBN: 978-1-64456-586-5 [AudioBook]

Library of Congress Control Number: 2023931206

INDIES UNITED PUBLISHING HOUSE, LLC
P.O. BOX 3071
QUINCY, IL 62305-3071
INDIESUNITED.NET

"In three words I can sum up everything I've learned about life: it goes on."
—**Robert Frost**

A SAFFRON SUN

The Darlings
Book Two

VERA JANE COOK

INDIES UNITED PUBLISHING HOUSE, LLC

Chapter One

1993

Like hot ash, the foreboding blood moon smoldered in the sky, making the night surreal, threatening. Dickie had the urge to stop and get out of his car, walk right up, and touch the moon, feel the fire, welcome the burn as he tried to embrace it, tried to understand it. There was a curse beneath its smile and whispers he couldn't hear, a witch's prophecy perhaps, an ambivalently beguiling spell put upon him that would blaze and fester in his memory like a wound.

His hand shaking on the wheel, he clenched it hard, held it steady. What had his mother said to him? That Lottie was dead? That she'd died in the fire that his wife had set? No, couldn't be so. It was preposterous, ridiculous, absurd. He wiped the tears from his eyes, eyes so sodden he could barely see two

1

feet ahead of him. Mostly he saw the glare, just the white miasmic glare of his headlights. He drove through quickly. He listened to his tires glide over the stones. The crunching sound was a welcome deterrent to the stillness of the blood moon night.

He finally saw his mother's driveway, appearing out of the macabre darkness, leaving the moon behind him, the bleeding moon, evincing the surreal, unnatural, and untimely death of the woman he loved.

His eyes still filled with tears, he made his way to his mother's door, praying she'd been fooling with him, praying this was all some cruel joke to get him to do what he didn't want to do. His mother's most contemptible desire was to break them up, he and Lottie. She thought a divorce would ruin him, the scandal of it. One can't be the brunt of scandal in a small town. Of course, what luck. The perfect solution appeared out of nowhere — death. Fate had intervened with glorious and deadly consequences. Fate would keep him in his loveless marriage. Why the hell would it matter to his mother, he wondered. Divorce was natural when the love was gone. Why the hell should she care if he took up with Lottie, his son Barnaby was a grown man, his daughter was practically out of the door, why the hell would she care?

"Hello, Mother," he said as he walked into the parlor where she stood in the center of the room, beside an old trunk. She gave every appearance of waiting for her ride to the train station, whereupon she would board the train and the trunk would accompany her, carried by a kindly old porter. For just a second, his fantasy soothed him.

"Son," she said and held out her arms. He went into them because he knew he had to. "Let's make this quick."

"Where is she?" he asked and followed her eyes to the trunk.

Dickie dropped to his knees. "No," he screamed. He put his hands to his head and cried deeply. "Please don't tell me she's in there, Mother. Please."

He looked up at her with beseeching eyes.

"I'm sorry, Dickie."

Dickie put his arms around the trunk and cried more bitterly. His mother's hand squeezed his shoulder. "But she was tall, this trunk couldn't hold her," he said.

"It held her," Lillian replied stoically.

"Can you open it?" he asked.

"It's best if we don't do that," she said.

"I want to see her one last time. Please."

"No! You don't want to see her, not like that, Dickie. You can't see her like that. Remember her the way she was. For God's sake, she was burned to death. It's not a pretty sight."

"Oh, God." Dickie wept some more before he was able to get to his feet. "Oh, God," he repeated.

"Go get your car and bring it round to the front door and open the back."

He looked up at her. "Maybe we should go to the police."

Lillian bent down and spoke in a whisper. "Only a matter of time before the whole town finds out about you and Lottie. Only a matter of time before they learn that Deborah finally discovered your indiscretion. Everyone knew they were the best of friends. Dickie, your wife had reason to want to kill Lottie."

"Whatever reason is there to kill someone?"

"Listen to me ... your wife's car was seen at Lottie's house, that makes her a suspect. Don't forget, she had motive. She'll be put away for Lottie's murder. It would be a slam dunk. She isn't innocent, Dickie. Lottie told me right before she died that Deborah set the fire."

Lillian choked up. She squeezed her son's hand. "Oh, it was awful. Poor woman." She got out a handkerchief and dabbed at her eyes. "We can't let anything happen to Deborah. We can't let her go to jail, for God's sake. We can't let a tragedy like that touch us and tear our family apart."

"We'll get her off." He looked at his mother, pleading with her even though he knew she was right. His family would be ruined by this.

"The mother of your children is a murderer? An arsonist? We can't have that, Dickie."

Dickie nodded his head and got to his feet. "Yes, you're right."

"We have to protect Deborah now. We must protect your wife, Dickie. It's not just about her either. Your children ... God, what will it do to them? They'll be ostracized just as you will be. Barnaby's legacy will be ruined. His clients will take their accounts away from him. Our family's fortune will dwindle. Everyone in this town loves and trusts you, don't destroy that."

Dickie got to his feet but not before kissing the trunk that held the body of his dead lover. He got his car and pulled it up to the front door as Lillian had asked. Then he heaved the trunk onto the dolly Lillian had provided. He hoisted the trunk into the back of his car and he and his mother drove off to the swamp where a multitude of sins could be hidden under the subfuscous twilight.

The blood moon followed them all the way out to Sutter's where the swamp waited, stinking and thick, a mud river. Dickie held his nose. He cried again and slammed his fist against the dash. The sky darkened, almost night but not quite.

"Damnit, I don't want to leave her here. I want her to have a coffin, a decent burial."

"We can't give her that, Dickie. Maybe one day."

"What difference does it make … one day? She needs it now."

"I'm afraid she doesn't need anything now."

Dickie took in a large intake of breath, despite the smell. He drove as far into the swamp as his flashy Escalade would take him. His mother sat in the passenger seat while he dragged the trunk as deep into the swamplands as possible, the shovel tied to his belt loops making him trip. He wanted to hurl the shovel into the Escalade's windshield. He wanted to scream out, fall to his knees and weep. But he kept walking. He buried the trunk under remote and bald Cypress trees by the water's edge, draped in Spanish Moss. He knew he would never be able to find Lottie's grave if he wanted to; the swamp was profuse in bald Cypress trees. There'd be no way to kneel at Lottie's grave and talk to her, no way to know where he'd hidden her because he didn't know where he was. He had walked a straight line from the car, straight out as far as he could go before the river stopped him, but he'd never be able to remember where he parked the car, or under which tree in this copious swampland of trees he had parked the car.

Two hours later, covered in mud and sweat, he emerged, still crying. His mother took his hand and squeezed it.

"Best to stay off the subject with Deborah. Let her go on pretending that she's not responsible."

Dickie looked at her as if he'd never seen her before. "Of course," he said. "I don't ever want to discuss this again."

"It's for the best," she said. "Wash the car first thing," she added. "Now, I've got to get to Greenville," she said. "Let's make haste."

He should have asked her why she had to get to Greenville so late in the day, but too forlorn, distracted, to care.

Deborah, refreshed after a bath, looked silky and sweet and smelled of rose oil. Filthy, Dickie stood in the front room with mud all over him. He took his shoes off at the door to avoid his wife's reprimands. Though she didn't seem to notice him as he walked in, dragged himself to the leather chair by the window and sat. But then she started making small talk, as if she'd sensed his presence. After their small talk, she babbled on about their son's wedding, discussing the guest list.

My God, he thought, she's just killed someone, and here she is going on and on as if she hasn't torn out my heart. Dickie responded in brief retorts though he couldn't bear to look at her. Perhaps he should confront her, maybe even put his hands around her throat and squeeze until her breathing ended. He went to the bar and grabbed himself a scotch. Behind him, he heard her, still going on and on about food, asking what he thought of serving fine little tidbits of filet mignon.

"For the wedding party?" he asked, knowing his voice sounded odd, woeful even.

"Of course, what have I been talking about for the last twenty minutes?"

"Steak is perfect," Dickie said. "But let's have fish as well, a lobster bake, perhaps." Resigned, his voice sounded so tired.

My God, he'd just buried his lover in swampland and here he is pretending his days and nights were still normal and included lobster bakes and tidbits of filet mignon, included the joy of his son's wedding, a joy he strove to find. He had turned to Deborah when he'd suggested a lobster bake and he had smiled, pretending that the love of his life wasn't lying in the muddy earth under a blood-red moon, emblazoning the night sky with its subtle mystery, a dead weight in his memory, threatening to crush him. Had he really done that, smiled at his wife? "I thought you didn't approve of this wedding," Dickie said. "You don't want our son to marry a Negro." Dickie stared at her with disdain; she disgusted him. "Isn't that right, Deborah?"

"Let's not dredge up the past. Could we persuade him not to go through with it?" She avoided his eyes and stared out the window. "Of course, I don't like it but he's not going to listen to me. I'd prefer a wedding over a surprise elopement."

"Your son is part Black, Deborah. You can't change that."

She ignored him. "My God, Dickie, go take a shower, you're filthy and you stink to high heaven. Where on earth have you been?"

He finished the scotch in his glass and climbed the stairs. He turned just once and caught the look on her face: it was unattractively vituperative, as if he were an incorrigible child and the dirt on his clothes was as commonplace as the sunrise. Disgusted, she stood shaking her head from left to right. He almost heard her saying, My God, Dickie, is that mud you're covered with? What on earth have you been doing?

I've been cleaning up your mess, he wanted to say.

Chapter Two

Lottie sat in the middle of the train she had boarded in Greenville, final destination Columbia, driven there by an indomitable Lillian, who kept telling her to enjoy her new life. Nearly midnight, she stared out of the window at a blood-red moon. She thought of Dickie and how much he would have loved the image of the moon. "It's stupendous," he'd say, "like an omen."

Yes, an omen of unforeseen events, shattering life as she knew it. She could kill Deborah with her bare hands, that murderous, crazy woman. Lottie was furious, but to be somewhat fair, she had been sleeping with Deborah's husband for thirty years, so did she have the right to blame Deborah? She understood her rage. But rage enough that she would burn down her closest friend's house, hoping she was in it? Can rage become so powerful that blindness ensues, and a person acts without reason? She'd never taken Deborah for a psychopath, but clearly, she was. Of course, she would have gone to the police if Lillian hadn't shown up and persuaded her to do otherwise. She would have seen Deborah carted off to prison. And then what? She and Dickie forever, the way it should have been?

She had been upstairs when Dickie arrived at his mother's house, hiding in a bedroom on Lillian's orders. She knew what Lillian intended to do, the vicious scenario she would enact. But did she really need to let Dickie think that he was about to bury his lover in a swamp, that her dead body had been stuffed inside a trunk, that his wife had started the fire that killed her? Lillian was so macabre, so overdramatic, but Lottie could not take the chance of denying Lillian the drama she'd created, wicked storyteller that she was, a modern-day Lady McBeth.

Well, so be it. Part of that scenario was true. She'd seen Deborah start the fire. She'd looked out from her bedroom window and wondered what the hell Deborah was doing in her backyard; about to call down to her, she'd smelled smoke and watched Deborah run off as if being chased by a Komodo dragon. Lottie had climbed out of the bedroom window once the fire went wild below her. She could smell it, she could even see it, certainly she could feel the heat. She couldn't go down; she could only go *out*. So, she'd jumped from the window and landed with barely a scratch in her backyard. Dickie would have been so relieved to know the truth. She had barely been hurt. She was about to call the fire department when Lillian showed up and told her that her circumstances were dire, she was near death and the fire department had already been called. She didn't feel near death, but she let Lillian carry her off, shove her into the backseat of her car, and made her promise to lie low. She'd followed Lillian's orders as if facing a high commander.

Lottie sighed, put her head back and closed her eyes; She must have been so confused.

Yesterday she was just a wanton woman who had been screwing the same married man for thirty years. So happens he was married to her best friend of even more than thirty years. She had been a part of their family, the spinster aunt their children loved. She was in essence, a bitch of a friend. Deborah finally discovered the truth, the horrible indiscretion and threatened divorce, a divorce Dickie would have welcomed because he fancied himself in love with Lottie. They'd be free to marry. But then, in storms Lillian, who refuses to let that happen. Ah, no, appearances are everything.

Lottie was well aware Lillian was protecting her son's reputation, but she didn't really care about Deborah's reputation. Oh, except where it concerned her son. She cared about his business going up in smoke, family money and all that; she feared people would pull their accounts from Dickie's company before he knew what hit him. No, Lillian did not want to be the brunt of gossip. Always be a mystery, she used to tell Deborah. And now Deborah would walk around with her dirty little secret. The mystery lady. Lillian should be pleased.

Straight out of one of Dickie's paperback crime novels that he loved. If only he knew the underhanded lengths his mother would go to get rid of his lover, that brazen, unscrupulous hussy who knew all his secrets and had stood by him for more than thirty years. In many ways, Lottie was more of a wife to Dickie than Deborah ever was. It takes two to tango, Lottie wanted to say when Lillian accused her of being a wicked adulteress. But one doesn't argue with Lillian Darling. One listens and obeys the queen's command. Why else would Lottie have agreed to just pick up and move to Richmond if Lillian hadn't pressured her into it? Lillian had blackmailed her into turning her life upside down, even going so far as to call it a new adventure, as if she were a twenty-year-old looking for thrills.

Richmond, Virginia, would have been a flight away but still doable. The distance would not have ended her affair with Dickie, but it certainly would have made it difficult. Perhaps that's all that Lillian had wanted, to make Lottie inconvenient. Then it became more macabre, more sinister. A dead Lottie is so much better than a faraway Lottie. How appropriate for Lillian that her daughter-in-law had provided the opportunity to kill off her rival.

A move to Richmond would have been a hardship for Lottie, she'd lived in Pickens all her life. Such a stupid move and everyone in Pickens would think that, but who would question it? Midlife crisis, they'd assume, run out of town for her wanton ways. Still, it was most ridiculous if anyone bothered to give it any thought. She almost didn't agree to it, she kept changing her mind, but she couldn't let Lillian turn the whole town against her. She'd be ruined if her affair with Dickie got out any more than it already had. She assumed it would get out real quick and spread faster than a plague of locusts if she'd stood up to Lillian and refused to relocate to Richmond. There'd be wagging tongues and sly looks instigated by Lillian after that, smoldering and festering like the fire Deborah had set. Lottie would be the brunt of every dirty joke.

"Deborah will gain sympathy and you will gain disgust," Lillian had said. Lottie had no choice but to let Lillian manipulate her and blackmail her into disappearing. "You'll be shunned," Lillian whispered stridulously. "The town whore, you'll be called. You will never be able to hold your head up again if you don't do as I ask."

Well, everybody has secrets. Deborah had an affair in her youth with Jeremiah Lennox, a Black man who could have stopped any woman's heart he was so handsome, so ambiguous in appearance. Hard to tell if he was Black, White or some dashing Mulatto who had suddenly materialized to undermine feminine virtue, or in Deborah's case, her marriage vows. Jeremiah impregnated Deborah, left her with a son, a son with an ambiguous comeliness like his father. Dickie had secrets for sure, being a cross-dresser. There, how's that for secrets? Well, for Lottie, none of it was a big deal. Being a cross-dresser just made Dickie tender and unusual. She loved that about him. But mostly, she loved the mystery that surrounded Dickie like the sweet scent of aftershave. Being a cross-dresser was an idiosyncrasy that would have caused Deborah a lifetime of therapy. But Lottie enjoyed the game, the covertness. The odd proclivity of Deborah's husband worked like an aphrodisiac on her but would have thrown Deborah into a whirlwind of despair she might never have escaped. Dickie's strangeness would have become her illness and, of course, her fault, her lack of something or other.

So, after thirty years of getting away with their affair, Deborah found out, finally found out, or perhaps she knew the truth all those years but refused to acknowledge it. No, Lottie didn't think she knew anything. Deborah thought Lottie was sexless, even assumed she was a lesbian. God, Deborah lived in her own reality, certainly not anyone else's.

Well, once the cat was out of the bag, Lillian had an excuse to drive Lottie so far out of Pickens, she wouldn't exist anymore. She'd remove the scent attracting the dog altogether. She'd put a real kibosh to Lottie's affair with Dickie. Before Deborah knew anything about it, it had never bothered Lillian that her son was screwing another woman. But once the ugly little truth surfaced, suddenly, Lottie was a threat to her son's perfect union. Lillian feared what his infidelity would have done to Dickie's reputation. So even though Lillian couldn't stand Deborah, she liked the packaging of her son's perfect marriage far too much to watch it go up in smoke. "Go up in smoke," Lottie sniggered. "Literally, I presume."

Before the fire, Lillian had used her wealthy network and gotten Lottie a job in Richmond, quite a good position managing a neighborhood branch of a large bank. She made it seem like an unexpected lottery win. "What a lucky break fate is bringing you, Lottie," she'd said.

But after the fire, Lillian had the perfect opportunity to get rid of Lottie once and for all. If her son believed her to be dead, he couldn't very well continue to see her. Lillian put a good deal of money in a new bank account for her in Columbia and swore that Lottie's secret life of wanton sex would never pass her lips, but only if Lottie remained out of sight. Lillian threw her money around for the control it gave her. She owned everyone in Pickens, and no one would cross her. They all professed to love her but did they really? Or did they revere what she could do to anyone who stood in her way about anything? The truth was, she scared Lottie to death.

"If you don't disappear, Lottie, I'll see you never hold down a job in this county or any other county in the south. You won't have money when I get through with you. You won't have friends or family, just people who will hate you for wrecking the marriage of my son and his lovely wife." Lottie didn't have a choice. She wasn't about to live in a town of gossipy, vengeful fools. She imagined every house she lived in would be burned down. Surely bricks would have been thrown through her window, crosses burned on her lawn. She couldn't live like that. She would have reluctantly agreed to Richmond, but after the fire, Richmond was no longer an option.

Lottie would still have been accessible to Dickie. Lillian knew her son would be fool enough to follow Lottie anywhere in the world, fool enough to wreck his marriage, destroy his reputation and even live without wealth, the wealth he was accustomed to. Lord knows, in Richmond, Virginia, even middle class would be a sorry sight for Dickie. Well then, wonders of wonders, along comes the fire, to hell with Richmond. Now Lillian had the perfect excuse to lay the entire issue of Lottie to rest, let everyone think she died that day. Of course, there'd never be a body, but if Lillian spread the rumor that she was dead, then who cared if there was proof of it or not.

The fire was Lillian's opportunity to absolutely assure the end of her son's perfidiousness. Lillian insisted that Lottie disappear where no one would look for her. Columbia was not exactly on the other side of the world, but it was one of the larger cities in South Carolina, certainly large enough to get lost in. Dickie rarely went to Columbia, preferring Greenville, or Charleston, so Lillian was not concerned he'd venture to Columbia and spot her on the street.

So, the narrative was that Lottie had perished, with or without a body; she was nowhere to be found, ergo, she must be dead, mustn't she? She'd probably be declared dead in a few years, anyway. But there she'd be, in Columbia, South Carolina, living a solitary life. She'd be able to afford a nice house and live rather modestly, but she'd be living without Dickie. That was the tribulation. He would mourn her death and she'd be about three hours away, forlorn as an old woman glued to her rocking chair and her aging cat. Happiness would be a memory.

But the light at the end of the tunnel was that Lillian was old, might die anytime now and then who would care if Lottie just reappeared to reclaim her lost life? Cruel to Dickie, cruel to her as well, but the money offered to Lottie to play dead was a formidable amount. She could not ignore that; an abundance of money could turn anyone's head. She'd be sad, but she'd be rich.

Dickie's tears after he'd come in the door of his mother's house and seen the trunk made her want to run to him and face Lillian's threats, tell him the truth, that the trunk was stuffed with old books to give it weight. That his mother was a power-hungry, meddling old biddy forcing Lottie to leave town, because Lillian didn't want his happiness, only the appearance of his happiness. Lillian was so much like Deborah, it was pathetic. Both with their own version of reality, their thirst for control. Well, she supposed she had been guilt-tripped into agreeing to Lillian's plan. Protecting Dickie and his family and all that. Not to mention Lillian's blackmail, the farewell package she had slipped into Lottie's hand at the train station.

Lottie had no idea how Lillian was powerful enough to come up with a new social security card for her, as well as a driver's license and a new identity as Lottie Cottonwood. Lottie was sure Lillian had had those fake papers for weeks. She was surely as underhanded as a legitimate crook. But however she'd acquired those phony papers, she'd acquired them. If Lottie remained in Pickens, she'd be notorious in a small town, an adulteress, a dangerous name. In Columbia, she had no history, she could be widowed. She certainly wouldn't have a wanton past following her around. She was middle-aged, no one would care about her. Lillian had taken her chances and blamed Lottie for wrecking her son's marriage, and Lottie had been so stupefied, she didn't deny it. She should have, she was stupid. Lillian didn't have proof that she and Dickie were sleeping together; she'd listened to a bit of gossip, a good guess is all. Her good guess could force Lottie into betraying herself and Dickie, could force her into lying, into taking the money, and running.

If Dickie thought Lottie had gone to Richmond

and was still alive, he would have gone there at every chance. But upon his mother's orders, he would not have divorced Deborah. Lottie's affair with him probably would have continued as it had for so many years, when he could get away, which would not have been very often, but it would be something and she would not be "dead" at least. She would be alive, laughing with him, drinking with him, and loving him as she always had. The fire changed everything. The fire made it possible to make a corpse out of Lottie, a disappearance, a tragedy, a mystery no one could solve, not even Dickie.

Lottie turned back to stare out of the window. The sound of the train rattling on the tracks made her feel she was being chastised. That life was behind her and the only thing ahead of her was an endless unknown. The moon had gone, vanished into the sky with all its dark omens, like the shadows from a sheet of sand.

Chapter Three

Billowy clouds floated in the sky, dollops of them, feathery and lazy, in disimpassioned indifference. Perfect for a wedding in South Carolina, a friendly blanched blue day. Flowers pungently effervescent, the scent of their perfume laying softly on the wind. Happy birds chirped their songs. Indefectible, the very day a gift from nature.

Guests languorously walked under colorful parasols spread out for them on a lawn so green it was hard not to lie on it, the freshly mowed smell emanating and lingering, intoxicating enough to throw decorum to the wind and roll all over it.

Prissy had chosen white lace for her parasol, beautifully matching her white lace wedding gown that trailed along the grass in an embroidered train. She was like a song, Dickie thought, a beautiful melody floating in the warm wind, haunting and romantic. Her rich black hair, piled on top of her head, her features defiant and perfectly striking, compelling, like majestic mountains that commanded notice. She walked as if she were floating over a gentle ocean.

Dickie smiled to himself as he watched her. Beauty, and brains, he thought. He fondly remembered when she'd been a child in pigtails, following Barnaby as he ran around trees and up hillsides. She always kept up with him and he always let her catch him. His son had loved this little girl forever, despite the fact she was their cook's daughter. Barnaby had no pretensions whatsoever. Certainly doesn't take after Deborah.

"Isn't marrying Prissy kind of like marrying your sister?" Dickie had asked his son, and his son had smiled and replied, "Never quite thought of her that way, Pops."

Dickie had known for years that he wasn't Barnaby's biological father, but he loved Barnaby with his whole being. Deborah was always going to take what she wanted, especially when she was younger, and even now, he supposed. She was who she was and that would never change. He forgave her long ago for her affair with Jeremiah. Besides, he'd never felt guilty for loving Lottie because of it. Dickie smiled to himself … his Deborah was the prettiest flower in the garden and the first to wilt and stink.

Priss and Barnaby had decided on marrying before her first semester at Tulane. They could have stayed engaged until she graduated but neither saw the sense in waiting. Besides, Barnaby didn't want Prissy running around New Orleans without a wedding ring on her finger. Barnaby planned on traveling to New Orleans some weekends and she'd come home when her course load was light, and summers were theirs, of course. Theirs for lying low and planning their family. They had been living together at the guest house on the grounds of his childhood home, acting like they were married, anyway. Prissy had officially moved in right after they had announced their engagement, right after Deborah had her hissy fit and forced into acknowledging her son was at least half African American, so what the hell difference did his marriage to a Black girl matter.

Lillian gave them the big house as a wedding gift, and she moved into the guest cottage, nearly as magnificent as the main house. A lovely white Colonial, it had three bedrooms and its own garage. The main house had six bedrooms "For their growing family," Lillian had said with a broad smile and a playful wink, but clearly expressing that not having children was not an option. Fair enough, they were hoping for a daughter when the time was right. "We'll keep trying until we get one," Barnaby told his grandmother, who seemed appeased by that.

Priss and Barnaby had a small engagement party and two months later, here they were at their wedding. An expense, perhaps, but certainly not one they couldn't afford. Deborah had been so taken up with the planning, she didn't have time to think about Lottie, to mourn the loss of her. But Dickie had time, he thought about Lottie practically every moment, grieved her constantly and had no one to share his grief with except his friend, Malcolm, better known, especially to Dickie, as 'Ginger Tea'.

Dickie promised himself he wouldn't think about Lottie at his son's wedding, he didn't want to feel sad.

Barnaby looked so radiant, like a smitten priest who'd found God by the edge of a riverbank, and he didn't want to spoil his son's day. Dickie forced a smile, forced a skip in his step, and greeted the guests as though he hadn't a care in the world, but his heavy heart threatened to explode from grief.

Dickie really wanted to be happy — weddings should be joyous events — but despite his best efforts, all he could think about was his loss, and thinking about his loss made him incredibly forlorn, to the point of losing control and starting up a real crying jag. He didn't want any blubbering here at his son's wedding, but his sorrow was close to the surface and tears triggered at the mere mention of Lottie's name.

Aside from Dickie's personal loss, Lottie had been a part of his family, his wife's best friend since they were children. His children had called her Aunt Lottie. He knew Barnaby was thinking about his Aunt Lottie, feeling deprived of her presence on this special day. He'd mentioned it just that morning, "Wish Aunt Lottie could be here, Pops. Happiest day of my life. I miss having her here."

He wanted to tell his son that his fucking mother was the cause, had set fire to Lottie's house, but he just forced a smile. "Me too," was all he said.

He hadn't been able to go near his wife. Deborah was as toxic as cyanide, a substance he fantasized holding over her face with one of her pretty lace hankies. He was sure she knew he hated her but, of course, he tried not to show it. They avoided any mention of the fire. No one knew for sure if Lottie had died in that fire. There wasn't any trace of a body. The person who'd set it was still at large. Well, still at large to everyone but him and his mother. His daughter, Leighton, had told him the fire was intentional, but there was little to go on about who had set it. Tittle-tattle had it that Jeremiah had stolen Deborah's car and driven it over to Lottie's house that day, but Leighton said he had no reason to burn down Lottie's house, and besides, he'd had an alibi for the time of the fire. His fingerprints were in the car but not on the gasoline cans discovered in the backyard. Dickie wondered if his wife hadn't taken up with Jeremiah again. What the hell were his fingerprints doing in their car? He didn't believe that Jeremiah had stolen the Cadillac, but he very well could believe he'd been sitting his sorry ass in it, on invitation from dear ole Deborah.

Leighton had a theory that whoever had burned down the house might have murdered Lottie first and taken her body elsewhere to dispose of it. Leighton talked to him about her theories, and he'd listened without reacting, without throwing himself in her lap and confessing to disposing of Lottie's body. He'd keep his mother out of it, of course, but he'd be sure to tell Leighton that his wife had set the fire, let Deborah sit her lush little gracious ass in jail as well.

Well, of course he wasn't going to do that. He'd live with his sin. His daughter, Leighton, took after him, that's why she became a detective. Dickie had a weakness for crime novels, but he'd never imagined he would be a perpetrator in a tale of murder, right there in Pickens, right in his own backyard. If Leighton solved this crime, he just might sit in a jail cell for the rest of his life because of his daughter's ability to fit all the pieces of the puzzle together. He wondered if this sordid, ugly little "film noir" had a finale he could live with.

Deborah kept lying to herself and telling anyone who would listen that Lottie had escaped the fire and took off for a new beginning. The foul expression on Dickie's face must have been apparent when she looked at him in all innocence and spewed that nonsense.

"My God, Dickie, there's no body, so how can she be dead? She took off," and then she'd laugh.

And Dickie would have his cyanide fantasy. Naturally, he never continued the conversation; his mother had told him to avoid it. He didn't have any theories about what happened to Lottie; he just had the painful truth.

"Took off without telling us, Deborah? Why would she do that?"

Deborah would give him a vacant stare. Maybe she was erasing her dirty little deed from her mind, having herself a true psychotic experience.

"Oh, well, you know. She wanted a fresh start. She just wanted to sever all her ties and have a fresh start. People do that."

Dickie would have laughed if he didn't want to believe his wife's fantasies. He pretended Deborah's speculation might have some merit, so he nodded his head and said, "Maybe."

Chapter Four

After what was a beautiful wedding ceremony on the rear lawn, officiated by the very minister who had baptized Dickie's daughter, Robinette, the crowd dispersed, some commenced into the gracious house, and some remained on the lawn. Inside the house, hors d'oeuvres were served by several young men in tuxedos while glasses of champagne, frothy and sweet, were sipped in vintage etched champagne flutes. Eventually, most of the guests moved back out to the lawn, where several covered tents and tables of food had been set up.

Dickie walked through the crowd greeting everyone with a firm handshake, a hug, and a smile, his mother's eyes on him. She knew of his misery, of course. He had been avoiding her since that night at the swamp. He couldn't really avoid her at Barnaby and Priss's wedding, though, so he walked over to ask if she was enjoying the food. She was sitting at a large table set up for the family under several towering maple trees and looked positively radiant, even at seventy-seven. Her white hair piled on top of her head, her lips as always, a pale pink, and her mesmerizing blue eyes a striking intrusion, a piercing into one's most covert secrets. The bodice of her pale green and yellow evening dress flaunted her freckled bosom offset by a diamond necklace with more sparkle than starlight.

"Yes, I must compliment Deasia. The filet, I believe, was brined in salt water. Very tender. The lobster is divine."

"I'm glad you approve, Mother," Dickie said and tried to smile.

Deborah was next to Lillian at the long table, chatting on and on to the guests around them, holding court as she usually did, telling everyone listening about Barnaby's first crush on the town's notorious prostitute when he was only ten years old. Everyone laughed but Barnaby, who merely smiled and took his wife's hand in a gesture of protection from whatever foolishness had fallen from his mother's mouth. Wasn't a soul on earth that didn't need protection from Deborah, Dickie thought.

"Better a crush on the town prostitute than on Ginger Tea." Barnaby smiled and his mother raised her eyes.

Ginger Tea had made it to the guest list but was not in drag. Deborah would certainly not have allowed that. It would have pleased Dickie no end for Ginger to entertain the guests, and Barnaby was all for it, but Deborah got her way. There would be no drag queens at her son's wedding. So Ginger was dressed as himself, as Malcolm Kram, recently divorced accountant at one of the state's most prestigious accounting firms and one of Dickie's closest friends. With his pinstriped suit and thick, wavy hair, he could have turned the head of every woman in the room, but that attention would have certainly gone unnoticed. For if Malcolm wanted to turn anyone's head at all, it would more likely be some sexy biker with tattoos.

Dickie had gravitated toward Ginger after Lottie's disappearance. He preferred to call it that even though he knew better. The whole town preferred to call it that, "a disappearance", avoiding even the slightest possibility that eventually someone would come upon Lottie's dead body. Dickie had felt so alone after he lost Lottie, and Ginger kept reaching out, making him laugh and filling the emptiness with his love of drag. Dickie critiqued his routines, laughed at the appropriate moments, and even sang along.

Ginger said that Lottie would have wanted them to be friends. Dickie gave in to his loneliness and took to visiting Ginger in the mansion he lived in. The mansion had belonged to his ex-wife, Rhonda. She'd let him remain there after she moved to Charleston with her female lover. What a soap opera: Leah had made his heart leap for years. Just so happens she was the mother of his daughter, Leighton. A teenage thing it had been. Now Leah is living with her lesbian lover in Charleston and he's pining over his dead lover — buried deep in a swamp over at Sutter's. Definitely a soap opera.

He and Ginger had a lot of belly laughs and laughter was the best medicine for Dickie; it made him feel he lived in an insouciant world. With Ginger, he was unburdened, wasn't lost in his head, in his gruesome thoughts. He and Ginger dressed up together in the guest house behind Dickie's main house, but Dickie never went out in public dressed as a woman, even though Ginger said he made the most perfect female, a dead ringer for Meryl Streep. The one and only time he'd ever gone out in public, he'd had the shit kicked out of him, wasn't likely to do that again. He'd done it for Lottie, though, because she wanted to show him off, she'd said.

Dickie took a seat in the middle of the table. Deborah was on his right and Lilian on his left at the long table under the maple trees while waiters served the food. Lillian would not allow anyone else to cater the wedding but Deasia and Jeremiah, especially not now, not while she was a silent partner in their restaurant and had put up the money for it. Deasia was in her family now, no longer the cook in Deborah's house. Lillian couldn't have her granddaughter-in-law's mother working as a domestic: she'd elevated the woman.

Dickie had to admit that the food was great, but he was annoyed to see Jeremiah at the family table. He'd had no choice. He couldn't contest it because Barnaby wanted him there, and rightly so; Jeremiah was his biological father. The two looked so much alike, no one could miss their familial connection. But maybe only Dickie took notice of it. Jeremiah was so youthful looking with his tall, toned physique and his chiseled features. He was always around town with young, pretty women, White or Black, it made no difference to Jeremiah any more than it did to the women who thought he was Pickens' answer to Hollywood's Morris Chestnut. Dickie made it a point to be civil to him, but he noticed Deborah didn't speak to Jeremiah at all, barely even looked at him, not even when he was the one doing the talking. Deborah aways looked away when Jeremiah was talking.

They'd both made mistakes in their marriage. But Dickie had to admit that his mistake was far more devasting than Deborah's. Deborah had been so young, and it had been so long ago, and it had been a short affair. Dickie assumed it had been a purely physical attraction, unlike his feeling for Lottie, which had been as deep and mysterious as the Edisto River.

Dickie didn't really know how Deborah felt about his affair with Lottie; she'd never really confronted him. She'd been furious at first and wanted to divorce, but miraculously, after she set fire to Lottie's house, she became the perfect little wife with enough small talk to keep his eyes open, to distract him at every turn. On some level, she must know that Lottie was dead and that she had been the cause of that. She was so good at removing herself from reality that she could have won an Academy Award.

He wasn't sure if Deborah knew how long his affair had gone on. Maybe now she felt she had nothing to worry about: Lottie was gone, so why ask for the divorce she didn't really want. She still insisted on sleeping with him, but he wasn't pursuing that. He really couldn't bear to touch her. It amazed him really, that he couldn't bear to touch the woman he had found so tantalizing in his youth.

He watched as his son rose to his feet and tapped his fork against his glass for silence, ready to make a speech. Dickie smiled. He glanced at Deborah, who was busy staring at her daughter, Robinette, furious that she'd worn a tuxedo and come to the party with Mindy Peach. "They look perverted," she had whispered to Dickie. He was sure his wife was plotting all sorts of ways to break them up. Maybe she'd run over poor Mindy and get away with that murder, too, just like she'd gotten away with Lottie's murder. Dickie downed what was left of his wine and reached for the bottle. "I am the luckiest man in the world because the most wonderful woman in the world agreed to marry me. My beautiful Pricilla Darling. As of today," he added. "She's a Darling."

Barnaby lifted his glass to Prissy and she smiled wide, her eyes sparkling. She reached out for her mother's hand and gave it a squeeze. Deasia had tears running down her face and had to blow her nose after Barnaby made a toast to her and Jackson, parents of the bride.

"'Whatever our souls are made of, yours and mine are the same.'" He bent down and kissed his bride. "Emily Bronte," he said. "Not my words but they are my feelings."

Barnaby then toasted Dickie, called him the best father in the world. Then he briefly acknowledged his mother and made a special toast to his grandmother. Lillian bowed her head regally. She looked like a brilliant peacock in her dazzling greens and yellows, Dickie thought. He observed his mother closely, her gracious smile. She was a warrior underneath her quiet Southern beauty, her soft-spoken lilt. Dickie almost giggled, wondering how people would react to her if they knew of her many talents, capable of

30

stuffing a trunk with a dead body, capable of sneaking off to the swamp and sitting there dry-eyed while her son dug a grave. Barnaby raised his glass high to his sister and grinned. Dickie enjoyed Deborah cringing because her son was highlighting how his sister was dressed, so mannish, and who she was with, not a young man but a young woman. How totally weird. Dickie clapped loudly. He wanted everyone to know he supported his daughter just in case anyone picked up on Deborah's disdain or shared her stupid opinions. And then Barnaby put his hand to his heart. "I want to make a special toast to my Aunt Lottie, who I wish like holy hell was here tonight, on the happiest day of my life. She always supported me, and I loved her as much as I love my pops and my mom. Thinking of you, Aunt Lottie. I pray I'll see you again." He lifted his glass high, and everyone did the same.

Dickie's mother squeezed his hand. Control of his emotions dwindled and heaving sobs came out of him. He put his head down and cried like a baby. He was embarrassing his wife, but he didn't care. Lillian leaned over and whispered in his ear, "Pull yourself together, Dickie."

Chapter Five

Later that evening, Deborah walked up behind him. He smelled her perfume before her arms draped around his neck. She sure was one for show, Dickie thought. Theirs was an irreproachable union, a marriage made in heaven, right, Deborah? He sniggered.

"Dance with me darlin'," she said with a wink.

Dickie stood to his feet. The song by Etta James, "At Last", had played at their wedding thirty-two years ago and danced to in the same euphoric rhythm as Deborah expected now.

"This pinning over Lottie has got to stop," she whispered in his ear. "You made a complete fool of yourself, crying like that."

He remained silent and continued to dance with her. It was expected that he twirl his wife around in his arms. The perfect couple, Deborah and Dickie Darling, always the perfect couple. Deborah was so into appearances. She had already made him dance with her twice. He forced the smirk off his face.

"You are going to be a proper husband to me tonight, you hear?" She looked up at him with her dazzling green eyes and winked.

"I don't know if I can do that, Deborah," he said.

"I didn't kill her, you hear me, Dickie?" she whispered. "I did not kill her. You've no cause to be angry with me."

He gave her a sneering smile.

"There's no body, Dickie. If I killed her, where's the body?"

He remained silent while he felt her knee in his crotch, her breath on his neck. Her perfume still had the lure it always had. Chanel, of course.

"Perhaps you think I've no cause to be angry at you. It doesn't matter. You no longer attract me, Deborah."

She laughed, which infuriated him. "Are you saying our marriage is over? Because I am saying it isn't. I know your feelings for me. Seems you can't hide your erection, Dickie."

"You are hallucinating, Deborah," he said and looked off over her shoulder.

Barnaby suddenly cut in and danced his mother off into the crowd. Prissy took Deborah's place in Dickie's arms. Dickie heaved a sigh of relief.

"You are my daughter now, Priss," he said and kissed her cheek, relieved to see Deborah twirling off with his son. "What a lucky man Barney is. You are by far the loveliest woman I've ever seen."

Prissy laughed. "You are as charming as your son," she said.

"I'm a man of truth. We both are."

Suddenly the music changed to a faster rock-and-roll classic, "Shimmy Like My Sister Kate" blasted out from the speakers. Prissy tried to follow her new father-in-law in a Lindy. Dickie was quite a good dancer and managed to get Prissy to imitate his fancy footwork, his spins. They laughed energetically as he dipped her.

"Hey, do you know that woman over there?" Priss asked suddenly as Dickie pulled her to her feet. She looked to her left.

Dickie strained his neck to see who she was referring to. "The tall, pretty blonde?"

"Yeah, that's the one. She keeps looking at you."

Dickie thought for a moment. "I think Barnaby used to know her from some summer camp he went to. I think he was her counselor." He closed his eyes for a moment. "Pamela Tilly, her name is. They became friends because she drives a motorcycle, or something like that. She used to be Robbie's friend, too. Everyone calls her Pam. She's a spitfire." He frowned.

"She's really staring at you, like she's trying to figure out who you are or something."

"Oh, she knows who I am, believe me."

Chapter Six

Leighton looked across the table at Sean, an escort Dickie had arranged so she wouldn't have to come alone to the wedding. "I can come with Mart," she'd told him, but as fate would have it, Mart was on vacation the week of Barnaby's wedding, catching what she hoped would be the perfect redfish, tarpon, and trout. She assumed he'd return to tell her all about it, lots of stories about the boat, "A real fishing vessel," he'd say, "and the river looked like a sheet of glass," and of course, he'd tell her all about the fish that took to his line like a beggar grabbing gold.

Leighton didn't like blind dates and had tried to meet up with Sean before the wedding so they wouldn't sit looking awkward, with nothing to say to each other. Unfortunately, her schedule had been filled to the brim. She was all caught up with two cold case murders, a suspicious fire, and the disappearance of Lottie Lacock. Sean was looking around the room and not at her, which she assumed was not a good sign but maybe it was just nervousness. When he did turn to her and smile, she found herself liking the attention, even though she was making a lot of assumptions about him. Such as, he would never find a female detective attractive, too aggressive a job for a lady who was better off being a librarian or the owner of a pet store. Sean looked as if he preferred completely androcentric women, whose world revolved around male opinions, male sports, and male sex as in *wham bam,* thank you, ma'am.

It's not that he looked as if he lacked imagination but more because he was so male looking, so rugged, not to mention abstruse. He had something of a pejorative smile, one that hid secrets. She thought he appeared a tad self-centered, probably because he was so attractive, the way he kept running his right hand through his hair. Well, she had to admit he had gorgeous thick brown hair. And why was he single at his age, she wondered, he must be way over forty. Dickie had said he was single, hadn't he?

Dickie had insisted she come to Barnaby's wedding even though she and Barnaby had barely uttered three sentences to each other since they found out they were related. They were speaking now at the wedding more than they ever had and she'd discovered he was immensely likable. Dickie insisted she sit at the family table, and she agreed, even though she knew Deborah was furious. Here she was, the secret daughter of Dickie Darling and his teenage crush, Leah Walker, better known as Leighton's mother.

Well, the secret had been out for a few months

now and much of the town knew her mother had gotten impregnated by Dickie Darling when she was a mere seventeen. Dickie had welcomed her into his family with open arms while Deborah smiled that rapacious smile, as if she were prey.

Barnaby and his bride were genuinely charming to her, and Barnaby asked her all kinds of questions to see how much they had in common. "Robinette and I are complete pushovers for science fiction, do you like science fiction?" She did like science fiction and told him so, and then the conversation slid into every subject under the sun to which they might have an affinity, arriving, finally, at the consensus that they indeed had a lot in common.

She noticed that Sean's habit of running his hand through his hair, brushing it nonchalantly off his forehead, revealing his eyebrows and most impressive, his blue eyes, dazzling like a garden full of periwinkle and morning glory, provided the color blue with even more reason to impress. "So, what's kept you so busy these last few weeks?" he asked, showing his perfect teeth, a treasure behind his lips, nearly hidden under his bearded face but certainly visible enough to appear quite kissable, the kind of lips you want a man to have if you have any intention of kissing him at all. She brushed the thought aside.

"I'm sure it's nothing you want to hear about, police stuff and all that."

He smiled again. "Quite the contrary. I think I'd find it remarkably interesting. I never miss a *Dateline* on television. I love a good murder mystery."

Now it was her turn to smile. "Quite the homebody then, aren't you? Television is such a sedentary pastime. Well, you're either a homebody or a serial killer."

Sean laughed loudly. "No end to the fascination of a Dahmer, Bundy or Green River Killer."

"Gruesome." She shuddered.

"You could say I'm a homebody, though." He let his eyes linger on hers for a moment and then he turned to survey the room again, leaving her nearly devastated to lose the heart flutters his gaze had caused, at least for the moment.

Leighton let her eyes drift away as well. She was sure she would never see him again after that evening. They would be cordial to each other, of course, but eventually their conversations would be limited to hello and how are you, brief encounters at the town supermarket.

"Well?" he said.

She turned to find his mesmeric eyes. "Yes?"

"You were going to tell me what has kept you so busy. What kind of policework? Are you working on a case? I hope that's not an inappropriate question."

She sat back and smiled at him yet again. That must have been her thirtieth smile, the perfect facial gesture when one is at a loss for words. He appeared to be genuinely interested in what she finally had to say, though; murder is meaty, everyone likes a good crime story.

"Not inappropriate. I assume a social studies teacher would be interested in crime."

Sean laughed. "Trying to get teenagers to understand the Constitution is never tame, but murder? That's really exciting."

"Yes, I would suspect that murder is exciting." She

laughed. "In books and movies. Crime scenes are not so exciting."

"No, I would imagine not," he said.

A silence fell between them for a few moments but then, suddenly, he leaned over the table and stared at her. "If you don't mind my asking, are you investigating the disappearance of Lottie Lacock?"

"You're asking me like you've got some interest in it … did you know her?"

He nodded his head and poured some wine in her glass and then his own as if he were trying to ply her with booze so he could retrieve information, as if he were a reporter.

"You're not a reporter, are you?" She gave him a serious look as if she meant what she said, but was really trying to flirt, to keep her eyes large and intently focused on him. She was sure she had forgotten how to flirt, but whatever she was doing seemed to work.

He stared at her with a shit-eating grin on his face, as if they shared a secret. She stared back until it became uncomfortable.

"Yes, the woman whose house burned down, apparently without her in it, was my cousin."

Leighton was surprised. "Your cousin? Really?"

"Her car was still in the drive and none of her possessions were taken from the house." Sean looked intently at her. "Odd, isn't it?"

Leighton sat back. She pointed a finger at him. "You could be a detective."

"Did she burn up in that fire?"

Leighton shook her head. "Nope. We would have found something. Bones, a partial body, something. We found nothing but a broken window she could have escaped from."

"So she's not dead?"

"Didn't say that, but without a body she isn't dead yet."

"Do you think you'll find a body?"

"I think someone murdered her in the house, set the fire, and then took her body out of the back door to dispose of. Either that, or he threw the body out of the broken window."

"Could he have buried her in the rear lawn then?" He raised an eyebrow.

Leighton shook her head. "We've turned the backyard apart. She isn't there."

"I guess we could say that's a good thing."

"Were you close with your cousin?"

"Not terribly close, but I liked her. She's my great aunt's daughter. My great aunt was a lot like my mother and Lottie took after her. My great aunt died last year, my mother, the year before."

"I'm sorry," Leighton said softly.

"Lottie came up on my side once, stuck up for me when I really needed support. I never forgot that. She was good to people she liked."

"So, I guess you really want me to find out what happened to her."

"You could say that. It would mean a lot to me." He looked away from her and then turned to meet her eyes. "Weddings are too joyful for talk of such depressing things, like the disappearance of my cousin, Lottie. Dance with me. Let's do something pleasant, like dancing." He grinned. "You can hum in my ear. I'd like that."

Leighton was surprised. Dancing with him was

unexpected but she got to her feet and let him lead her onto the dance floor. She would not sleep with him, she told herself as she felt his arms around her. They had nothing in common, it would go nowhere. She trembled from the effect of his breath near her ear.

"You're a feather in my arms, Leighton," he whispered.

More like a weight in your life, she thought.

He stepped back and looked at her. "I'm glad Dickie introduced us."

She smiled. She wouldn't see him again, she was sure. "Me, too."

Chapter Seven

Robbie couldn't believe what she was seeing: at a table near the bar was Pamela Tilly. She knew Pam had been invited, but didn't think she'd come. Sure, she knew Barnaby, but not that well. Robbie had asked Barney why the hell he was inviting Pam Tilly to his wedding, and he'd told her something stupid like he wanted a ride on her Kawasaki Ninja. "She's a cool woman," he'd said. Robbie had raised her eyes and called him a jerk.

Pam was sitting with Boyd, her date for the wedding, no doubt. Robbie couldn't imagine why she was dating a boy who'd tried to rape her back in high school. At least that's what she'd said, but no one believed her. Boyd had been a straight-A basketball star, not the type to try to rape a girl, if there is a type for rape. As badly as Robbie wanted to approach Pam, she held herself back. No use making a fool of myself, she thought.

Robbie clinked her fork against her glass and put Pam as far out of her mind as she could push her. It was time to bring attention to herself, which is what her mother would accuse her of doing. She would truly embarrass her mother by giving a short speech about life with her brother, Barney, and while all eyes were on her, everyone could admire her tuxedo. Next to Barney, she supposed she loved Deasia and Prissy most. As might be expected, she wouldn't say that; her mother would be furious. Robbie was supposed to love her mother most, but she might mention that her father was the light in her life and her mother was what was left when you flicked off the light. She wouldn't say that, either. Far be it from her to embarrass her mother even though her mother thought nothing about embarrassing her.

Robbie rose to her feet. She thought she looked smashing in her black tuxedo and her cufflink white ruffled shirt. She wore a bowtie which she assumed her mother found most distasteful. "My God, you're not going to wear that," she'd said earlier. Robbie had replied, "And why shouldn't I wear this?" Her mother's reasoning had been that she looked like a boy.

That was ridiculous: no way did she look like a boy. She was wearing makeup, red lipstick, and thick mascara, even blusher. Her mother didn't get anything, didn't get that Robbie looked so cool, and that many women wore tuxedos. She'd just seen Diane Keaton in one on some award show and she had looked amazing. She had to admit, though, it was the juxtaposition of her tuxedo and Mindy's shorter-than-short dress that gave them away as a couple. If she were there alone, no one would have even speculated. Her mother was so bourgeois. There were millions of gay couples all over the place, not to mention perfectly straight women who wore tuxedos. Robbie surveyed the room, she knew everyone, and everyone knew her, so maybe not many tuxedo-wearing women in this place, this town. Maybe tuxedos on women were just a bit too progressive for Pickens. But she didn't really think anyone cared about her sexuality, except as gossip over a backyard fence. But as for really caring about it, why should they?

She glanced at her mother, who looked stoic. She managed to come up with something sweet to say and lifted her glass in her mother's direction. Deborah smiled and blew her daughter a kiss. Robbie wondered how difficult it was for her to do that.

She noticed Leighton, who seemed to think she was "interesting". Well, why wouldn't she think that Robbie was "interesting"? Leighton's mother was certainly "interesting"; she was gay and ran off to live in Charleston with her female lover. So many gay people in the world, Mother. Look at Leighton's mom. Robbie had wanted to do her final English exam on all the gay artists who had fled to the isle of Capri in the nineteenth century, but her English teacher had threatened to fail her if she did, "Why in God's name does that interest you, Robbie?" So, she wound up turning in a paper on George Sand, ignoring the fact that she might have been trans. She just completely ignored the obvious to spare her teacher a heart attack. Well, what did she expect? This was, after all, small town South Carolina. In only a few weeks, she'd be leaving for Europe and then on to New York. The start of her life would begin there, in New York, where wearing a tuxedo was no shocker, no less a shocker than prostitutes in Times Square.

Not unexpectedly, Mindy was having a hard time with it. She didn't want Robbie to go away; she didn't want Robbie more than a twenty-minute car ride from Pickens. They'd argued about it, but Mindy had to back down, either that, or be accused of trying to hold Robbie back from her dream of being an artist. Robbie had already told her she'd probably never move back to Pickens and Mindy would have to move to New York if they wanted to be together. "Oh, yeah, what am I going to do in New York, Robbie, pimp myself out on Eighth Avenue or hand out towels at the Plaza?" Mindy didn't think she had any talents that would help her survive anywhere, much less New York. Mindy just wanted to be a lucky girl and find herself taken care of. It made Robbie sad: she'd hardly be the person to take care of Mindy; she'd chosen to be an artist, whether she'd be successful or not remained to be seen. Besides, she'd be an art student at NYU for the next few years, not much money in that and certainly not much time for Mindy.

After Robbie's toast, Mindy excused herself to go to the lady's room and Robbie wanted a cigarette. She walked all the way down to her grandmother's guest cottage and took a seat on the porch rocker where she couldn't be seen from the rear lawn; the cottage was set back and hidden by a maze of trees. She felt private and alone. She'd never have a wedding; was that what her mother was thinking too?

After only a moment, Robbie heard something, perhaps the sound of breath, a dog maybe. In any case, someone was about to violate her privacy and hoped it wasn't her grandmother. She put her hand over her eyes to block the sun and peered out in front of her.

"Hello, Robbie."

Robbie looked up to find Pam's lips around a cigarette and her hands around a lighter. She flicked the lighter closed and took a deep drag.

"I followed you, kept hoping to get you alone."

"What on earth for?"

"Mind if I join you?" Pam took the other rocker without waiting for Robbie's reply. "It's good to see you. What's it been? Three years?"

Robbie remained silent. She didn't know what to say. She and Pam had parted under not-so-great circumstances.

"Saw your father inside dancing. He's still so cute."

Robbie turned to her. "I noticed you were here," Robbie said. Perhaps she shouldn't have said that. "I mean, you're wearing a satin jumpsuit, who could miss you?" She did not want Pam to think she'd been looking for her, but Pam was an eye-stopper, the kind of girl you had to look at, a beauty magnet. Her jumpsuit was quite becoming, low-cut and her pants flowed like a kite being held in a breeze.

"I'm back from college now, for the summer."

"And that's important because?"

Pam laughed. "Wow, still holding a grudge?"

Robbie wished she'd leave but not really. She wanted to wish it, but she was so happy to see Pam that it took all her strength not to show it.

"I hardly remember you," Robbie said. Pam stared at her.

"I never thought I'd get a moment alone with you. Your girlfriend is rather clingy, isn't she?"

"Mindy? Not so much."

"I've missed you. I know I couldn't reach out or anything, not without being shot." She giggled. "But anyhow, I wanted to. I knew how mad you were, and you had every right to be but for the record, I really loved you. You were just so young, Robbie. I'm almost three years older than you."

Robbie didn't want to go there, didn't want to rehash the pain of the past, the longing, the grieving. "Almost? Are you for real? You don't think I look older than I am?"

Pam laughed. "I heard young boys discover each other's sexuality at early ages so maybe you weren't so advanced."

"Won't Boyd wonder where you are?" Robbie asked sarcastically.

"I needed a date for the wedding."

"So, you asked a boy who attempted to rape you in high school?" Robbie's tone was incredulous. "I didn't think you were the type to be so hard up."

Pam laughed loudly. "Boyd isn't who you think he is."

"I'm sure not."

Pam looked off, took a deep drag off her cigarette and blew the smoke in Robbie's direction.

"I remember everything about our friendship." Pam looked at her and smiled.

"How's your mother?" Robbie asked quickly, blowing the smoke away. She needed to avoid any memories of having her body discovered by an "older girl."

"You were only fifteen, Robbie."

"I asked about your mother."

"Haven't you missed me just a little?"

Robbie got to her feet. Pamela Tilly had broken her heart, smashed the split pieces and spat on the remains.

"Not especially."

Pam looked off and continued to smoke in silence for a while as Robbie watched her. "My mother took off a few months ago. She went to Columbia," she finally said. "She's a real estate broker there, doing well, I hear. I haven't seen her since she left."

"Shame," Robbie said sarcastically.

"Look, I had to break off with you. My mother went ballistic when she found out about us. You were fifteen, Robbie. Didn't matter that you looked my age. It should have mattered that you weren't."

"And you were eighteen and looked my age." Robbie had said that loudly, she hadn't meant to.

"I was going to start college. Jesus, you weren't even a senior in high school." Pam threw her cigarette on the ground. Neither spoke for several minutes.

"Don't think I've forgotten about Boyd, Pam."

"Boyd? My God, Robbie, he's not important."

"You still went out with him then and he's your date today. You must have a thing for rapists."

"I went out with Boyd because your grandmother caught you and me making out in this very cottage and told my mother. I had no choice but to appease her, make her think I liked boys, which I don't."

"Bastard had an alibi for the night you said he raped you." Robbie looked at the ground.

"His father lied for him. Boyd knew he would."

"How many men in your life you going to accuse of attempted rape?"

Pam looked at her and shook her head. "Robbie, I've been sidestepping rape all my life, whether anyone wants to believe it or not. That stuff with Boyd wasn't real. Sean Dowd didn't succeed in getting into my pants, neither did some creepy boy I met in college who thought rape was what he owed to girls who wouldn't succumb to his charms of their own volition."

Robbie looked off. She couldn't begin to understand Pam's experiences, she'd never had to fend off boys. "Did your mother ever leave Sean?" Robbie asked, breaking the silence between them.

"Sean? Yeah, he went back to Greenville. Sean, the asshole. He never left me alone."

"He's here tonight. I guess my father invited him."

"Yeah, I saw him dancing with some pretty blonde."

"That pretty blonde is a cop and she's my half-sister."

Pam leaned back. "Wow. I don't know what's more shocking, that he's dancing with a cop or that the cop is your sister."

"Half-sister. Sean ever come on to you again?"

"Yeah, he did."

"Why didn't you tell your mother, for God's sake?"

"I did tell her."

"Yeah, finally."

"I didn't want to hurt her."

Robbie watched the night begin to fall. The sun was still there, fading in the darkening sky.

"I wish I could say it was good to see you."

Pam laughed. "I know you don't mean that."

"I didn't know you were invited to the wedding."

Of course she knew, and she was almost too excited to speak knowing it. She'd searched for Pam the moment the guests started arriving.

"I'm a friend of your brother's, Robbie."

"Oh, did he know about us?" Robbie turned to her.

"No." Pam stood up and moved close to Robbie, who was leaning against the porch rail. "Do you remember this cottage?" she asked.

Robbie looked up at the sky. The air had suddenly turned cooler. She didn't want to go there with Pam. Her grandmother had still lived in the big house then and the cottage was vacant. The cottage was where they'd meet up, where they both discovered they were gay. It's where they talked about loving each other, exploring each other's bodies, falling off a goddamn cliff and landing in a foreign country.

Suddenly Pam reached down for Robbie's chin. She leaned over and kissed her hard on the lips. "Well, I guess it means something that you didn't sock me for that kiss."

"Go away, Pam," Robbie said. "Please."

But Pam didn't go away. She reached out and pulled Robbie into her arms. "Whatever you feel, I'm feeling it, too. I thought about you a lot in college."

Robbie put her arms around Pam and pressed hard against her body. She found Pam's lips and pressed hard again, as if she could drink her under her skin.

Pam reached in her pocket and handed Robbie a sheet of paper. "I wrote this before I came out here. Just in case, you know, you were interested."

"What is it?"

"Just stick it in your pocket. Read it later."

"Don't think a kiss means anything. I've just had a lot to drink and so have you. I've never forgiven you, Pam."

"Just stick your tongue back in my mouth, Robbie, and stop talking."

Robbie went back to the table where they had all been sitting, shaking, the way she shook after she and Pam finally broke apart. The shaking hadn't stopped. Robbie sat quickly and reached for her wine. Mindy sat beside her.

"I went out to look for you. My God, where were you? You were gone at least forty-five minutes."

"Needed a smoke. I was just walking around."

"Oh," Mindy said.

Robbie felt someone take the seat beside her and she turned and found Leighton there smiling at her.

"Nice speech," Leighton said.

Robbie thanked her and grinned. "Why do I get the feeling you want to ask me some questions. You look so serious. You look too serious for my brother's wedding."

"Your brother's wedding is not really appropriate …"

"Ask away, Leighton, it will take my mind off my mother's insipid opinions … and other things. I know you've been wanting to speak to me."

"You were very fond of Lottie, weren't you?"

Robbie turned to her. "As opposed to how I feel about my mother?"

"Not necessarily."

"I loved Lottie, my Aunt Lottie. I don't know what happened to her. I truly don't, but I would give anything to know where she is."

"Where she is? Then you don't think she's dead?"

Robbie shook her head for several seconds. "No, not dead. I can't let myself go there. She disappeared and we don't know what happened to her."

"Was she unhappy?"

"Lottie was never unhappy."

Suddenly Sean appeared at their table grinning at Leighton. "Can't leave you alone for five minutes without you going back to work. I appreciate that you're trying to find my cousin, but this is a party, not an interrogation room." He pointed a finger at her.

"This is Sean Dowd," Leighton said to Robbie, "a friend of your father's."

Robbie ignored the hand he extended. "Yes, I remember you. Marlene Tilly's boyfriend."

Sean flinched. He nodded. "Well, not for a while," he said.

"Did Dickie put you up to this?" Leighton said it with a smile and stared at Sean. "He didn't mention that you were Lottie's cousin, you know. He could have told me that. And who's Marlene Tilly?"

"No, no, I swear. Dickie did not put me up to anything. I didn't want to tell you I was Lottie's cousin at first because I didn't want to ruin a perfectly wonderful social day. I didn't want to talk about a crime, but I am concerned about finding my cousin, so I was really looking forward to meeting you. I intended to put off telling you for another time, though. But my curiosity got the best of me. I had to talk to you about it. It just came out 'cause you're easy to talk to."

"I see," she said. "And Marlene Tilly is?"

He smiled. "We lived together, a while ago. We broke up. That's it."

"She isn't here, is she?" Leighton looked around.

"No, but her daughter is," Robbie said, staring intently at Sean.

Leighton could have sworn Robbie was boring her eyes into him but then dismissed it. But it sure doesn't feel as if she likes him, Leighton thought.

Chapter Eight

"Why didn't you tell me you were Lottie's cousin right away?" Leighton turned to look at him, to study his profile, which revealed a stalwart chin. They were sitting on the lawn watching the wedding guests dance, picking up the remnants of their chatter and their laughter. People were mingling, some were still eating. The music was low and slow and seemed far away.

Sean had his feet up on a chair and casually held a glass of scotch in his hand. He turned the glass around and she heard the ice cubes clink together.

"I did tell you, not at first maybe, but I did tell you."

"Were you close?"

"Going to interrogate me?"

"Of course not."

He reached out for her hand and held it. "I'd like to see you again," he said.

Leighton nodded. "Okay."

He smiled and told her he was free the following Saturday night. "You like seafood?" he asked.

She nodded. "I do."

"Going to take you to the best seafood restaurant in the south."

"We going to Atlanta?"

He laughed loudly. "We won't be traveling more than ten miles from where we're sitting."

They turned and their eyes locked: a romantic moment under the moon and the stars, as if they were destined lovers, finally meeting, finally giving way to the fate that was theirs, a fate to which they had finally succumbed. It must have been the magic of the moment, or the alcohol. The warm air between them brought the aphrodisiacal perfume of evening. She felt so sacchariferous, like cotton candy, as if her teeth would curdle if he kissed her.

Leighton quickly dismissed her thoughts; they were so inane. Too much sugar was not a good thing. Sean was just that, too much sugar. She wouldn't let herself go down that road. Beau had been too good a catch to appear in her life again. Besides, Sean Dowd was probably just looking for information.

Of course, Sean walked her to her door and kissed her goodnight and she didn't lose any teeth. It was one of those soulful kisses. Yes, she could call it that. His tongue was a tease, nothing he bombarded her with, just a gentle tease for a later time. But something about him was as ambiguous as words falling from one's mouth, words that could or could not be said to wound, depending on the way they were taken and the way they were meant.

The next morning, Leighton awoke feeling lightheaded. She knew she had to call Dickie. She wondered why he didn't tell her that Sean was Lottie's cousin. Dickie was a man of so many secrets. He didn't tell you anything beyond the superficialities, the discernable and obvious facts.

"So how did you enjoy your fella last night?" Dickie came through the phone with a smile in his voice."

"Sean Dowd?"

"The very same. Charming, isn't he?"

"Lottie's cousin?"

"I see he told you."

"Yes, eventually. But you should have told me. Why didn't you?"

Dickie laughed softly and said he wanted the two of them to get to know each other. He didn't want to intervene with talk of Lottie. "It would have depressed both of you to dredge up such a gloomy tale. That's all you'd talk about. Sorry I didn't get much time to socialize with you at the wedding, but if I had, I still would not have told you."

"Well, I think you should have told me at some point, Dickie."

"Why? He's trying to find out what happened to Lottie and so are you. He would have told you at the appropriate moment, which apparently he did."

Leighton felt a wave of disappointment. He'd put them together to solve the disappearance of Lottie Lacock and not because he thought they'd like each other?

"Your daughter doesn't seem to like him."

"Robbie? I'm sure she likes him. Whatever gave you that idea?"

"I'm observant."

"My other daughter is convoluted."

"He seems like a ladies' man," she told him. "Your Sean."

"Not so, not so," he said. "My Sean? He isn't my Sean at all."

Leighton wondered how the hell he'd know if Sean Dowd was a ladies' man or not unless, of course, there'd been gossip, but then Dickie told her that Sean lost his wife several years ago and hadn't remarried.

"He lived with Marlene Tilly for a few years, remember her?" Dickie added.

Leighton shook her head as if he could see her and then snapped out of her thoughts. "Can't say as I do," she said.

"He never married her. There was some rumor about Marlene's daughter. I don't think there was any truth to it. Lottie didn't believe it, either."

"What was the rumor?"

"That he tried to seduce the kid. Look, Marlene's daughter is a strange little girl. I wouldn't believe anything she says."

"You think the girl is lying?"

"Well, I just doubt Sean would do anything like that. He's not that kind of man. He's a teacher, for God's sake."

"Hmm. Where's Marlene these days?"

"She moved to Columbia recently, sells real estate there. Of course, she believed her daughter."

"Well, of course."

"I saw her daughter at the wedding last night. Barney always liked her. She's got a motorcycle. The girl used to ride him around town on it."

"Oh? Can't be all bad then."

"Yeah, she's a friend of Robbie's too. But I don't think they were close."

Leighton intended to investigate this further. She refused to fall for a man who'd tried to get a teenage girl into bed.

"What was his wife like?" she asked.

"Pleasant enough. He has two kids, boys. He's raising them himself with the help of their grandparents, his wife's folks."

"Really?" Somehow that news made Sean seem more attractive, less suspicious. Being a father gave him a very approachable quality. "And Marlene Tilly, what's she like?"

"Nice enough. Sean cheated on her … well, at least Marlene accused him of it. Her daughter told her she saw him with some pretty brunette. Not the kind of woman to stand for that, not to mention what her daughter told her about him coming on to her. Their relationship was doomed. Marlene is older than he is, too."

"Really?" Leighton asked. "By how much?"

"Well, he's a few years younger than I am, and Marlene and I are the same age. Nine years or so."

"Hmmm," Leighton said. "Likes older women and is potentially a real bastard, cheated on his girlfriend and tried to get his girlfriend's daughter into bed."

"Look, Leighton, don't believe that rumor. I don't believe it, neither did Lottie. I would never introduce you to a man like that."

Leighton bit her nail. She had to get to the bottom of it, anyway.

"You think she's dead?" Dickie asked suddenly.

"Lottie? Who would have wanted to kill her?" she asked and heard him sigh. But he didn't give her an answer.

Dickie sighed again as he put down the phone. He felt bad that Leighton thought he was so sufficiently lacking in character he'd fixed her up with a cheater and a man who would try to seduce a teenage girl. Truth was, he didn't believe that Sean had cheated on Marlene, and he certainly didn't believe that Sean would go after a teenager. Marlene had been so shaken over her daughter's accusations that she didn't know what to believe. Women had thrown themselves at Sean most of his life, especially after his wife's death. He was a likable, handsome man. Women noticed him. Women wanted to take care of him, but as far as Dickie knew, Sean wasn't seeing anyone else but Marlene while living with her.

Sean would not have lied to Dickie about it. Sean was nearly in tears when he told Dickie what Marlene's daughter had accused him of, but the truth was that Sean was devastated that Marlene believed her daughter, and that became reason enough for Marlene to break up with him. It's her daughter, Dickie had said. That's all he needed to say, that explained it. How could she not believe her daughter? He couldn't tell Sean that Pam was a wild card, a real little witch and more than capable of feeding her mother a bunch of bull. He couldn't tell Sean why he knew that. Pam Tilly was capable of lying, cheating, and attempting to ruin other people's relationships. She told her mother she spotted Sean with another woman, a young and glamorous woman, of course. The girl had her own agenda. Pam Tilly was out for Pam Tilly. She'd been at The Red Lady the night Dickie and Lottie had gone to see Ginger's drag show. Pam had seen him there, but he did not take much notice of it at the time, trusting he was unrecognizable. But she'd approached him after he was back walking around town. "You sure make a beautiful woman," she'd said.

He remembered how he reacted, how completely exposed he felt. He stuttered. He smiled uncomfortably while she stood in front of him grinning. Then the girl tried to blackmail him. She wanted a thousand dollars not to tell his wife he was a drag queen. Dickie told her to go to hell, he wasn't a drag queen; people didn't understand cross-dressing, certainly this evil little girl didn't. If Pam ever told Deborah, he never heard about it. He assumed Deborah would not have believed her, anyway. But the point was that one couldn't trust anything that came out of Pam's mouth. "Look, Sean," Dickie had said at the time, "Pam Tilly is a liar, a fabricator of facts."

Truth was, he really thought that Sean would like Leighton, that they'd be good for each other. He knew Leighton was sad, still pining over Beau. Dickie thought she needed a distraction, someone to care for, someone who might care for her in return. Of course, he didn't want them to solve Lottie's whereabouts, that would be disastrous, but he assumed that if they liked each other, they were likely to get off the subject of Lottie Lacock soon enough.

Chapter Nine

Robbie stretched her arms out wide the morning after the wedding. She'd slept a full eight hours in euphoric slumber. She was still tingling after seeing Pam. Sharing that kiss had been unexpected, but it brought it all back – the attraction, all those declarations of love. No longer angry, she was excited. It felt, at least for Robbie, that their affair had started all over again, their affair – their crazy love affair. That had been their song, "Crazy Love." How could what they were feeling for each other be anything else but crazy love? Their passionate secret meetings at her grandmother's cottage, where they laughed almost as much as they explored their sexuality, made Robbie's heart rush when she thought back on it.

Pam's little love affair with Boyd didn't work out, but that wasn't surprising, he'd tried to rape her one night out at Hagood Mill, Pickens answer to Lover's Lane. Boyd turned out to be just another horny jerk.

Pam had been so upset when she told Robbie about it, wringing her hands, and crying. Robbie told her that he'd be sure to try it again if she gave him the opportunity. Pam tried to make excuses for him, said he'd been drinking that night, so maybe he didn't have any control over himself, but he'd had no right to her body, drunk or not.

"How'd you prevent him from doing it?"

"Kicked him out of the car." Pam smiled. "He was a bit drunk, so he fell on his ass."

Sorry for her, Robbie imagined that some boy trying to rape you was pretty devastating. After that incident, Robbie had jumped at the chance to put herself back in the picture. Why not? Pam told her she didn't care about making her mother happy anymore, said her mother was just going to have to deal with the fact that she didn't like boys. She begged Robbie to take her back, and of course, Robbie did.

"I was just trying to make my mother happy," she told Robbie in tears. "I didn't mean anything I said to you about not loving you and all that. I wanted to mean it … it would make life so much easier if I didn't want you so much, but I do."

Unfortunately, Boyd wouldn't take the hint and kept tagging after Pam like a puppy dog. Pam never reported Boyd to the police, but Robbie insisted she at least tell her mother about Boyd's failed attempt to rape her. Her mother persuaded her to go to the police, but they never did anything. It was a good thing she went off to college because Boyd would never have stopped pursuing her. It seemed wherever Pam was, Boyd would show up.

Pam probably had a hundred lovers at the U of

South Carolina, and Robbie wondered if they were male and female or just female. Boys flipped for Pam, she was one of those All-American pretty blondes, and even though she said she didn't like boys, she lapped up the attention.

But she had a particular radar for scouting out girls who were gay and seduced them just as easily. Girls being her preference, Robbie was sure. Girls succumbed to Pam's toughness, that wise-cracking quality that had a seductive humor about it. Robbie thought of her as a marauder in sheep's clothing, beguiling as a lonely beach in the Caribbean, especially after hearing the rumor that Pam had blackmailed some girl out of a thousand dollars. She said it was payoff for keeping her mouth shut to the girl's parents that she slept with girls.

Naturally, Robbie didn't trust Pam after that first break up, not altogether. She needed to and wanted to, but Pam was a wildcard, and she didn't disappoint. She came back to Pickens for Thanksgiving break and told Robbie that she was seeing someone she'd fallen madly in love with, and left Robbie in a state of shock and anger.

Sudden and unexpected, Robbie was stunned that Pam would just ditch her like that again, not twice in just a few months. Especially after she'd been there for Pam when she was so upset about Boyd trying to rape her. Furious at this betrayal, and then so hurt, she couldn't move forward for a long time.

Robbie remembered the night she had been at The Red Lady with Mindy and had seen Pam in the crowded room; she'd turned away quickly to avoid Pam noticing her. Seeing Pam was devastating enough, made worse because she was with someone, a tall, dark girl who was hanging all over her. Robbie had been relieved when the show started, and all eyes shifted to the stage. Thankfully, she hadn't seen Pam again until her brother's wedding.

Aware she might be making a mistake, Robbie intended to break off with Mindy, had to break off with Mindy; it just wasn't fair. Seeing Pam had brought it all up again, those feelings she'd quickly interpreted as "love". Maybe Pam didn't have anything to do with her breaking up with Mindy, but she'd do it anyway. Mindy wouldn't move to New York, and it wasn't right to ask her to wait for Robbie to graduate. Robbie didn't plan to return to Pickens anyway. She wanted to live in New York. It just wasn't fair to Mindy; she'd never leave Pickens. Their relationship had no future.

Robbie couldn't find the piece of paper that Pam had given her, the handwritten invitation to take up where they left off. She had read it quickly on her way back to the wedding party. Pam had written that she still loved her and asked to see her the following day. Robbie hoped the note hadn't fallen out of her pocket and Mindy had picked it up. She remembered being a little bit drunk by the end of the evening.

Pam was staying at her mom's house until it sold. It had been on the market a month or two. Robbie knew that because she'd often driven past the house and seen the For Sale sign. Of course, she would be there at the designated hour. They'd make love the way they used to, and she was so excited she could barely breathe. She'd never find the passion she'd had with Pam with anyone else: it just burned too fiercely.

It would be a million years before that happened again.

She didn't notice Mindy's car when she drove up to Pam's and pulled into the drive. Before Robbie could get to the front door, there was Mindy, fuming and scowling at her.

"You dropped this on the ground last night," Mindy said fiercely and held out the piece of paper Pam had slipped her. "I was gracious enough to pick it up. I was about to give it back to you when I couldn't help but notice the signature."

Oh, shit, Robbie thought, embarrassed and not knowing what to say, she said nothing, just stared at Mindy's glaring expression.

"Just saying hello to an old friend, Mindy," she finally said.

"You used to go with her."

"'Used to' being the operative words here."

"She said she still loved you in the note."

"So what?"

"What are you doing here, Robbie?"

"I told you, calling on an old friend."

"Are you breaking up with me? Because you better be breaking up with me if you're going to sleep with her."

"Of course, I'm not going to sleep with her. Where did you get that idea?" Robbie didn't know why she didn't tell her the truth, but she wanted to get rid of her. She was on pins and needles to get inside that house so she could feel Pamela Tilly's naked body against hers once again. However, she didn't want to get into it here at Pam's front door with Mindy. It wasn't appropriate somehow. She'd have to explain too much, deal with Mindy's tears probably.

"Then turn around and come with me. We'll go to the movies."

"She's expecting me, Mindy. I'm not going to do anything with her."

The door opened and Pam stood in her sailor-boy pants and a little midriff top that showed a tan and a very flat stomach. She stared at Mindy.

"What do you want?" she asked.

"What do you mean, what do I want? I'm Robbie's girlfriend."

"Well, so am I," Pam said and smiled at Robbie.

"Not in the way I am," Mindy said and stood her ground, folded her arms in front of her and scowled some more.

"If you don't mind," Pam said. "I have invited Robbie to my house for lunch to hash over old times." She looked flirtatiously at Robbie. "Maybe even bring them back again."

"She's spoken for," Mindy said.

Pam hunched her shoulders up. "Okay."

"Go home, Mindy," Robbie said. "I'm just visiting with an old friend."

"Sure, Robbie, sure, keep lying to yourself and lying to me."

"I'm not lying, Mindy."

Mindy stared at Robbie and then reached over and kissed her. "Well, okay, I trust you're telling me the truth and if I find out you're not, I don't know who I'll kill first, you or her." She glared at Pam.

"I wouldn't mess with me, little girl. I've got five women in my past with black eyes and broken noses." Pam gave Mindy a pinched look, as if she had a pain somewhere.

"Don't threaten me, Pam Tilly. I can hold my own."

"C'mon, Mindy." Robbie reached out and took Mindy's arm. "I'll call you later. I promise."

"You're not going to sleep with her, are you?" Mindy asked as Robbie walked her back to her car. "It's over between us if you do."

"Of course I'm not," Robbie said. She watched Mindy drive off with a screech and a face that would have sent little children running for cover.

"What was that all about?" Pam asked as she held the door open for Robbie and they walked inside.

"You threaten her," Robbie said.

"How nice."

"Do you really have five women in your past with broken noses and black eyes?"

Pam smiled. "You know I'm a badass, Robbie."

Robbie stood close to Pam. "Mindy is jealous. Can you blame her? You're a hot woman, Pam." Pam smiled and ran her fingers down Robbie's arms. Robbie's tank top was tight and made her look busty. Her short shorts showed off her long legs. Pam's fingers found the inside of her thigh and soon her mouth was on Robbie's.

"Hey, what happened to the girl you fell in love with?" Robbie asked. "Do I have competition?"

"Oh, she turned out to be a jerk."

"She did, huh?"

Pam winked at her. "Remember where my bedroom is?" she whispered low.

Robbie turned around and ran up the steps with Pam close behind her.

Their lovemaking was intensely passionate, the way it used to be. When they finally came up for air, hours later, Robbie's hair was plastered to her forehead and Pam's stomach was so wet it shone.

"Now that was a workout." Pam smiled.

"Beats the Stairmaster."

"Want a coke?" Pam asked.

Robbie nodded and Pam threw her sailor-boy pants back on and went downstairs.

Robbie looked around Pam's room. It hadn't changed much in three years. She still had a big photograph of Jodi Foster on her mirror; she'd loved Jodi Foster. Her closet door was open, jean jackets, fancy scarves, and high-top sneakers on show, and some pretty evening clothes, the kind you'd wear to a five-star restaurant. She wondered who was taking her to fancy restaurants: Pam certainly didn't have the money to pick up the check, at least not to Robbie's knowledge.

The quiet afternoon was suddenly pierced by screams, Robbie recovered from the shock, grabbed Pam's robe, and raced down the stairs.

"Holy shit," Pam said. She was out on the patio, eyes gawking, naked from the waist up.

Robbie ran outside, shocked by the fear on Pam's face.

"My mother is going to kill me," she said.

Robbie followed her eyes to the garden, where every flower had been ripped out. Someone had pulled out every flower in the entire garden by its roots. The bushes, too, had been uprooted.

"My mother said the garden is what's going to sell our house," Pam said, practically in tears. "Who would do this?"

Robbie shook her head, but she was thinking of Mindy and wondered why she was thinking of Mindy.

"My mom said our garden was a top selling point. Those pink roses were breathtaking." She looked at Robbie helplessly.

"I'll get our gardener, Hector, to replant it all. It will be okay."

"I think that little bitch, Mindy, did this."

"Look, Hector will fix it."

"Hector has the money to do it?"

Robbie told her he had access to cash for all repairs on their house. "He just withdraws what he needs. It's for anything."

Pam stared at her. "How much you think is in there?"

"A few thousand. I don't know for sure but my mom trusts Hector to take what he needs. He's been with us forever. Besides, my mom goes over his expenses with a fine tooth comb every month."

"I'll need at least a thousand dollars to replace this garden."

"Okay," Robbie said. "I'll ask him to withdraw the money and give it to you to buy the flowers and Hector will plant them. Does that work?"

Pam threw her arms around Robbie. "You're a lifesaver," she said. "Do I have to pay him anything, you know, like for his time?"

Robbie did not have the answer to that. It wasn't fair to ask him to do it for nothing.

"I'll tell him to give you a break."

Pam stepped back. "I don't have money for something like that, break or not. He's got to replant the whole damn garden."

"Well, I'll ask him to charge my mother. She might not notice."

"Really?"

Robbie slowly nodded.

"Like I said, you're a lifesaver." Pam threw her arms around Robbie and held her close.

Chapter Ten

Marlene showed her five houses before she spotted Cottonwood, so named on the spot because it had to be hers, had to have her phony new name. It just shouted "Cottonwood."

"Stop the car, Marlene," Lottie said.

"Oh, honey, that's not for you, it's too big."

"Stop the car, or I will throw myself out of it."

Marlene came to a stop. "Ten months on the market, seven bedrooms and the kitchen is an eye sore. It's not for you."

"How much?"

"Out of your price range."

"Got the keys?"

Marlene sighed deeply. "C'mon, they're in the lockbox."

Lottie was falling in love, regardless of knowing she was being a fool. It was random, coming upon this house. It was also random that she had walked into the first real estate office she saw and there, behind a desk, was Marlene Tilly, her old friend from Pickens. After they'd screamed and hugged, Lottie gave her some bull about having married a man named Carter Cottonwood who, unfortunately, had passed on. Lottie had all this money and so much time on her hands. "Staying in Pickens was just too painful. I needed something new." Lottie dabbed at her eyes. "So here I am."

"I only left Pickens three months ago," Marlene said.

"Yes, I heard you broke up with Sean."

"Well, what did you expect? Oh, Lottie, let's not get into that. Let's leave that subject alone."

"That's a good idea."

"I hadn't heard you married. You must have lost Carter soon after the wedding."

"Yes," Lottie said. "A damn shame. It was so sudden."

She stared at Marlene, the quintessential real estate broker — pretty, blonde, perfectly and elegantly dressed. She hated lying to people, especially people she had history with, but she had no choice.

Marlene wiped away a tear. "So sorry for you, Lottie," she said.

"Ah, well, had my moment in the sun, had to move on." She followed Marlene up the stone steps to the back door. It was like walking into a fairy tale, an enchanted house greeted her. There she stood in an elegantly remodeled kitchen in beautiful shades of blue and steel appliances. Lottie sighed deeply and put her hands to her heart. "This is not an eye sore," she said.

Marlene smiled. "Well, I don't like blue. It's too blue. I was just trying to talk you out of it."

"I love the color blue." Lottie gave her a big grin.

"Well, like I said, I was just trying to discourage you. What are you going to do with a house this big?"

Lottie grinned at her. "What do you think I'm thinking of doing with it, Marlene Tilly?"

"Bread and Breakfast, am I right? Is that it?"

Lottie's wide smile further widened as she continued her tour in silence. She started with the front room and silently marveled at the three large oval windows with so much sun streaming through that one had to squint. The fireplace was what Marlene called a large French cast stone fireplace with an antique parchment finish.

"It's got golden highlights." She turned to Lottie, her smile now ear to ear. "On a shell and foliage motif." She repeated her smile. "The owners said be sure to say that."

The high ceiling had wide crown molding and the golden wood floors were wide planks, the kind of floors that show age and history and all those good things old houses can boast of.

"They leaving the furniture?" Lottie asked

"Some of it."

"Elegant," Lottie whispered. "I love it."

Marlene smiled. "Love, is it?"

Marlene watched as Lottie inspected every nook and corner of the old but gracious house and followed her up the stairs and back down again.

"You can't live here," Marlene said. "You'll be so lonely. Unless, of course, you really do open a bed-and-breakfast?"

"Look at all that sun."

"Southern exposure, Lottie."

"Unfortunately, I can't cook. I'd have to hire a chef. A bed-and-breakfast has to offer food, doesn't it?"

"I would think."

"Well, I mean, if I open a bed-and-breakfast, I assume I'd serve breakfast and lunch, at least. Maybe even dinner. Who knows?"

"Why yes," Marlene said tentatively. "Well, if you're serious, then maybe this is meant to be."

Lottie turned to her. "Yes, yes, meant to be. I think it is. I think fate's led me here."

"I can cook. I can cook like Beau McArdle ... you remember him, Lottie?"

"Yep, poor man, Leighton's husband, gone too soon."

"You interested in having me cook for you? This is fate for sure if you are."

"Sure enough is fate," Lottie said. "What about your real estate business?"

"I can't do both? Real estate is part-time, anyway. Cooking is part-time, too."

"Well, I got me some thinking to do," Lottie said. "At least, I'm going to look into it."

Lottie had no idea why she bought the house. It was beautiful, true, but it was big, daunting, even. She'd had a moment of insanity. She fell instantly in love. She took a small mortgage and paid the rest, mostly cash. Marlene was quite impressed.

The house was on a quiet street in Wales Garden,

walking distance to Five Points for shopping and fine restaurants. She was surrounded by a canopy of trees and there were gardens in front of every house on her street that commanded attention. Everyone who passed stopped to admire, to marvel and sniff the flowers. Lottie had not seen anything more beautiful, certainly nothing like this in Pickens. This was an expense, but if she opened her bed-and-breakfast, it would make her money.

The house was blue with cream trim, seven bedrooms in all. What in God's name ever possessed her to purchase a house with seven bedrooms? Perhaps, the sheer beauty of it, she thought. Maybe she just wanted something to do. Maybe she did it because she could afford it. But it would take at least a year to fill it with furniture.

But it did not take a year, it hardly took a month. It helped, of course, that she was able to purchase most of the furniture already in the house. One evening, she arranged the living room to her liking, old world and comfortable as a cottage in the English countryside. Except it wasn't an English cottage, it was enormous, seven bedrooms for God's sake. The prior owners had left the beds, seven charming beds with tufted headboards and fine old mahogany side tables. She scoured the countryside for estate sales and antique shops that could be persuaded to come down in price. Before she knew it, the house looked lived in and full and quite charming. The downstairs windows were draped in silk with subtle neutral colors and the upstairs bedrooms all had lace on the windows and fine old quilts on the beds.

A good deal of the house decorated with appropriate antiques, she sat by the fire, sipping a nice, hot cup of tea and summoning up the nerve to go through with the bed-and-breakfast, revving up to it, you might say. She imagined herself running the inn and smiled, confident she was making the right decision to go forward with the idea. It was a perfect image, something she may have always wanted to do if she'd thought long enough about it. Why, it was selfish of her not to be sharing her beautiful home. What a perfectly sound decision. Yes, it was. She could not look for a job at a bank, an uninspiring, boring bank, when this opportunity was sitting in her lap.

She made plans, visualized herself running a real, bona fide B & B. She'd serve a hearty breakfast, a light lunch, and a sumptuous dinner. She'd have people around her all the time. The problem was that Lottie was not a good cook. Her specialty was minted peas with lamb, and she made a fair jambalaya, but the buck stopped there. She usually overcooked the peas and dried out the lamb, but at least one might enjoy her jambalaya, which was often quite tasty, but she couldn't serve the same meal day after day. Well, she could enroll in a culinary course and learn to make all kinds of homecooked Southern meals for those travelers who loved the quaintness of Wales Garden. But she didn't think being a chef was in her genes. She wondered if she should take Marlene seriously.

Lottie remembered that falling out she'd had with Marlene a few years ago, the falling out they'd hinted at when Marlene had first shown her the house, an uncomfortable conversation they'd dropped quickly enough. At the time, it had been a painful confrontation. Lottie had taken Sean's side and told Marlene that her daughter was lying, must be lying, that Sean wouldn't do anything like what he was accused of doing, coming on to a teenager, for God's sake. She'd known Sean all his life and he just wouldn't do that. Marlene seemed not to hold a grudge, though, she wasn't acting angry at all. Lottie just hoped the conversation wouldn't come up again, but maybe they should clear the air.

Marlene showed up on her porch a few days later fully prepared to cook. Lottie was stunned and quite impressed, sure to hire her on sight. "Look at you," Lottie said, "reminding me of Julia Child."

Marlene had an apron on that said "Wine me and Dine me." She looked professional, as if she could cook anything from a three-minute egg to potatoes au gratin and beef a l'orange, which had been Dickie's favorite. She held up a spatula and had that "I am a gourmet cook" look. She was certainly a formidable woman, strong and tall like Julia Child, certainly not a woman to mess with. She must surely be Lottie's age; they'd gone to the same high school but weren't close at the time. Marlene was perfectly put together, but Lottie noticed that though Marlene was pretty, she had lots of lines running every which way on her face until they culminated at her mouth, which turned up in what looked like a perpetual smile.

Lottie clapped her hands when Marlene pulled a chef's hat out of her purse and put it on her head. Under her adorable "Wine me and dine me" apron, she had on designer pants and a long shirt with polka dots. Her hair was perfectly cut, short and thick. Lottie would definitely ask who her hairdresser was. At the end of a leash, a little red-haired dog sat at her feet, looking up at Lottie with her inquisitive brown eyes.

"That your sous chef?" Lottie asked.

Marlene gave her a saucy look. Across her shoulder, was a large bag which Lottie assumed contained all her personal cooking apparatus.

"You are a riot, Marlene Tilly."

Marlene looked at the dog. "This is Roxie," she said. "She's no trouble, fully housebroken ... most days."

"What have you there?" Lottie asked and pointed to the bag on her shoulder, choosing to ignore a paw shake with Roxie.

Marlene stepped back and grinned at her. "Why, I assume you want to audition me, have me cook for you, see if you like my style. I am known for Cajun, but I make such a fine meatballs and spaghetti, Southern style, of course. I put cinnamon in my meatballs, can't beat the flavor." Marlene grinned and walked inside the now fully decorated home.

"Oh, not to mention paella." She turned to her and raised an eyebrow. "Oh, you can request anything, but I have several specialties. This is going to be such fun, Lottie. Your guests are going to come running back for more."

"Yes, yes, I imagine it could be fun."

"We'll meet people from all over the world."

"Well, I hope there's some Europeans that are interested in Columbia, South Carolina."

"You'll need the perfect wine list. I can help you

with that too."

"That would be nice. I like wine, but I'm not an expert."

Excitement mounted in Lottie, but something was incomplete, something shrouded the space between them. Something she'd promised herself she wouldn't mention, but it wasn't right not to.

"Marlene," she began. "I swore I wouldn't bring it up, but I think I need to. Do you still resent me for sticking up for my cousin?"

"Oh, God, Lottie, no. That's water under the dam."

Lottie nodded. "I just wanted to clear the air between us. I know it was a painful time for you."

"Look, Lottie, he's your cousin, I get it."

"And Pam is your daughter, naturally, you believed her."

Marlene nodded her head. "Of course," she said.

"So, you going to audition for me?" Lottie assumed they'd made peace.

"I sure am. Take me to your kitchen, I'll whip something up to die for."

Later that evening, Lottie sat in her parlor, relaxed and relieved that Marlene wasn't holding a grudge. Who wouldn't believe her own daughter? But Pam was often not truthful. In high school, she'd accused another student of attempting to rape her. Turned out the kid's father had taken him on a trip — he wasn't even in town when he was supposedly trying to rape Pam. That should have been reason enough not to believe her. But a mother's blindness, Lottie assumed.

Lottie had hired Marlene on the spot: her coq au vin had been spectacular. Marlene needed nothing else but what she'd found in Lottie's kitchen. Not to mention the red burgundy that flavored the sauce, which she found in the liquor cabinet and the final touch, the cognac.

Roxie had stayed quietly curled up in the chair while Marlene cooked, but once she knew the stew was done, she jumped up, took center stage in the kitchen, and demanded to be fed with a few high-pitched barks.

"You don't give her dog food?" Lottie asked, not really used to dogs, except for her neighbor's dog back in Pickens that used to find his way onto Lottie's porch to lie in his favorite wicker settee, making Lottie's favorite yellow cushions damp and hairy.

"Oh, sometimes," Marlene said. "She doesn't like eggs or fish, so she eats dog food then. I keep a can around for occasions like that when I make something she doesn't like."

Lottie raised her eyebrows, but she was fond of Marlene; even Roxie was getting to her. The dog had a way of staring at her with an intelligent expression as though she spoke five languages and was reading a book on the mysteries of human nature.

After dinner, she and Marlene agreed on a suitable price for each meal she cooked for the bed-and-breakfast. They shook hands at the end of the evening and Lottie watched her drive off in her sleek new convertible. Lottie knew she didn't need the money, company was what she needed. There they were, two middle-aged women alone, creating all the possibility in the world for them never to be alone again.

"What do you think of Lottie Cottonwood's bed-and-breakfast?" she asked Marlene when she saw her the following week. She had gotten all the information she needed to run a bed-and-breakfast and she'd have all the paperwork in place in a month or two.

"I think it has a little poetry to it, but I might just call it Cottonwood's."

Lottie nodded, "Yes, I thought so too."

"You're going to have to do something with that backyard. Guests will want to sit there in the evening shade. We're going to have to make it attractive."

"Before or after I put in the bathrooms?"

"Bathrooms?"

"Small ones for each room. I don't think people want to share a bathroom."

"Your ex-husband must have been loaded, Lottie."

Chapter Eleven

Leighton pulled Beau's Corvette up on Deborah's drive. She hadn't the heart to sell it though Lord knows, enough people had made an offer on it. Beau had treated that car like his firstborn. He'd washed it every weekend and polished it frequently. He'd put the top down and drive around town, never losing the straw hat on his head, despite the wind, the sun deepening the redness on his left arm, and he'd flex his vocal cords to whatever country western tune was blaring from the radio.

Leighton noticed Deborah on the porch as she drove up. She was reading a magazine and her long tanned legs were bare to her beautifully shaped thighs. Leighton wondered if Deborah had anything to do with Lottie's disappearance or murder; her car had been seen at Lottie's house right before the fire, possibly during the fire. That did not sit right with Leighton. It didn't exactly incriminate Deborah, especially since Deborah had said her car had been stolen, but Leighton was suspicious. The car was later found abandoned at a Country Food Mart parking lot in the part of town Deborah would never be caught dead in. Perhaps someone had stolen Deborah's Cadillac and murdered Lottie, but why? It seemed farfetched. Leighton couldn't find one single soul or one single rumor that intimated that Lottie had any enemies. It could have been random, but as there were no other random murders in Pickens, it didn't seem likely.

Leighton braved Deborah's eyes on her as she climbed the porch steps.

"To what do I owe the pleasure?" Deborah crooned, sweet as sugar.

Leighton took the seat beside her. "Just a few questions, Deborah."

Deborah threw herself back in her chair. "Oh, my God, but you have questioned me to death."

"Thought you might think of something you hadn't thought of before."

"I can get Heaven to bring out some sweet tea with lots of ice."

"That would be fine, much appreciated on such a hot day."

Leighton watched as Deborah rang a little bell and after a moment, a young girl appeared in her black uniform and white apron. The girl was tall and gangly and looked no more than sixteen. Deborah told her to bring out a pitcher of sweet tea with lots of ice and some of those little lemon cakes. The girl gave a brief curtsy and a smile. Leighton thought it was all too *Gone with the Wind* for her. Very few people in

Pickens now had their help wear uniforms, much less curtsy after a request.

Leighton settled into her seat and stared at Deborah, who had not closed the magazine but kept it aimlessly open across her lap.

"Where were you when your car was stolen?" Leighton asked casually.

"I told you a million times, I was shopping on Mill Street, parked my car in front of The Chic Shack, came out and, the car was gone."

"But the car was found clear across town."

"Yes, because it was stolen." Deborah sounded completely exasperated and Leighton almost smiled at her theatrics.

"How long were you in The Chic Shack?"

"Long enough to have my car stolen." She took in Leighton's serious expression. "I bought a pair of slacks and two new blouses. I tried them on and then had to wait over ten minutes for some fool woman to count up all her dollar bills and lose coins to pay for some ridiculous pair of shorts in cash." She made a face. "Who the hell wears cargo shorts anymore?"

"Do you have a receipt for your purchase, Deborah?"

"Oh, I never keep receipts." Deborah laughed. "Everything fits me perfectly."

Leighton almost asked to see her purchase, but she didn't. It would be going a bit too far without any solid evidence. She'd need a court order to search Deborah's house and she knew she wouldn't be able to get it. "Did Lottie have any enemies?" she asked instead.

"Lord, no."

"Who do you think did this to her?"

"Did what to her?"

Leighton sat back as Heaven brought out a tray with the pitcher of sweet tea and lemon cakes.

"Well, burn down her house for one."

Deborah looked off. "Who knows? Maybe there's an arsonist in Pickens."

Leighton took a deep breath. "Maybe there's a murderer in Pickens."

"Murdered? There's no body."

"Well, she either left town or she was murdered."

"You can't have a murder without a body."

"Doesn't mean she wasn't murdered. I mean, her body could still show up."

"Oh, my God. Who would murder poor Lottie?"

"A jealous wife or girlfriend?"

Deborah laughed and took a sip of her tea. "Lottie was not exactly a femme fatale … she was no Marilyn Monroe. She was past having boyfriends."

"I don't think that matters. Passion is often blind."

Deborah had an odd look on her face. "I suppose so," she said.

Leighton's instinct told her Deborah knew something she wasn't revealing. She had to look deeper into Lottie's love life.

"Was she seeing anyone?" Leighton asked as she bit into the tangy cake.

Deborah laughed. "Didn't I just say she was past having boyfriends?" Deborah stared at Leighton, whose eyes had never left Deborah's. "Anyway, your guess is as good as mine. If she was seeing anyone, I did not know about it."

Deborah turned abruptly away and nibbled on her

cake in short quick bites. Leighton didn't know for sure, but thought she had upset her. Sitting there, drinking tea and eating cake, she thought of her mother. Odd thing to think about, but her mother just popped into her head, her mother and all her secrets.

"Did you know my mother well?" Leighton asked.

"My husband did, long before we were married. But you know that, don't you, Leighton?" Deborah smiled innocently. "What the hell does Leah have to do with Lottie?"

Leighton ignored her, just went on to talk about the weather, her gardens and how wonderful Barnaby's wedding had been.

"Oh, yes," Deborah said softly. "My son could not have found a more perfect bride. I've known that girl all her life, you know. We adore her."

"One more observation, Deborah."

"Yes?"

"Your fingerprints were found on the gasoline cans used to start the fire."

Deborah made an odd sound and threw her head back. "How many times do I have to say it? Lottie and I were friends. I always helped her clean out her garage and I touched every damn thing in there."

Leighton smiled again. "Yes, I see. Well, that explains it, doesn't it?"

They finished their tea, discussing everything but Lottie Lacock. Deborah rambled on about her gardens, the design tips she'd discovered in *Magnolia Magazine* and how excited Robinette was about leaving for Europe.

A trip to Charleston to see her mother was better than a phone call: a phone call didn't reveal facial expressions or twitches or downcast eyes.

Besides, Leighton loved visiting her mother and Rhonda. Rhonda was the quintessential Southern hostess and planned elaborate surprises, even for short visits. Leighton wondered what little party or expensive restaurant she'd be whisked off to, what historical tour she'd be given. Perhaps that Russian monastery she'd wanted to see last visit, but never got to.

Her mother was happy. She and Rhonda weren't hiding in Charleston as they'd had to in Pickens. Perhaps Charleston was more sophisticated, less opinionated than Pickens. In any event, they just lived their lives and had a small group of friends, many of whom were paired with same-sex partners. She always had the feeling after visiting her mother that her mother's life had become blissful, untouched by tragedy.

They sat out on the porch listening to Southern summer sounds. It was late in July, and the lilies were in bloom, the yard abundant with butterflies. Their dog, a large golden mutt, lazed on the grass.

"How is Aspen?" Leah asked.

"He's with Mart. Mart takes great care of Aspen," she said.

"Bet he'd take great care of you if you let him."

Leighton cocked her head. "We're friends, mother."

"Uh hum," Leah said.

Leighton looked away. She wondered if she should mention Sean. She wondered if it were premature to think of him as a boyfriend. They'd only had two dates, if she counted the wedding. Their dinner date had been pleasant enough, out with a man whose company she enjoyed. After the wedding, he'd gone back to Greenville saying he'd call her, and he did call to ask her out again, but the potential for a life partner? She wasn't even sure of the potential of a sex partner; the chemistry was a bit off. She found him quite attractive, but he had not initiated any intimacy, which was fine by her, she wasn't ready for it, wasn't sure if she'd ever be ready.

"I'm seeing someone," she said anyway.

Leah turned to her. "Oh?"

Leighton nodded. "Not much to say about it yet. I've just begun to see him."

"Lives in Pickens?"

"No, Greenville."

Leah put her head back. "Didn't think there would be anyone to date in Pickens." She laughed. "But you're full of surprises."

Leighton laughed with her. "Sometimes."

"Well, come on, name? What's he do? Spill it."

"His name is Sean Dowd. He's a high school social studies teacher and I don't know much else. Oh, his wife died a few years ago and he never remarried. He's got young children, two small boys."

Leighton's mother made no response, might've recoiled a bit. But her interest in who Leighton was seeing ended there.

"Anyway, I'm not here to talk about me. I need to ask you a few questions."

Silence filled the space between them, and the breeze ruffled Leighton's hair, reminding her of

Beau's touch. Her mother's head fell back, her eyes closed, as if she were still thinking about Sean, though that would be odd. Had she known him at any point, Leighton wondered. She'd like to ask, but she was on another mission.

"How well did you know Lottie Lacock, Mom?"

"Not very well at all. Malcolm Kram knew her quite well and he'd talk about her every now and then."

"Marshall Kram, alias Ginger Tea?"

"One and the same," Leah smiled.

"What did he say?"

"Oh, nothing important."

"You know she's missing, right?"

Leah nodded. In her silence, Leighton detected something unsettling. "What do you know about it?"

"Nothing, Leighton."

Leighton sat forward and studied her mother, who had those frown lines on her forehead, those deep-in-thought lines. "What are you debating? To tell me something I should know or to tell me something I shouldn't know?"

Leah sighed. "I have no loyalty to Deborah, but you know I'm fond of Dickie."

This got Leighton's attention and she sat up straighter, leaned closer in.

"Please tell me what you know, Mom. I need the information."

Leighton heard her mother sigh before she started speaking. "The day of the fire, Deborah had been to see me."

"Why? You two weren't friends."

"She thought I was having an affair with her

husband."

Leighton shook her head as if to clear it. "Well, you had an affair with him."

"Yes, dear, when I was seventeen. I was certainly not sleeping with him when I returned to Pickens. I'd already met Rhonda."

"Was Dickie having an affair?"

Leah nodded. "He sure was, ever since he married Deborah, I believe."

"Wow." Leighton sat back in her chair. "Dickie?"

"Yes, Dickie."

Leighton peered at her mother. "And you told her who the woman was?"

"Yes, I told her it was Lottie Lacock," Leah said softly. "Deborah's best friend. She thought it was me. I couldn't let her think that. She might have shot me. She was angry enough."

"And Lottie was dead or gone right after you told her?"

Leah nodded. "I guess you can jump to conclusions." She stared at Leighton.

"How did you know about the affair?"

"Malcolm knew, and he told me."

"Shit," Leighton said. "Both Deborah and Dickie are lying to me, covering up something."

"Well, I wouldn't jump to conclusions, they might not be involved with Lottie's disappearance."

Leighton gave her an odd look. "And lightning doesn't follow thunder," she said.

Chapter Twelve

It was all too bizarre. According to Leighton's mother Dickie had been having an affair with Lottie for thirty years.

"Lottie knew he cross-dressed?" Leighton asked after Leah told her about Dickie's odd proclivity for women's clothes, and her mother had nodded.

Leighton thought back to when Dickie and Lottie were attacked as they left The Red Lady, that drag bar hidden away in the backroads between Pickens and Greenville. She knew Dickie had been wearing women's clothes that night, but Leighton hadn't thought much of it at the time, she thought it was a joke, a prank they were pulling for Malcolm's benefit. She should have called him on it, but she never did. The police dropped the whole thing, most likely because Lillian Darling didn't want it known that her son wore women's clothes, even for fun.

"You're a cross-dresser," she said to him. They were sitting on a bench in the middle of town, right in front of the new bookstore. She'd spotted him as she stopped for a light on her way to The Chic Shack.

He didn't look at her. He kept staring at the two books he had just purchased.

"I thought you knew that," he finally said. "You knew I was nearly pummeled to death at The Red Lady, and you knew why."

"No crime in it, Dickie, but I thought you just did it as a one-off, like a joke. Is it something you're into, like a fetish or something?"

"It's really a private matter." He looked at her stoically. "You didn't put the pieces together until your mother told you?"

Leighton looked off. She hadn't put the pieces together. She didn't want to think of her biological father that way, as strange.

"She also told me that you were having an affair with Lottie, nothing light about it either. It had been going on for thirty years, so don't try to shrug it off."

"I wouldn't think of shrugging it off. I loved her."

"As in I loved her, so I'd never kill her?"

Dickie turned to her. "I wouldn't harm a hair on Lottie's head."

"Why didn't you divorce your wife if you loved Lottie so much?"

"First, it was about the children, then it was about my mother. She'd never allow me to divorce Deborah. She said Deborah was good for business."

"Your mother runs your life?"

Dickie turned to her. "You could say that."

Leighton stared right into his eyes, boldly confronting him. "Do you have any idea why Lottie would disappear right after Deborah learned of your affair? Did you have an argument?"

"No."

"My mother told Deborah about your affair and an hour or so later, Lottie's house was in flames. Coincidence?" she asked.

Dickie turned to her, his eyes like little blue bullets glaring.

"Do you see any connection, Dickie?"

"My wife did not kill Lottie." He said it wearily, not angrily, she noticed. He stood to his feet. "I'll be going now. If you want to question me, you'll have to arrest me."

"Nobody said she killed him," Leighton called after him. "And no one has cause to arrest you, but it's an odd coincidence, wouldn't you say," she yelled out.

Dickie didn't turn around, just kept walking as if he hadn't heard her. She watched as he got into his car and drove off. She'd have to go back to Deborah with this new information, that she had just learned of Lottie's indiscretion minutes before the fire. She didn't know how Deborah would have gotten Lottie off the property, but she was certain she'd set the fire. Maybe she wasn't guilty of the whole crime – removing Lottie's body – but Leighton would bet her pension that she was guilty of setting that fire. Deborah would have needed help disposing of Lottie though. Perhaps all she had to do now was figure out who would have helped her. Could it possibly have been Dickie?

She got up and walked into The Chic Shack, a

clothing store that Deborah had said she'd been in right before her car was allegedly stolen. As Leighton questioned the shop girls, none of them remembered seeing Deborah that day, but it had been busy, and it was hard for them to pinpoint exactly what day their customers came in the store. There were no credit card records to prove Deborah had purchased anything on that day, but if she paid cash, there wouldn't be a record. All Leighton had was inconclusive information, nothing that would stick in a court of law. She left The Chic Shack convinced Deborah was lying – but how to prove it?

Guilt about questioning Robbie bothered Leighton somewhat, but the girl was close to Dickie, might possibly know something important. She called and asked if they could meet at a small coffee shop over in Easley.

Robbie was already there when Leighton arrived and slid in opposite her at the table. After a bit of small talk, Leighton braced to ask some uncomfortable questions. After the waitress had poured them each a cup of coffee, she leaned in toward Robbie.

"Your father and Lottie were having an affair. Were you aware of it?"

Robbie flicked her eyes at Leighton. "I suspected it."

"Did you know your father was a cross-dresser? I know that's a delicate question, but I have to ask it."

"Why? What does it have to do with anything?"

Leighton sighed as she added more cream to her coffee. "I want to understand their relationship. Your parents' relationship."

"I was there the night he was nearly beaten to death. That's when I found out that he liked to dress like a woman." She leveled her eyes at Leighton. "My mother wouldn't know how to comprehend Dad's hobby." She drew air quotes saying the word hobby. "Lottie probably knew everything about my father."

Leighton sat back. "How long did your mother know about their affair?"

"Seriously? If my mother knew about it, she would have shot Lottie in the back." As if realizing what she'd said, she quickly added. "I'm not being serious. My mother would not have shot her."

"Just burned her house down?" Leighton raised an eyebrow.

Robbie stared at her. "My mother would not have done that either."

"Would you have done it?"

"What? No, of course not. I didn't know they were having an affair for sure until you just mentioned it."

"I'm sorry to tell you, really I am." She put her hand over Robbie's.

Robbie sat back with a defiant stare. "My parents aren't murderers. They may be many things but not murderers. You do know that, don't you?"

Leighton removed her hand and sighed. "I want that to be true as much as you do."

"It is true," Robbie said.

"Yes, unless it's proven otherwise."

"Well, speaking of crime. You might as well know that your boyfriend is a sleaze."

Leighton's head came up sharply. "Sean?"

"He used to come on to Marlene Tilly's daughter.

I'm sure that's why she threw him out."

Leighton was disappointed to know that Sean's reputation was all over town. "How do you know that?"

"I know Marlene Tilly's daughter."

"Was this ever reported? The girl must have been a teenager."

Robbie shrugged. "Pam told me he had a restraining order against him by his first wife. I guess that was reported."

"Pam Tilly told you that?"

"Yeah."

Leighton's heart beat fast. "He seemed so nice," she said and laughed slightly.

Robbie grinned. "Ted Bundy was nice, wasn't he? Good looks, boyish smile."

"Well, Sean is not a psychopath."

"Not as far as we know." Robbie leaned forward. "Look, Leighton, I'm sorry, but you haven't been seeing him that long, have you?

"No, I haven't."

"Fair warning then ... get out before you get in too deep."

Leighton sat back in her chair and changed the subject. "Hear you're going to Europe?"

Robbie smiled and her eyes lit up. "I leave tomorrow."

"Going alone?" Leighton asked, seeing how excited she was.

Robbie shrugged. "Mostly," she said. "Some kids from the Art Club are going, but I plan to ditch them."

Chapter Thirteen

Aimlessness consumed Deborah. That aimlessness drove her back into a book she still couldn't finish, a garden that Hector took such good care of, there was nothing for her to do but stare at its florid perfection and sip her sweet tea. Life was too good, and its goodness was about to suffocate her.

Her daughter was in Europe, running around "looking at masterpieces", as she put it, dining in the Testaccio neighborhood of Rome, and showing off her perfect body on the beaches of Grande Plage in Biarritz. Deborah had to admit to feelings of envy. She had never run youthfully around Europe. Oh, she and Lottie used to fantasize about it when they were girls, but she went and got married when she was so young, and Dickie hated to fly. Lottie went to Europe once on some tour with her book club group. It made Deborah smile. Lottie had come back speaking about ten words of Italian that she'd drop every time they went to

Mezzogiorno, known for their sumptuous cacciatore. Not a waiter in the place understood a word of what Lottie said. Deborah smiled to herself, Lottie had refused to eat anything that didn't include tomato sauce, fusilli, or shaved parmesan for months after she'd returned from Italy. Ten pounds heavier, she went back to soups and salads.

"You ole fool," Deborah whispered.

It pained her to think about Lottie. She hadn't let Lottie enter her thoughts since the day of the fire but every now and then, something would remind her of Lottie's big laugh or her long stride in those Capri pants she wore with what she called her Earth sandals. Now the engagement party was over, and the wedding was past, and she had nothing to distract her from wondering where Lottie was.

"She wasn't inside her house when I set that fire," Deborah said softly. She could not have been, she thought. Else she would have come screaming out the door. She would have chased me down the block and beat me to a pulp and even when I accused her of sleeping with my husband for thirty years, she would have laughed in my face and told me I didn't make him happy, and she did. "Wouldn't you, Lottie?" she whispered.

But if Lottie was in the house, then what the hell happened to her? Deborah clung to the thought that Lottie had gone out … but then why the hell hadn't she come back? It was certainly a mystery Deborah had a sinking feeling about. She knew Lottie told her everything, well, at least almost everything. If Lottie were planning to disappear, then Deborah would have known about it.

There are just some things you can't do to your friends, things that are worse than betrayal. You can't disappear on your friends. You can't leave an empty hole, a frigging ache where there was once laughter and confidences. You can't feel alone when you have a friend. "You fucking left me alone," Deborah whispered. "Oh, I hate you for that, Lottie. I hate you for that."

Big tears ran down her face leaving mascara lanes on her cheeks, assailed by the emptiness, the physical absence Lottie had left her with. She called for Heaven to bring her a vodka tonic. She knew what Heaven would think, of course. Her mistress was becoming a drunk, one of those sad drunks who kept dredging up the past, letting her tears mingle with the alcohol, telling old, tired stories, scattered memories of what once was. She'd always hated drunks like that.

She'd had three vodka tonics by the time she saw Dickie heading across the lawn. She hadn't expected him. She didn't want to be caught crying about Lottie. They didn't speak about Lottie. She didn't want to admit it, but Lottie was a wound, an absence she couldn't fill, furious to be left with the pain of loss, furious at Lottie.

"Deborah?" Dickie whispered as he crept up to her. "Deborah, is everything all right?"

She would lie to him, tell him she had just finished a sad book, but she was too drunk to lie. She was too drunk for defenses.

She looked into his eyes. "Leah told me Lottie was supposed to be moving to Richmond. She told me the day I visited her that Lottie was moving to Richmond. Did they look for Lottie in Richmond, Dickie?"

Dickie nodded. "They're still looking for her in Richmond, but they haven't found her there," Dickie said softly as he knelt before her.

Unexpectedly Deborah reached out her fists and pounded Dickie on the chest, "She was my friend, Dickie. She was my friend, you had no right to her."

"I'm sorry," Dickie whispered and grabbed her hands. He held them down in her lap.

"I miss my friend," Deborah wailed, a sorrowful sob.

Clearly surprised, Dickie took her hands to his lips. "Lottie?" he asked, and tears sprang from somewhere deep inside her. He reached out and held her tightly. His tears mingled with hers.

"Oh, Deborah," he whispered. "I needed you to mourn her. I needed it so much." He kissed her hair and stroked her cheeks and her shoulders. He kissed her deeply on the mouth.

Deborah picked her head up sharply. "You think she's dead? You don't think she just started a new life somewhere?"

Dickie shook his head. "We need to accept it," he said. "Lottie is gone."

When Heaven brought Dickie's vodka tonic to the porch, she found them both crying, holding hands, and crying.

Suddenly Deborah sat up straight in her chair. "No, Dickie. No. No. She isn't dead," her eyes red and her mascara dripping. "She isn't. She's going to come back to us. She is. I swear it. I feel it so strongly."

Dickie held her tighter and wept more loudly.

Chapter Fourteen

Both young women, profoundly serious, very studious, tipped their heads this way and then that way at a nude portrait by Lucian Freud, and then Robbie felt Pam's hand across her ass, and she giggled.

Robbie turned to her. "Really, you're going to seduce me in the British Museum?"

"I don't have to seduce you anymore, you're mine now." Pam let her hand wander just a bit lower.

Robbie smiled at her. She knew that was the truth. Pam had withdrawn fifteen hundred dollars from her mother's checking account, secured a ticket to Heathrow Airport and come knocking on Robbie's door at the Sherlock Holmes Hotel so she could push her way inside, throw Robbie on the bed and run her hands through Robbie's hair, down her legs and in between until the panting and screams of delight left them too exhausted for dinner.

Robbie smiled, remembering the pleasure. "Glad

you came?"

"Is that a double entendre?"

"It's whatever you think it is."

Robbie dragged her toward the Egyptian Sculpture Gallery. "C'mon, I want to see the Rosetta Stone."

"Oh, no," Pam cried. "That's miles away. Don't make me sorry I got a passport."

Robbie stopped and squeezed her hand. "You didn't have a passport?"

"What would I have a passport for? Anyway, I have one now, just in case you want to whisk me off to Africa."

"Not a bad idea," Robbie laughed as she said it.

"I'm sorry, I can only stay five days."

"Yes, I know, your soccer game."

Pam shrugged. "The girls would kill me if I didn't show."

Robbie grabbed her hand and squeezed it. "C'mon, I want to walk around Bloomsbury. We can come back here."

"What about the Rosetta Stone?"

"We'll be back," Robbie said as she hunted for the exit.

"Well, considering you've walked me all around this museum for the last few hours, what's another few miles?"

Robbie pulled her through the crowds, and they finally found the exit. It was cool for a London summer and they both wore tight jeans, leather jackets and scarves around their necks, tied the European way, needless to say. Robbie was already fantasizing about living in London, in some glorious flat near

Shoreditch, a dead certainty Pam would room with her, pursue her passion for the stage, and they'd sip tea at four and learn how to drive on the left side of the road, and Robbie would set up her easel around Leicester Square.

"We need to live here," she said, still holding Pam's hand.

"Before or after you tell Mindy you've reunited with the love of your life and you're never going back to her?" Pam stopped walking and turned Robbie to her. "I mean it, Robbie, tell that bitch to lie under a truck."

Robbie smiled. Mindy, of course, knew nothing about the passion that had flared up again between her and Pam. Unless, quite reasonably, she'd assumed it that day at Pam's door. This time with Pam, though, it was more intense, maybe because they were older, connected in a way she couldn't ever be with Mindy. She and Mindy weren't kindred spirits, the way Pam was. Pam made her weak in the knees. Pam didn't even have to touch her to take her to that place of no return: she only had to stand in front of her with that lidded look when she was about to let go and it would be over for Robbie, any chance of having a sense of the world around her would be long gone.

"I'll have to tell her," Robbie said.

"Well, for God's sake, wait until you get back to Pickens. I don't want any hysterical Southern belles showing up in London to toss my sweet behind from The Shard to the ground below."

"We should go see The Shard ... I think it's taller than the World Trade Center."

"Where thou goest, go I, or something like that."

"What about when I goest to New York?" Robbie asked.

"Take me with you," Pam said with a wink. "I've heard so much about New York. The place to be if you're in the theater, of course. I aimed to go to LA, but I could be swayed East."

Robbie looked at her sadly. Pam was kidding. "Oh well, we'll write and call, and I'll see you on holidays. This time I won't let you dump me."

"Do you have to go? Can't you transfer to a South Carolina college?"

"Sure," Robbie said, "like I'm really going to get the same exposure to art that I would in New York City, Pam. Really, New York City? I count my blessings."

"I guess you're right," Pam said.

Robbie shrugged. "We'll work it out," she said.

Pam turned to walk backwards in front of her. "Look, Robbie. I still have my father's inheritance. It's enough for me to get an apartment in Manhattan, and it will tie me over until I get a job."

Robbie grabbed her by the shoulders and stopped walking. "Your mother will kill you," she said.

"It's not my mother's money, it's mine."

"What about soccer?" Robbie grinned.

"I'll play in Central Park, right?"

"Wow," Robbie said, taking her hand. "Really?" She kissed her right there in the middle of the crowded street. Then they ran for a bench in Queen Square park and sat. "When will you come?" Robbie asked. "I mean if you're serious about this."

"Soon," Pam said. "I'll give you some time to find us an apartment and then I'll come. Oh, my God, we'll live in Greenwich Village. That's the best place in the world to live, Robbie."

"What about college, don't you have another year?"

"I'll transfer. NYU has the best theater department, right? I'm sure they'll accept me."

"Wow, the two of us in New York. Wow."

Robbie turned her face to Pam and kissed her again. Unbelievable … the two of them with a life together in New York.

"You're mine, now," Pam whispered.

Robbie kissed her again. "I always have been."

Chapter Fifteen

Deborah reclined on the porch, thinking about how nice it was to have Dickie sleeping beside her again. She'd missed the way his hands would find her arms in the morning, the touch of those hands, those fingers on her skin were always so soft. They'd usually lie like that, entwined, she on her back and he on his stomach. If it were a morning after a slow, cozy, fornicating, lovemaking evening, Dickie would spend extra time caressing her all over before he'd let her out of bed. That morning he'd even kissed her with his stinky breath. She didn't mind, she knew he couldn't really stay away from her. She wanted him back with all his flaws, stinky breath being the least of them.

She didn't understand his attraction to Lottie. Personally, Deborah always thought Lottie was inferior in the looks department. Well, she did have a big personality, but Dickie was into aesthetics, into women other men harbored desires for.

Deborah was beautiful, and had no illusions about men when they looked at her. Not a one of them cared whether she could bake a cake or solve the diameter of an isosceles triangle. They only cared about the fantasies they hid behind their smiles, those pornographic yearnings that included a bare-assed Deborah on her back, or on her knees or her belly, whatever; men's fantasies were so simple. Ha! dream on you foolish men, my Dickie is the only man between my legs from now and forever. But then, she thought of Jeremiah and wondered if she'd make an exception for a man she'd had a history with, one to whom sex was a superior ability.

Oh well, she quickly put Jeremiah out of her mind. She put Lottie out of her mind as well, especially when it came to Dickie. She separated the friend, Lottie, and the Lottie who'd betrayed her. She knew she was crazy, wild with anger, that day she set fire to Lottie's house, but she didn't kill her. God, there was no body. She didn't kill anyone. She breathed a sigh of relief. The good Lord was smiling on her, she might have killed Lottie, but Lottie wasn't there, so she obviously didn't kill her. But if Lottie showed up in front of her that very moment, she'd throw herself on the ground at Lottie's feet and beg forgiveness. Without doubt, Lottie would do the same and then they could continue being best friends. She wouldn't let Dickie destroy that friendship, she just wouldn't. Besides, Dickie loved her, not Lottie. Lottie was just a big ole barrel of laughs. She was sure that had been the attraction, Lottie's gift for gab.

Deborah looked out over the grounds and watched

as Hector walked toward her, finally coming upon the porch steps but stopping just below. Deborah smiled at him. He must have just finished planting those new lilac bushes out by the driveway.

"Good morning, Hector," she said and grinned wider. "I suspect you'll want a glass of something cold. You're sweating like the dickens."

He handed her his invoice and bowed his head a bit. "I had to use funds from next month," he said and hunched up his shoulders. "That was a big job. Expensive job."

"The lilac bushes?" she asked.

Hector shook his head. "No, no, the whole garden at Mrs. Tilly's. I couldn't save a lot of it. Had to replace some bushes and flowers, cost more than I thought it would, took me five days to get it right."

Deborah raised an eyebrow. "Whatever are you talking about? What does Mrs. Tilly's garden have to do with my garden?"

Hector took a step back and gave her a look of surprise. "You told me to repair it all, someone had ripped everything out. Someone did real damage there, tore it all up by the roots, couldn't save it, saved what I could but couldn't save it all. It was a shame. It had been the prettiest garden in Pickens. Next to this one," he quickly added.

Deborah looked at him as if he had three heads. "I didn't tell you to fix that woman's garden. Why would I tell you that?"

"Miss Robinette, she told me you'd approve it, you and Mrs. Tilly being best friends and all. I thought you told her to tell me." Hector's eyebrows came together, and he looked nervous.

"Robinette told you to replant Marlene Tilly's garden? I barely know that woman, Hector."

Deborah stood to her feet and called him back as he started back down the steps.

"I will not pay for Marlene Tilly's garden, Hector, and I will not pay you for your time there. We'll have to wait for Robinette to explain herself when she gets back from Europe. In the meantime, you'll have to eat that cost somehow because I won't pay for it."

Chapter Sixteen

Dickie had been sitting in Lottie's backyard for over two hours. He'd found an old chair in her garage and brought it out to the center of her half-acre lot. Under a white Ash tree, he remembered how proud Lottie had been of that tree. She'd planted it herself about twenty years ago and now it was full and shaded, the only perfect thing left in what was once resplendent and precious because Lottie had loved it. She had nurtured her gardens, spent hours rearranging the backyard patio with potted plants, sweet little white wicker chairs with the prettiest flowered cushions, making everything without flaw. The backyard had reflected how she felt about color and design. Now the damn police had dug the whole thing up, heaps of dirt every which way. He planned to tell Leighton that the police should replace what they had destroyed. Lottie still owned the house; they didn't know she wasn't coming back. He felt so sad sitting there staring at everything she had loved. The yard she was so proud of looked like a war zone now.

He let out a long low sigh. He was so despondent. He was back where he belonged, though, back to holding Deborah's hand, taking up half the space in bed and letting everyone think they were so delightful, so perfect a couple. Dickie didn't really know if he loved Deborah or he was just used to her, she was so conniving and opinionated, but the other day when she'd been grieving over Lottie, he'd felt a kinship with her. He wanted her close to him. He wanted to crawl up inside her and feel that grief, maybe so he wouldn't have to endure his own. Well, he was alive, and Lottie wasn't. He would never stop missing her, but he was in the here and now with Deborah. He had to bounce back and take up where he had left off — as Deborah's husband. She loved him to death, he knew that. He had to go on.

He picked up the chair and took it back into the garage. The house looked fire-damaged but repairable. Lottie had been insured and could restore the house if she were living. She could move back in, and he could meet her there as before, as he had been doing for so many years. But the thought hit him hard: she wasn't coming back to restore her house. Her house would probably go to some distant relative, maybe even her cousin, Sean. Maybe Leighton and Sean would marry and move into Lottie's house so that every time Dickie walked by, he'd know the love was back in those charred walls. It would be a happy house once again. He turned his back and walked away, the house so sorry looking now; it was in pain. He was in pain. He felt like the house, so forlorn and lost and empty.

The minute Deborah spotted him walking up the drive, she got to her feet and put her hands on her hips. That was his Deborah, never a moment devoid of drama, Dickie thought.

"You will not believe this, Dickie. Go get the car, we have to drive over to Marlene Tilly's house."

"What won't I believe?"

"Marlene's garden was all tore up and our daughter had Hector fix it."

"What's wrong with that?"

"At our expense?" She almost screamed it, her eyes all pinched in, and her face getting that stayed too long in the sun look.

"Robinette volunteered Hector to fix it?"

"No, not volunteered, apparently, she was going to get me to pay for it, thought I wouldn't notice, I imagine. She knows me better than that. Nothing gets past me, Dickie."

Dickie smiled to himself. No, nothing but my thirty-year affair with your best friend.

Dickie pulled up behind Pam's little Kawasaki. "You know, Marlene moved to Columbia? I'm sure she doesn't know anything about this."

"Her daughter is staying here until she sells the house, isn't she?"

"Well, I'm quite sure that's Pam's motorcycle. She must be home," Dickie said.

"Then I have to take this up with Pam." She gave

Dickie a stern look. "The little witch."

They walked up to the front door and rang the bell. Dickie looked around. "She's not answering. Might be the girl is out, someone might have picked her up."

But just as they were about to leave a young man came to the door. "Can I help you?" he asked politely.

"We're looking for Pam," Deborah said.

"She's in the back," the young man said and went back inside.

As they walked around to the back, they heard music playing. They were surprised to find Pam on her knees planting tall phlox. She looked up as they approached.

"Mr. and Mrs. Darling, how are you?" She turned to them and smiled, wiping the sweat from her brow.

"I see Hector did a fine job," Deborah said sarcastically, and looked around.

"Oh, yes, thank you so much. I'm sure my mother will be pleased. These gardens will sell the house," she said and rose to her feet. She removed her garden gloves and continued to smile at them. "I think it even looks better now, even though it doesn't have as many flowers."

"Pamela, I will not pay for Hector's work here, whatever he spent on the flowers and his time here is your responsibility." Deborah walked up close to Pam. "Whatever gave you the idea that I would pay for your garden?"

Pam looked as if she were about to cry. "Robbie told me he'd do it for me and wouldn't charge me a dime."

"Robbie said that?" Dickie asked. "Doesn't sound

like our daughter, she's more responsible than that. She'd ask our permission first."

"Well, her girlfriend tore up my garden. She felt responsible for that." Pam put her hands on her hips and stared at Dickie.

"What are you talking about? What girlfriend?" Dickie asked.

"Mindy Peach."

Dickie looked at his wife. "Most unusual," he said. "I doubt if Mindy would tear up anybody's garden," he said. "She's a nice young woman, why would she do something like that?"

"Mindy got even madder when she found out I was joining Robbie in Europe, that's why. She's got a terrible temper. I have to hope she won't come back here and tear this garden up, too."

Deborah looked even more confused. "You were in Europe with my daughter?"

"Just England. I had to come back after five days. My soccer team was playing Asheland, and I promised the girls."

Just as Deborah was about to tell her that none of it mattered because she was responsible for the cost, the young man who had answered the front door came out with a pitcher of lemonade.

"Oh, this is Boyd. These are the Darlings," she said to him.

Boyd said hello and then went back to helping Pam plant the phlox.

"You will have to pay for your own garden," Deborah said. "Do you understand?"

Pam laughed. "I think you'll have to take that up with my mother. I don't have the money for something like that."

"Do you have your mother's phone number in Columbia?" Deborah asked.

"I'll write it down for you."

Deborah and Dickie waited for Pam to return with the phone number while her friend Boyd sang along to the radio and ignored them as he covered the roots of the tall phlox with dirt.

"Do you believe what she said about Mindy?" Deborah said as she slid in the passenger seat of the Cadillac. "Mindy wouldn't do that," she said. "I mean she's a cheap little thing, but she's not a criminal. What possible reason could she have for doing something like that?"

"I can't imagine," Dickie said, thinking that Pam might be blackmailing his daughter the way she had tried to blackmail him. Maybe it's about being gay, he thought.

Chapter Seventeen

Mart walked through the screen door and into Leighton's kitchen carrying a six-pack of beer and a large bag of potato chips. Leighton reached out for the six-pack and Mart put the chips on the counter. He reached for a bowl off a shelf and filled it with the chips. He held the bowl out to Leighton, and she helped herself to a handful.

It was such a comfortable relationship with Mart; she'd known him for so long now. They'd been partners going on five years. Leighton had known his wife before she died of cancer and she and Beau had been there for him, and then when Beau died, he'd been there for her.

"Thanks, Mart'" she said putting the beer on ice. "I've made a chili."

Mart smiled, "with meat, I hope."

"Yeah, I'm off the vegetarian thing for now but I'd love to try and stick with it. It's healthier."

Mart grinned. "I'll give it a try."

"Yuk, fish chili?" Leighton made a face.

"No, fish stew," he said.

"Oh, that sounds doable. Unfortunately, I prefer *beef* stew."

Mart laughed as he flipped off the bottle cap from his Budweiser. "You'll never change, Leighton."

It was pouring outside, rain coming down so loud it pinged against the roof so their usual place to recline out on the deck was off limits, sure to disappoint Aspen because Mart always threw things for him to catch, his rope toy and his rubber fire hydrant. Reluctantly the dog followed behind Mart when he took his beer into the sunroom, still wagging his tail and hoping for a reemergence of that bright yellow ball in the sky.

Aspen found a comfortable place on the rug near Mart's feet and promptly went to sleep. They were almost like a couple, Leighton, and Mart, but not quite, there was no romance between them, but every now and then, Leighton had to admit to an attraction, but it was something she would never act on. She was sure Mart thought of her as a mother figure, not the most romantic of ways to be considered. Well, they were two years apart in age, she being the oldest. However, if they were an item, those two years wouldn't matter, especially since Mart looked at least fifty with his full head of prematurely grey hair. They spent a lot of time together, as if they were a solid duo but the notion of anything romantic between them would have made them both laugh themselves silly and deny that they could ever be anything other than friends.

"Let's let the chili cool a bit," Leighton said as she sat opposite him on the couch. "How was your date?" she asked.

"I like her," Mart said as he reached over and grabbed a few chips out of the bowl Leighton had placed in front of him. "I mean, she's nice."

"Great," Leighton said. "Pretty?"

"Yeah, I guess so."

Leighton laughed. "Well, I'd think you wouldn't have to guess about a thing like that."

"I'm going to see her again next weekend."

"Where are you taking her?"

Mart hunched up his shoulders. "Don't know."

"There's a country bar serves great burgers and plays cool music just over in Marietta. You can even line dance after dinner. It's great fun."

"I was thinking maybe a movie and dinner at The River House."

"Sweet, that'll work."

"Tom Hart is investigating the Rabbit Trail murders. I like the guy, he's so relaxed, great sense of humor. I hear he's moving over to Pickens."

"Rabbit Trail murders?" she asked. "I haven't heard anything about that."

"You will. I think they want you on the case. It's cold. Two or more of the bodies been up there a few years."

Leighton sat back in her chair and put her feet up. "So, Tom Hart is relaxed?" She found that amusing. "I haven't officially met him, but I hear he's unconventional. I haven't yet heard that he's relaxed, though."

"Yeah, I know, whatever that means," Mart said.

"He's handsome." He looked at her and grinned. "Divorced," he added.

"Are you trying to fix me up, Mart?"

"Me?" He put his hands on his chest and raised his eyes innocently. "Oh, no, ma'am, I am not." His grin became wider.

"Best not be." Leighton gave him a toothless smirk.

Mart took a long sip of his beer. "He mentioned the other day that there was a shortage of single women in our town, so I guess he'd like to meet someone."

"Well, then, I hope he does."

Mart sat forward and scrutinized her for a few moments. "Well, you'll be pleased to know that I couldn't find any restraining orders against Sean Dowd." He wore a frown, and his lips were in an odd position.

"Then why aren't you smiling?"

"Not sure."

Leighton raised an eyebrow. "Then the girl is spreading lies about him, making people think he's a wife beater."

Mart nodded his head. "Could be."

Leighton tried to understand. She couldn't figure out why Pam Tilly would lie about something like that. She'd asked Mart to investigate Sean, she didn't want to be the one to dig up any dirt on him, but apparently there hadn't been any dirt to dig up.

"You want me to question the girl?" Mart asked.

"No, this is my call. I need to get a reading on Pamela Tilly, an unofficial inquiry."

"Well, there was something else."

Leighton looked up quickly.

"The girl's mother filed a police report a year or so ago, said Dowd was inappropriate with her daughter. The daughter was still a teenager at the time, and he was her mother's boyfriend."

"I know about that ... I just didn't know the mother had actually filed a report. Anything come of it?"

"No, she withdrew the charges, so they were officially dropped. Pam's mother broke up with him. My guess is she believed her daughter was being seduced by this guy. Anyway, he moved back to Greenville. Nothing else on him. No more police reports of inappropriate sexual behavior."

"How does he know Dickie?"

"I'd guess through Lottie."

"If the girl is lying, then she's really trying to kill his reputation."

"What she's accusing him of could be true." He looked at her stoically. "I mean, we don't know."

"Then you don't think she's lying?"

"Why would she?"

"Don't know, maybe she liked him in an inappropriate way, he rebuffed her, and she got back at him by telling her mother he was coming on to her. Maybe she was angry at her mother about something."

"How serious are you with this guy?"

"You think he's a perv, don't you?"

Mart shook his head. "I don't know, Leighton, I'm just thinking of you. I don't want you to fall for a perv, okay? Just in case he is."

Leighton laughed and took his hand. "Got it, Mart, and thank you."

"There's something else you should know."

121

Leighton lifted her eyes to his. "Yeah?"

"Pam Tilly also went to the police about a kid she went to school with, a Boyd Baxter, said he tried to rape her. Her mother dragged her down to the police station on that one, too."

"Really?"

"Yeah, but the kid's father gave him an alibi, said they were off camping together, so he wasn't even with Pam that night."

Leighton pulled her lips in and put her head back. Why was the girl lying? If she was lying. "Maybe that's how she gets back at the male sex for not finding her attractive, she accuses them of rape."

"Well, speaking as someone of the male sex, not finding Pam Tilly attractive is a long shot."

"I guess," Leighton said.

"Oh, by the way, those impressions of the tire tracks on Lottie Lacock's lawn?" Mart leaned toward her.

"Yes?"

"They're from a Mercedes S class. Mercedes Original Silent they're called."

Leighton stared at Mart, trying to figure out what he was talking about.

"What's that mean exactly?"

"Well, the car could be a Mercedes luxury sedan. The tires used on that model are usually MOS."

"Do you know how many Mercedes there are in Pickens?"

"I'm not sure, mostly Fords in Pickens." Mart stared back at her. "You look strange. Why do you look like that?"

"Lillian Darling drives a 1993 Mercedes sedan,"

Leighton said. "I need to check her tires."

"Really? Well, that's interesting." Mart sat back and took another long swig of his beer. "Killer Lilly?" he said with a broad grin and Leighton joined him in a boisterous laugh.

Chapter Eighteen

Leighton pulled in behind the Mustang and the Kawasaki in Pam's driveway. She got to the door just as a young man was coming around the side of the house.

"She's in the back," the young man said. "I assume you're looking for Pam?"

"Who are you?" Leighton asked.

"Who are you?" he said.

Leighton smiled. "Police." She took out her badge and showed it to him.

Startled, as if a bear had crossed his path, the boy regained his composure. "What do you want with Pam?"

"Just want to ask her a few questions. Now, who are you?"

"Her boyfriend."

Leighton laughed. "Your name?"

"Oh, Boyd Baxter."

She recognized the name right away and wondered why Pam would hang out with someone she'd accused of raping her. It didn't make any sense.

"Okay, thank you, Boyd Baxter." Leighton walked to the back of the house after watching Boyd drive off. She found Pam on a lounge chair soaking in the sun. The music from her radio was loud.

"Pamela Tilly?" Leighton yelled out.

Pam jumped up. "Oh, my God, you scared me."

"Can you turn down the music?"

Pam reached over and turned off the radio. She sat up and stared at Leighton. Leighton held out her hand. "Leighton McArdle," she said. "Special Investigator's Unit."

"Did Deborah Darling send you?"

Leighton was clearly surprised. "No, why would she?"

"She thinks I owe her money for this garden. I don't. Robbie Darling promised me her mother would pay for it. I don't owe her a damn thing."

"Well, I'm not here about that. I'm here to ask you a few questions about Sean Dowd."

"Oh." Pam's face changed, like a rain cloud caressing a perfect sky, darkening the sheer pleasure of what it once was. "Why?"

"Well, you accused him of inappropriate behavior."

"Yeah, so?"

"You want to tell me about it?"

"He came on to me. What more is there to tell? This was a while ago. Why are you rehashing this now?"

"Did he attempt to rape you?"

Pam laughed. "What do you think, he was trying to dance with me?"

Leighton smiled, despite herself. "Could you have misinterpreted his actions?"

Pam glared at her. "I highly doubt it."

Leighton dragged over a white plastic chair and sat in front of Pam

"Well, do you think you might have misinterpreted his actions?" Leighton repeated.

Pamela moved close to her. "Well, you tell me, Detective, what you would think of a man who stood before you stark naked and winked?"

Leighton was shocked. She couldn't imagine Sean exposing himself like that. "How did you get away from him?" she asked quickly.

"I ran."

"Well, what happened?"

"He didn't catch me. I ran into my room and turned the lock. He didn't stop coming after me, though."

"You mean he didn't stop his inappropriate behavior?"

"No, he didn't. And my mother thought he was the living end. He was an awful man. I had to let my mom know, eventually. I mean, he kept flirting and trying to touch me."

"Do you think you might have misinterpreted his actions?"

Pam looked at her as if she had three heads, "are you for real?" and laughed.

Leighton felt sick to her stomach. "You told the police what you told me?"

"I sure did. My mother made me tell them."

"What did the police do?"

"They questioned him and let him go. He told them I was the one lying, that I'd stood in front of him naked, but he never stood in front of me naked. Wow. It was a real 'he said, she said.'" She stared into Leighton's eyes. "That man was my social studies teacher in tenth grade," she said. "Can you believe it?"

"Did the incident happen in your mother's home?" Leighton asked.

"Yes, most of the incidents happened in our home." Pam had emphasized the "s" on incidents. "I used to catch him staring at me like I was lunch. My mom would go right on talking and not seem to notice."

"More than one incident?"

"Yes, several more. Is that all?"

Leighton sat back. "Did you ever have sex with him?" she asked slowly.

Pam gave her an odd look. "Surely not."

"I realize he was your mother's boyfriend, but he's a handsome man. The young girls in his class must all have crushes on him."

"Not all the girls." She glared at Leighton. "Listen, I'm gay. I'd have no interest in sleeping with him."

"I just saw your boyfriend leaving," Leighton said. "I didn't think lesbians had boyfriends."

"My boyfriend?"

"That's what he told me."

"We are platonic friends. He rewrites reality to suit his purposes. I don't like Boyd that way any more than I liked Sean Dowd that way. Any more than Boyd likes me that way. Get it? We tell people we're boyfriend and girlfriend. It's kind of a joke."

"I see," Leighton said. "Bit of a strange joke considering you accused Boyd of attempted rape."

"I mean, what am I supposed to do to get rid of men that come on to me, shoot them?"

"Don't own a gun, do you?" Leighton smiled: Pam had avoided her accusation against Boyd.

Pam did not see the humor in Leighton's question and glared at her. "Are you done?"

"Tell me, why would you be hanging out with Boyd … didn't he try to rape you in high school?" Leighton went back to it, sure the girl was hiding something.

Pam was speechless for a moment. "I lied about that," she said.

"Hmm," Leighton said. "So, you could be lying about Sean?"

"I'm not lying about Sean. Are we done?"

"For the moment."

Pam lay down, dismissing Leighton, and turned the radio back on.

Leighton drove home not knowing what to believe. Pam had lied about Boyd, must have been angry with him about something, but accusing him of rape was detestable. Leighton wasn't sure at all if Pam was telling the truth about anything, so it was unlikely she was telling the truth about Sean. Leighton leaned to believing Sean; if he said he didn't come on to the girl, then he didn't.

Chapter Nineteen

Lottie was stunned; the grand opening for the bed-and-breakfast was the following weekend and Cottonwoods was booked solid. Most of the guests had requested dinner, and because it was Labor Day weekend, she knew Marlene would be busy whipping up her gourmet delights; walnut banana pancakes for breakfast, for instance. Of course, for those who wanted simple eggs, they could get poached or scrambled eggs with Marlene's homemade cinnamon raisin buns.

It seemed so perfect. They would offer tea sandwiches for lunch, along with a Waldorf salad. Lottie asked Marlene to make beef a l'orange on Saturday night, and a duck breast with plum, raspberries, and strawberries on Sunday. Friday night, there would be a light dinner of Chicken Florentine and for those non-meat eaters, there was a hearty bowtie pasta with a sage butter sauce, or seared salmon with a pepper crust. On Labor Day itself, Marlene had come up with a Rosy the Riveter cake to serve at teatime.

Lottie was beside herself; she was also a nervous wreck. What if her guests did not like their room? What if the air conditioning broke down or the bathrooms had leaks? The construction workers had worked overtime to finish the bathrooms in time for the opening, but what if they had done a faulty job because she had rushed them? She would be able to tell if her guests were unhappy, and would bend over backwards to please them. She wanted to be the best proprietor in the whole damn south. Then she worried that she'd become notorious, and word would get back to Pickens and that dreadful Lillian Darling would crucify her. Then she told herself she was being silly and was able to relax, at least for a moment or two.

She'd advertised in a travel magazine she'd come upon while getting her hair done. The guests were all from Georgia, which she found amusing. They seemed to know one another and must be traveling together, for the group took all seven rooms, except for hers, of course, tiny and end of the hall but quite charming. She'd had a photographer come to the inn and take photographs she could use for advertising, and she had to admit that the Queen of England would have wanted to come to Cottonwoods; the pictures were beautiful. She was able to afford a half-page ad that showed a photo of the sitting room, one of the guest rooms and the patio. You just wanted to walk into that photograph and start enjoying yourself.

Lottie was thrilled with what she had done with the

backyard. She and Marlene had designed it together, choosing the white wicker lawn furniture and the colorful flowers that sprouted up everywhere, the lush orange and pink azalea shrubs were Lottie's favorite and Marlene was crazy for the weigela shrubs that lined the walkways. They had put in a bar, and piped in music for the evenings, gentle jazz as Lottie called it. Who wouldn't like that?

The long mahogany bar was under a pergola where mixed drinks would be served, and their wine list was carefully selected with a fine mix of reds and whites. Lottie had hired two people to work the bar for the weekend, and they promised to make themselves available to her when she needed them at any time of the year. It was all over town that Cottonwoods was rumored to become the hottest spot in town. People made reservations at the restaurant weeks in advance even though they weren't staying in the guest rooms. Cottonwoods had gotten into a local newspaper in the Where to Dine section for the opening weekend, and reviewed the following week.

Lottie's heart beat rapidly as she sat out on the porch, she was so excited, anticipating the weekend. She wasn't prepared for Marlene's dramatic entrance, as if she'd just had an encounter with a hurricane, shattering the peaceful afternoon breeze.

"For goodness' sake, Marlene, what is with you? You scared me to death."

"You will not believe this … I am so furious I could spit."

"Well, please don't spit on the porch, one of the guests might slip on it."

"We're not expecting anyone until Friday."

Marlene scowled at her. "Plenty of time to wash the floor."

"Like I said, what's with you?"

"You're not going to believe this."

"You said that."

"I just got off the phone with Deborah Darling."

Lottie was so shocked she didn't hear a thing Marlene said for several seconds. Finally, her heart hammering, she asked, "You didn't mention me, did you?"

Marlene was startled for a moment. "No, you two have a falling out?"

"Marlene, I'd really prefer you not mention me to Deborah. I don't want her to know where I am just yet."

"Yeah, sure."

"Now, what happened?" Lottie asked, still somewhat apprehensive, but Marlene had never been friendly with Deborah, so she had nothing to worry about; they didn't talk to each other, had never been more than acquaintances.

"I told you," Marlene said. Someone ripped up my garden and my daughter had Deborah pay for it somehow."

"Lottie scratched her head. "How'd she do that?"

"Who knows? Anyway, Deborah won't pay for it, so it looks like my next commission check is going to Deborah. Though I probably should refuse to pay her. I should take it out of my daughter's hide, have her work it off and pay Deborah back herself."

"Who'd rip out your garden?"

Marlene shrugged her shoulders. "Who the hell knows?"

"God," Lottie said, "that's a hell of a thing to do to someone."

Lottie was so busy having the guests sign the guest book as they registered that she didn't notice until the following evening that all the guests were men. She and Marlene relaxed in the backyard after their sumptuous dinner on Saturday, stretched out their legs and treated themselves to a Margarita. The meals had been extraordinarily successful, and the dining room had been filled with conversation and bursts of laughter. Lottie stared around her.

"Well, looks like the boys are having a good time."

"Where did you advertise, Lottie?"

"Gay Travel."

Marlene sprang up, as if a fire had been lit under her. "Oh, my God, that's why we have a backyard full of homosexuals."

"Oh, so what," Lottie said. "Their money is good."

"How could you?"

Lottie glared at her. "Well, I thought it meant happy travel, fun travel, not homosexual travel."

Marlene sighed deeply and sat back. After at least five minutes, Lottie heard her laugh. "Well, I have never seen so many pretty men in one place in my life. So aesthetically, it's very pleasing, having them here." She turned to Lottie. "They're fun too, aren't they? I never heard men have so much fun together, carrying on the way they do."

Lottie sat back and closed her eyes. She wondered why she hadn't put it together, the meaning of the word 'gay' as homosexual. She got it now, though. No wonder they're called 'gay' – they give new meaning to the words 'a good time.'

Just then, a man walked up to them and introduced himself as John. He sat on the edge of Lottie's chaise. "I have never liked beef a l'orange before in my life, but my, yours was so good that I just salivate thinking of it. And that breakfast you girls served was to die for. I'll never be able to eat a pancake anywhere else but here. I'm going to tell all my friends about Cottonwoods."

The young man smiled. His good looks were striking, his hair was almost black but not quite, his eyes changed color, sometimes nearly blue but then mostly green, like Caribbean waters, his eyelashes long as feather dusters. "You two make a delightful couple," he said.

Marlene and Lottie looked at each other and raised their eyebrows.

"See that handsome older man over there?" John asked with a broad smile. "That's Peter, my better half. Isn't he dashing?" He giggled as he got to his feet. "I like older people."

The two women gave him a friendly grin. He reached out his hand and squeezed Lottie's arm. "Honey, I am going to keep you in business. This is the most delightful inn I've ever been to." He bent down and kissed Lottie's cheek. "I shall spread the word."

They watched him walk over to Peter and grab him around the waist. Lottie heard Marlene laugh and turned to her. "What's so funny?" she asked.

"He thinks you and I are an item," she said.

"I'm sure they all think that."

"Bother you?"

"Nope."

"It bothers me. I am against homosexuality. It's so wrong. I really don't want anyone thinking I belong to that clan. I mean, I can appreciate these men, but they do go against nature."

Lottie turned to her. She had a feeling that Marlene's daughter was gay; she'd seen her at The Red Lady with some girl hanging all over her. She stared at Marlene for a moment. She didn't want to be rude, but she found Marlene's comment distasteful.

"Forgive my boldness, I'm going to say something very delicate …

"You're going to ask me if my daughter is gay aren't you?"

Lottie nodded.

Marlene looked at her seriously. "Who knows what she is? Though she did have an affair with Dickie Darling's daughter a few years ago … but that doesn't define her, does it? These kids today go through lots of changes before they wind up being who they're supposed to be. If my daughter doesn't give me grandchildren, I'll never forgive her, though."

That news about Robbie surprised Lottie, a bit of gossip she hadn't heard. "She had an affair with Robbie?"

Marlene nodded. "Yeah, Robbie was just a kid. The old lady told me, you know, Lilian Darling. She caught them in the act of being unnatural."

Lottie laughed. "Unnatural? That's a strong word to use about people acting absolutely naturally as far as they are concerned."

Marlene stared at her. "I see you're one of those

liberal people."

Lottie laughed. "You best be adopting my politics, Marlene, if you want your daughter to start confiding in you. Leopards don't change their spots."

Marlene gave a pout and sat back. "God made it so opposites attract."

"Well, I'm sure they do, just look at Deborah and I."

"Oh, my God, you two weren't … " She gulped and gaped at Lottie.

Lottie laughed. "Oh, stop staring at me. No, we weren't, but my point is that same-sex friends can be opposites and attract. What does that mean, that chemistry has to be between a man and a woman? Chemistry is hard to define and not limited to heterosexuals." She studied Marlene's prissy look. "Nothing wrong with being gay, you know?"

Marlene raised an eyebrow at Lottie. "Tell that to God."

"I don't speak to God," Lottie said.

Marlene smirked at Lottie. "How did I know you'd say something like that? Anyway, aside from having absolutely no sexual morals, she's also a thief, my daughter. Stole fifteen hundred dollars out of my bank account."

"If you allow her access to your bank account, then in my mind, you stole from yourself."

"I am just learning all new things about you, Lottie, most specifically, you make no sense. C'mon, Roxie," she called.

Roxie came running from across the yard where she had been accepting food from two men and beguiling them with her bag of tricks, laying down, sitting, and dancing on her hind legs. She stood before her mistress and snarled at her.

"Oh, my God, Roxie, stop snarling at me," Marlene said in disgust. "C'mon, we're going home."

The dog jumped up on Lottie's chaise and refused to budge. Lottie laughed. "Your little mutt has other plans." Roxie gave her mistress a mouth full of teeth and a low guttural growl.

Marlene sat with a disgusted grunt. "Goddamn dog runs my life," she said. "Stop growling at me, Roxie."

Chapter Twenty

Leighton spotted Lillian's Mercedes in the drive. It looked newly washed and polished; its teal blue body picked up reflections of tree branches that swayed in the mellow breeze and made a swishing sound, like musical notes, as they gently tapped the car. She bent down and stared at the tires. It was there, clear as day, MOS.

Leighton looked for the boy who drove Lillian around. She thought his name might be Ethan. He worked at Clemson University as a security guard and had been one of the waiters at Barney's wedding. She'd briefly spoken to him, and he'd told her that he lived near campus and did odd jobs for people. Then she noticed him walking toward her.

"You need some help?" he asked.

She took him in as she spoke, everyone was a suspect in Lottie's disappearance, and he had access to the car.

"I'm Lillian's granddaughter," she said. "Just here for a visit." She smiled politely, aware the young man was grinning at her as if she were a double scoop of chocolate ice cream. It was the way men grinned in bars when they were on the make for a woman. She almost laughed out loud; the kid couldn't be much more than twenty.

"I'm her driver," he said.

"Oh? Don't see you driving her anywhere." She gave him a mischievous grin.

He laughed. "Oh, you're a sassy one."

"Sometimes."

"I do odd jobs, too. She wants the fence painted, she calls me." He kept his eyes on Leighton and the grin in place. "And the roof repaired, the gutters cleaned, she calls me." His grin even wider. "I mow lawns, too."

"Do you know if you were driving her anywhere on the 30th of May?"

"Memorial Day weekend?"

Leighton nodded, a little uncomfortable at the way this kid kept leering at her.

"I was hanging out with my friends that weekend, Mrs. Darling didn't need me, said I should go play."

"Thank you, Ethan." Leighton walked toward the house when he called behind her.

"I never charge a pretty woman for mowing a lawn," he shouted.

She smiled to herself. The kid was a real Romeo. Lots of hair, including too much of it on his face, lots of muscles and lots of bullshit coming out of that mouth.

An attractive woman led Leighton into Lillian's

parlor, gave her a little polite curtsy, and told her that Mrs. Darling would be down shortly. Leighton remembered seeing the woman at Barnaby's wedding and remembered her name as Carla. She'd been very attentive to Lillian. Leighton recalled an introduction, surprised, because most people did not bother to introduce their help to anyone. But certainly, Lilian was not like just anyone. Still, the woman had curtsied, a show of respect Leighton did not welcome. Curtseying, to Leighton, was archaic, except in the theater.

Leighton surveyed the parlor; it was quite lovely and not at all old-fashioned. Like most people her age, she supposed the elderly lived in outdated musty spaces, usually overcrowded with art in ornate gold frames — dog portraits, ancient ancestors, and scenes of quiet rivers. Their couches thick with dizzying flower patterns facing wing chairs with antimacassars on the arms standing stoically, and old coasters painted with little bulldogs lying in wait.

Quite the contrary though, Lilian's parlor was sparce, light, and open. The fabric was all beige and white linen and the paintings on her walls were original Duchamp, O'Keefe, and Matisse, to name a few that Leighton recognized. When the truth come out about Dickie being her father, Lillian had consistently promised to invite her for lunch to discover everything about her new granddaughter, but up to that point, she hadn't yet extended the invitation. However, Leighton was quite sure that Lillian knew all there was to know about her.

Lillian entered the room and Leighton stood, a spontaneous reflex she did not have time to control, but it was proper to do so she supposed. Lillian walked right up to her and kissed her on the cheek.

"My dear, to what do I owe this delightful surprise? Sit. Sit."

Leighton sat quickly. "I'm afraid I'm here to ask you a few questions."

Taken aback, Lillian said, "Of course, my dear, what would you like to know?"

"Your cottage is quite lovely," Leighton said and added, "as nice as the big house."

"Thank you." Lillian sat forward in her chair and stared at Leighton. "I must say, though, Barnaby and Priss have made gracious improvements."

"Well, I'll get right to it," Leighton said. "We have impressions, tire tracks on Lottie's lawn from the day of the fire. We got them from her rear yard."

Lillian stared at her, as if waiting for her to say more. "What has that to do with me, my dear?" she asked after a moment.

"They're from MOS tires, usually found on a Mercedes sedan.'"

Lillian shook her head. "Well, I do own a Mercedes sedan but it was not my car. I was never on Lottie's rear lawn. I mean, why would I drive on her rear lawn?"

"Well, that was my question. Does anyone aside from you drive your car?"

"Well, Ethan does, he's my driver."

"Yes, I spoke to him outside. He said he was off that day. It was the 30th, Memorial Day weekend."

Lillian shrugged her shoulders. "Well, then I guess he was off."

"And you were nowhere close to Lottie Lacock's

house on the 30th?"

"Why would I be?"

"No reason, I suppose, but you don't recall what you did that day?"

"I didn't say that."

Leighton sat forward. "Then where were you?"

"My son and I had lunch together. He was here until about four. After he left, I took a nap. When I woke up, it was dark. I watched some television and fell asleep."

"Dickie will be able to verify the hours he was with you?"

"Of course."

"I do remember it was so hot that day. I must have taken a few naps myself." Leighton grinned at her.

"Would you like tea, my dear?"

Leighton shook her head. "I can't stay. Perhaps another time?"

"Yes, of course." Lillian gave her a somewhat condescending smile. "My dear, aren't there other Mercedes sedans in Pickens? I couldn't possibly have the only Mercedes in this town, could I?"

Leighton chuckled. "I'm afraid you do, Lillian."

"Most unusual. But it was not my Mercedes. That I can assure you."

Leighton nodded her head a few times. She knew she had nothing to go on. No reason to suspect Lillian Darling had driven her car on Lottie's lawn. And for what purpose? There was none. No reason to suspect that Deborah had set the fire just because she'd found out about her husband's long affair, no reason to suspect that Dickie had carted off the body and Lillian had driven it away. Ridiculous. No reason at all to think that. She must be way off track.

"Does anyone else drive your car, Lillian?" She knew she had asked that before but thought Lillian might remember someone if pushed.

Lillian's face was flawless as she raised her eyes and smiled. "As I said earlier, dear, just Ethan."

Leighton walked out to her car and surveyed the property. She wondered if Ethan could have driven off with Lillian's car without her knowing. If Lillian and Dickie had lunch in the dining room, they would not have seen the car leave the grounds because the dining room windows faced the back and were at the other end of the cottage. So, it was possible that Ethan could have driven off in Lillian's car, but why would he cart off Lottie's body? For that matter, why would he murder her, unless it was a rape, or a robbery? But nothing had been stolen.

Ethan came up beside her as if out of nowhere. "Lose something?" he asked.

Aware she had been looking around, it must have appeared that she was looking for something.

"An earring," she said. "I found it." She touched her earlobe and smiled.

He smiled back. "You look like her," he said.

"My grandmother?" she asked from the open window of her car. Ethan nodded, his grin so wide, Leighton wondered if his face hurt. "Thanks, I guess … she's over seventy, though."

"A pretty beautiful over seventy. You know she was a knockout at your age." Ethan put his elbow on the door. His face was too close to hers and she leaned back.

"And how would you know that? You don't look a

day over twenty."

He laughed and tapped the side of her car as he stood back. "Rumor," he said. "Known to be the most beautiful woman in the county once upon a time. Too bad we get old, huh?"

Leighton looked to the heavens and drove off. "God's revenge for our sins," she said into the rear-view mirror.

Chapter Twenty-One

Leighton walked into the station reluctantly; it was late in the day, and she would have preferred being on her back deck with a beer and her feet up on the railing, her mind as empty as her bank account two days before payday. Not so lucky, she'd been called to the station. Earlier, she'd questioned both Dickie and his mother about the 30th of May and they both gave each other alibis. Well, maybe it was the truth and they'd lunched together at the house, "in the dining room" they'd said. So, if Ethan happened to borrow the Mercedes, they would not necessarily have known. But she could not come up with any reason to suspect Ethan guilty of anything except being an overly flirtatious and somewhat vexatious young man.

A rape over in Greenville was tied to the Rabbit Trail murders, and a meeting set up. Mart, sitting on top of his desk when she walked in, was deep in serious conversation with Tom Hart, the new chief of detectives.

Detective Hart was indeed a good-looking man, just as Mart had mentioned. He was tall and well-toned and his hair attractively dark and thick. He wore his suit casually. His neatly pressed shirt was minus a tie, and his sneakers somehow didn't seem out of place: blue and somewhere between Keds and Versace. She smiled at him and noticed how naturally it came. He returned her smile with a scrutinous exploration of her face.

"Detective." She returned his stare.

Detective Hart gave her a lengthy handshake. "We've got ourselves a cold case, Detective," he said. "Right up your alley." He looked directly into her eyes and then quickly shot his glance to Mart. "Bodies found on the Rabbit Trail."

"The Rabbit Trail murders?" Leighton asked.

"Yep," Detective Hart said, turning back to her. "I hear you're a great cop. Great instincts." He looked at Mart. "I think we've got ourselves a serial killer here."

"Which means he's still out there," Mart said.

Leighton nodded. This one sounded serious. "Can you brief me before the meeting?"

"Well, It seems that a woman in Greenville was raped last night and left for dead in the woods at the Swamp Rabbit Trail," Tom said. "Some hikers heard her moan and investigated the sound. She'd been stabbed repeatedly with a simple hunting knife and whoever left her dying in the woods most likely believed he had killed her. He might have been frightened off, or it might have been a mistake and he thought he was done with her. But if the woman lives, we have a victim who can hopefully identify her rapist." Tom sat on the desk and looked at her, inviting questions.

"Have you spoken to her?" Leighton asked.

Tom shook his head. "At the moment, doctors are refusing any questioning by police. She's had a near-fatal stab wound to her chest and needs rest and quiet. She's pretty much sedated."

Leighton responded with a nod. The Swamp Rabbit Trail was in Greenville, not their jurisdiction, but they often worked together with neighboring counties when the crime was murder or rape. "You think this is local?" she asked.

"Yeah," Mart said. "I think our guy might be from Transylvania, Anderson, or Oconee, maybe even Pickens County. But he's highly likely to be from Greenville."

"This victim is a Clemson University student, blonde and pretty. She was last seen in a bar in Greenville, but no one we've questioned so far saw her leave with anyone," Tom told her.

"You have the identities of the bodies you found on the trail?" Leighton asked.

"Yeah," Tom said. "Dental records provided the identity of the two deceased victims. It seems that all three women were blonde, and all of them Clemson University students. The bodies of the two deceased girls have probably been up there for as long as two years. Both were stabbed with the same type of knife used on our latest victim. We had the lab conduct bone weathering, which ascertained the Clemson University student's murders had been at least a year apart. So, we've got a murder in '91 and another in '92."

"About four years ago, there was another murder up there, same MO," Mart said. "So, approximately 1990 or 1989."

"Was that woman a student?" Leighton asked and Tom shook his head. "Could be related, though. The deceased was blonde, around thirty."

"But why'd he wait over a year after the first victim to kill the other two?" Leighton asked.

"Maybe becoming a serial killer is a process." Mart smiled and looked at Tom.

"Yeah," Tom said sarcastically, "If it's the same guy, it looks like he's killing a woman a year."

"Anyone see any similarities between these murders and Lottie Lacock's disappearance?" Leighton asked.

Tom shook his head. "We don't have Lottie's body, Leighton. We have no proof she was murdered."

"And she wasn't blonde or young," Mart added.

"So, our Rabbit Trail killer favors a type," she said.

"Yep," Tom said, "blonde, most likely pretty, and young."

"That sure fits a lot of men," Leighton said.

Of course, she thought of Ethan. He was around lots of female students, and he was a womanizer. Unfortunately, being a womanizer didn't make him guilty of murder and it didn't even make him guilty of rape, just made him a jerk. Ethan was just one of hundreds of young men who could be a suspect at this point.

Chapter Twenty-Two

Leighton sat at the bar of a new restaurant everyone wanted to try; the chef was from New Orleans and gaining quite a reputation. Leighton was waiting for Sean after work. He was driving in from Greenville, so she guessed he hit some traffic because he was late. She ordered a glass of white wine and admired the décor, the low-lit chandeliers, and the plush, comfortable booths, color of a gray catbird, reminding her of that blanket she'd splurged on last week; its softness had been worth every penny. The restaurant was one Sean wanted to go to, Southern French cuisine, a favorite of his. They agreed to meet there one night during the week when it wouldn't be so crowded but despite the early hour, people were arriving and several people stood in line for the maître d'.

After she'd taken about three sips of her wine, she was aware of someone standing over her and crowding her space. She turned to find Ethan's wide grin.

"Oh, Ethan, you startled me ... what are you doing here?"

He looked down her low-cut blouse. "Same as you, I suppose, waiting for my date."

"This place is pretty expensive, how do you afford it?" She didn't mean it as an insult, but worried that it had come out that way.

"I've got assets." He said it with a smile; he hadn't taken her comment negatively.

"Oh." She was surprised. She couldn't imagine what his assets would be. "I guess you've got a secret trade, something that brings in the dough?"

The muscles in his jaw tightened and he moved closer to her. "Yeah, would love to show you what that is sometime."

The movement and the way he'd spoken, so low and intimately, made her uncomfortable. She shifted on her stool. She was after all, a cop, which obviously meant little to Ethan. She was a woman, and that's what mattered.

"An improvement," she said as she noticed he had shaved his beard.

"What? Oh, yeah, my beard. My girlfriend didn't like it." He leaned into her again and let his eyes take ownership of her face.

She leaned back just as Sean walked in and found Ethan hanging all over his girlfriend. He slid on Leighton's other side and stared at Ethan. "Her boyfriend has arrived," he said and smiled broadly, winking at Leighton, and then kissing her on the cheek.

Ethan looked up and showed a mouthful of teeth.

"Lucky man," he said. "She's got great legs."

Sean gave Leighton a befuddled look; his expression suggested he thought this kid was a jerk.

"Pretty eyes, too." Ethan leaned in close to Leighton's face again with a wide smile.

"Thanks for admiring my girlfriend's body parts, but I'm told women aren't always comfortable with those kinds of remarks." He stared at Ethan.

Ethan sucked in his breath. "Okay then, I won't mention her ass."

Leighton watched Sean's face redden, as he looked at Ethan, ready to kill him. "Get lost, kid," he said. "I don't think Leighton is interested in your appraisal."

"Hey, I was having a talk with her, we know each other, right, sugar?"

Sean got up and put his hands on the lapels of Ethan's jacket and dragged him outside. "Asshole," he shouted.

Leighton got up and ran after them. "Sean," she called. "Let him go, he's just a stupid kid."

Sean knocked Ethan into the front of a car, shoving him into the front fender and yelling at him to mind his manners. Leighton kept telling him to stop but he ignored her. She tried to grab him from behind, but he was so angry he didn't notice. She almost cuffed him when suddenly a woman ran up to Sean and slapped him on his back. "Let him go," she screamed.

Distracted, Sean stepped away. The woman went to Ethan and pulled him off the car. "Are you alright, sweetheart?" she asked.

Ethan straightened up and stared at Leighton. "You best control your boyfriend," he said with a good amount of anger, clearly embarrassed.

Ethan put his arm around the woman and they walked back into the restaurant. Leighton noticed that the woman looked to be in her fifties. She was dressed in expensive clothes and had had one facelift too many. Through the window in the bar, Leighton watched her touching Ethan's face and kissing his cheek.

"Not his mother," Leighton said.

"What's that?" Sean asked.

"I think I just discovered his secret trade." She looked back through the window of the restaurant and took in the woman's taut face.

Chapter Twenty-Three

Irresoluteness consumed Leighton where Sean was concerned, but it didn't just happen that night in the restaurant; her ambivalence had been building for a while. It would have been there even if she hadn't witnessed his temper. She didn't know what to believe about his relationship with Pam and she wanted to feel more certain about it. She couldn't countenance any kind of intimacy with him without knowing in her soul that he would never attempt to seduce a teenager, much less his girlfriend's daughter.

What Robbie told her about the restraining order against him was also troubling. Whether it was filed or not wasn't as important as had there ever been a reason to consider filing it? She questioned whether Sean was a violent man, whether he threatened his wife in some way. It wasn't about his going off on Ethan, but more about his lack of control. Yeah, Ethan needed putting in his place, but not thrown against a car so many times he could have been seriously injured. They should have just found a table and gotten away from Ethan and his inappropriate behavior. That's what Beau would have done, that's what any man would have done with just a modicum of maturity.

Truth was, she missed Beau and wasn't ready for another man. Despite thoughts that she was betraying Beau by seeing Sean, which was ridiculous, she continued to date Sean, ignoring her troubling doubts about his character. She enjoyed him, and she had no proof at all that he had attempted to seduce a teenager or had beaten his wife. It was all just hearsay. She was certainly lonely for a man's attention, but not just any man, a decent man.

There was a sexual attraction between her and Sean but what does that mean really? Sexual attraction was just chemistry and stupidity and not necessarily a good thing or anything to take seriously. She certainly wasn't acting on her sexual attraction to him; she was avoiding it. Her emotions difficult to understand at the moment, she told herself she wouldn't make any decisions to take their relationship to the next level until she could sort it all out. How patient Sean was willing to be was another issue.

She eliminated Ethan as the Rabbit Trail murderer. Something she'd seen in his eyes the night Sean pummeled him wasn't the expression of a serial killer. He was afraid of Sean, more like a scared kid about to get the shit kicked out of him. Ethan's vulnerability didn't equate with a murderer. He was just a cocky little bastard who didn't know when to shut up. She'd also learned something about Sean that night: that his rage was triggered way too easily.

Sean was eager to hear all about her strategy for solving the Rabbit Trail murders but she didn't like to talk about her work. Every now and then, she and Mart discussed a case out of hours, but he was her partner. Normally her work was off limits. Sean was frustrated that she wouldn't include him in any progress the police were making. She didn't want to resent that he seemed intrusive; he didn't appreciate that her work was private, and not dinner talk, but unfortunately, she did resent his attitude of entitlement to know whatever she knew. He was more obsessed with the Rabbit Trail murders than she was. The anger he'd shown toward Ethan worried her, but was it reason enough to stop seeing him? Men often overreact when threatened, when they feel another man is interested in what they have determined as 'theirs'. Besides, everyone has a bad day, makes mistakes – that's how she justified it. The assumption was their relationship would deepen and they would sleep together at some point, but that point had not yet arrived. Leighton knew she was prolonging it, perhaps scared to death of the intimacy and relieved he was being a gentleman, not pushing himself into her bedroom. But he was a man, and not likely to accept her excuses not to have sex forever. She knew they would either make love pretty soon, or they'd simply drift apart. The other day he had laughed about it, "You're not a lesbian?" he had asked and she looked at him as if he had three heads, but it was a stupid thing to accuse her of, a threat – prove to me you aren't and sleep with me.

She was observing him, trying to determine his truthfulness, and discovering things she didn't like about him, discovering, too, an ambiguity she didn't yet understand, some disturbing questions and no answers. Had he come on to Pam Tilly when she was just a teenager? Had he used violence against his wife?

She took a trip to Greenville's library and discovered from some articles in the local town newspaper that Sean was pretty much a hometown hero, favorite teacher of the year, and an avid hiker. She found a picture in an old copy of *The Greenville Gazette* of Sean and his wife and their friends, Dorothy, and Ed Sanders. They looked as though they'd been camping in the woods; on the ground in front of the two couples were a canteen, a backpack, and a hunting knife. She took a mental note of the hunting knife, the weapon used against the deceased women found on the Swamp Rabbit Trail and the newest victim. Most people who went camping or hunting carried a knife of some kind. She wondered whether she suspected Sean was capable of these murders ... which had to be ridiculous. Yet there he was on what appeared to be the Swamp Rabbit Trail.

If Sean's wife had been like most women, she would have confided in someone if Sean had been violent. Perhaps that someone had been Dorothy. She found a phone number for Dorothy Sanders and set up a meeting with her for later that day. She left the library quickly after researching only one copy of *The Greenville Gazette.* She told herself she could always come back for more information: meeting with Dorothy was more important.

Chapter Twenty-Four

Leighton had not expected Dorothy to look as she did. Glamorous, she was quite a contradiction to the photo of the messy young people she had found in the *Gazette*. In the photograph, they had all been dressed in jeans and T-shirts and looked to have been roughing it in the two tents behind them. The date was the summer of '83, so they'd been a decade younger. Certainly, no one looked glamorous out in the woods, but in person, Dorothy had striking dark hair, beautiful dark eyes and dressed like someone with a fat bank account. Her jewelry was large and showy and, apparently, she had a weakness for very red lipstick.

She led Leighton into her comfortable and stylish older home, seated her in the living room where a pot of coffee waited and some delicious-looking cookies with chocolate chips and nuts.

Leighton sat and smiled at the woman. "Thank

you for seeing me, Dorothy," she said. "I really appreciate it, especially since this is not an official visit."

"Did you know Ashley?" Dorothy asked as she handed her a cup of coffee.

"No, I didn't know her."

"You would have loved her. Everyone did."

"This is more of a personal journey for me." She looked at the woman across from her. "You see, I've just begun to date Sean Dowd."

Dorothy brought her head up sharply. "Oh," she said. "I thought you were a detective?"

"I am. I am a detective, but as I said, that's not why I'm here." Leighton sipped her coffee and looked at Dorothy over the rim. "It's personal."

Dorothy smiled at her. "Well, I hope I can be of some help."

Leighton put down her cup. "I don't know if you're aware, but Sean was accused of improper behavior with a teenager. I'm trying to find out if there's any truth to that, or if it's just a nasty rumor."

Startled, Dorothy put her head back. "Oh," she said.

"Did he strike you as that type of man?" Leighton asked.

Dorothy handed the plate with the cookies to Leighton and Leighton took one.

"Thank you," Leighton said, and wondered why she had to give her question any thought.

"I think I understand what this is about." Dorothy finally said and looked at her. "That teenage girl with the crush?"

Leighton was clearly surprised. "Pam Tilly?"

"Yes, I think that was her name." She cleared her throat and looked back at Leighton. "A question of she said, he said?"

Leighton nodded. "Exactly."

"My money would be on Sean. I don't think he'd come on to a teenager. He was a teacher, for God's sake."

"What do you know about it?"

"Nothing, really."

"Whatever you remember might be helpful," Leighton said.

"Well," Dorothy sighed deeply before speaking. "After Ashley's death, about two and a half years after, maybe less, Sean met a woman from Pickens. I don't know if it was love or not, but he moved in with her. I think it was unbearable for Sean to lose Ashley the way he did, and he needed comfort. She was an older woman and very maternal. That's how Sean described her, maternal. He also said she had a great sense of humor. He used to say how much he enjoyed her company. I felt she was good for him." Dorothy smiled affectionately, as if the memory had been a pleasant one. "Well, she was apparently good for him at the time, and he was very fond of her. So, I was supportive of his new relationship. I didn't want him to be alone, despite the fact I didn't like him."

"You didn't like him?"

Dorothy shook her head. "No, not really. Not at all, actually. It took a couple of years after Ashley's death for him to even speak to me or me to him.

"May I ask why you didn't like him?"

"Just chemistry, I guess."

Leighton sighed. "And this woman he started to

see had a teenage daughter?"

Dorothy nodded

"And this daughter accused Sean of improper behavior?"

"Rubbish," Dorothy said quickly. "I can't believe that about Sean. I can't imagine him trying to get one of his students into bed. He's too intelligent for that."

"Though I hear the girl is gay, which makes it unlikely she'd be interested in him."

Dorothy looked at her and smiled. "And that means what, that she's gay? She's young."

Leighton studied her expression. "I assume she wouldn't come on to a man if she were gay."

"That is not necessarily true." She took a sip of her coffee. "Sometimes people use their sexuality to get what they want, and their sexual preference is secondary. Anyway, I don't know if the girl was gay or not." She looked at her hands. "I mean, how would I know that?"

"No, of course you wouldn't," Leighton said.

"I will say that people's sexuality is often more complex, not necessarily one way or the other. Young people tend to be adventurous, wouldn't you say?"

"Yes, they can be."

"I do know Pam threw herself at Sean, at least, that's what he told me, and I had no reason to doubt him. He said she was obsessed with him, not the other way round. He used to complain about her to me. He was furious that she wouldn't leave him alone. He said it ruined his relationship with the girl's mother. He could have been lying, but I believed him."

"Sean told you that she wouldn't leave him alone?"

"Yes, he did."

"Why do you think he didn't go to the police? She could have gotten him in a lot of trouble."

Dorothy looked at her as if no one had thought of that as a solution. "Well, she was so young, I guess. I'm sure he didn't want to do that to the girl's mother, you know, file a complaint against her daughter? Maybe he was hoping he could put a stop to it on his own. But even after the girl's mother threw him out, the girl would come up here on that motorcycle of hers and sit in front of his house waiting for him to come back from wherever."

"Did he let her in?"

"I wouldn't know that. It's what he told me."

"Well, then, how do you really know that she was after him and not the other way around?"

Dorothy hunched up her shoulders. "What was she doing in Greenville in front of his house instead of in Pickens, where she belonged? She came here because she wanted to have an affair with him, I'm assuming."

"Or she was already having an affair with him, and she was just waiting for him to get home and let her in." Leighton realized that Dorothy didn't really know if something went on between Pam and Sean or not. She assumed that Sean wouldn't come on to a teenager, but she didn't know anything concrete. She had a blank look on her face, as if she were trying to figure out something.

"Could she have been blackmailing Sean, threatening to go public about their affair?" Leighton asked.

"What affair? You're assuming they had an affair."

"I'm looking at all the possibilities," Leighton said.

"Well, if she was telling everyone who would listen that she was sleeping with her teacher, I guess she'd already gone public about it?"

"Dorothy, did Ashley have a restraining order against Sean? Was he violent toward her?"

"What? No. He has a temper but only when he gets into a heated argument about politics. He's passionate about issues, as you might know."

"I've seen his temper," Leighton said.

"I don't think he's a violent man," Dorothy said. "Not really."

"Did Sean and Ashley have a happy marriage?" Leighton stared at her.

Dorothy looked away. "If you want my opinion, the girl had a wild crush on him, and he didn't reciprocate. So, she just spread lies, vindictive lies."

"You didn't answer my question."

"I assume they were happy," she said, turning back to Leighton.

"I see," Leighton said.

Dorothy looked shaken as she stared at Leighton. "He's never been the same since Ashley's murder. None of us have been."

Leighton's head jerked up and she nearly jumped out of her seat. "What murder?"

Dorothy raised one eyebrow. "I thought that's why you might be here. Sean was a suspect for a while, but he was cleared pretty quickly. He was at a parent's evening at the high school the night Ashley disappeared. Several people saw him and spoke to him there."

Leighton thought back. She remembered something about a woman being murdered in

Greenville a few years ago. Tom had recently mentioned that there had been an earlier murder on the trail; perhaps he was referring to Ashley.

"Where was her body found?" Leighton asked.

"About five miles from The Steak House. That's where she was going to pick up some food. They found her body near a woody incline that leads to the Swamp Rabbit Trail. She was found just off the trail in the woods." Dorothy rubbed her forehead. "I wished I'd gone with her. I'll never forgive myself for not going with her."

"Ashley was murdered?" Leighton asked softly. "I had no idea."

"It was a terrible shock for all of us."

"My God," Leighton said softly. "I didn't pay much attention to it at the time, it wasn't in my case file, but I do remember hearing about it, and her murder just came up again."

"It happened four years ago."

"Sean told me that his wife died of cancer."

Dorothy shook her head. "He doesn't tell people she was murdered. He can't really deal with it. You might have seen an article about it in the library ... didn't you tell me you'd just come from the library?"

Leighton had stopped her research after finding the photograph of Ashley with Sean and their friends. She'd stopped looking for anything else. She had been too eager to question Dorothy.

"Have the police given you any updates on Ashley's killer?" Leighton asked.

"Not yet," Dorothy said. "Not even after four years."

"Forgive me for asking and changing the subject so

abruptly but did Sean ever come on to you?"

Dorothy laughed. "Absolutely not." Dorothy laughed again.

Leighton looked at her oddly. "That's funny because?"

Dorothy looked away. "He wouldn't come on to me."

Sean's fascination with the crimes she was working made sense to Leighton, his desire to find out what happened to Lottie, not to mention his wife.

"Did you know Lottie Lacock?" she asked.

"Of course, wonderful woman. Sean is devastated about her disappearance, he fears she met Ashley's fate."

"You said Ashley's body was found on the Swamp Rabbit Trail?"

"Yes, in the woods. Why do you ask?"

"Recently a woman was attacked and left for dead there. Two other bodies were discovered on the trail. It's possible they were raped."

"Ashley wasn't raped, she was brutally murdered. I didn't know about the other two women. So, it sounds like a serial killer?" She looked up and Leighton noticed the tears in her eyes.

"Yes, the remains were just recently discovered. Ashley was blonde, wasn't she?"

Dorothy smiled dolefully. "She had the most beautiful blonde hair, a golden color."

"This killer has a type, blonde … college age."

"Ashley looked young. She often wore her hair in a ponytail, and she was very petite. I imagine someone could mistake her for a college student, but she was in her mid-thirties. Ashley was a very beautiful woman,"

Dorothy said just above a whisper.

"I'm sorry to dredge this all up."

"Have they caught this bastard?"

"Unfortunately, no," Leighton said.

Leighton thanked Dorothy for the coffee, the cookies, and the information. She felt differently about Sean now, sorry for him. Not only had his wife been a victim, but he was as well. His life had obviously been torn apart by his wife's murder. Pamela Tilly was not in the least bit sensitive to the trauma he had suffered. She had made things worse for him.

Leighton started her car and drove back toward Pickens. If Pam Tilly had come on to him, it would have put him under enormous pressure. Whatever comfort he got from Pam's mother was shattered by Pam's accusations. He was clearly still feeling those losses. Convinced he needed to talk to someone, Leighton would find a way to recommend a therapist.

Chapter Twenty-Five

Robbie had been back from Europe about a week and had no idea where Pam was, she had literally disappeared off the face of the earth. She wasn't answering her cell phone and she hadn't called to say where she was either. It was as if she'd vanished into thin air. Robbie would be leaving for New York in less than three weeks, and she needed to see Pam, to make plans. She'd had to deal with her mother's fury over the Tilly's garden and now this – a vanishing act from Pam. She wondered if she'd been kidnapped before she'd even made it on the plane in England. Robbie wondered if she should go to the police. Instead, she went to Mindy's. For all she knew, Mindy had chopped up Pam and thrown her pieces to the wind.

Robbie held a small package out to Mindy as she walked inside her house, a beautiful blue scarf she had bought in Harrods, wrapped in soft pink paper. A gift that, guilt-ridden, Robbie picked up at the last minute.

"Everyone over there is wearing them, they're almost like ascots but they aren't. Open it," Robbie said. "Try it on."

"Get out of here, Robbie. I wouldn't have opened the door if I'd known it was you."

Robbie stood and stared at her. "Look, I'm sorry about everything. I never meant to hurt you, Mindy. Please, let's get past this."

Mindy had a serious expression on her face. She threw the gift at Robbie, and it landed at her feet. "I don't want it." she said through her teeth.

Robbie cautiously sat in one of Mindy's old club chairs and stared up at her. "Listen to me, I'm so sorry. I never meant to hurt you, I swear. It's just that seeing Pam again was so unexpected." The urge to run through the front door gnawed at her. "I never got over her, Mindy."

"Perhaps you should have gotten over her. She's a psychopath," Mindy said.

"She's not a psychopath."

"You're blind."

Robbie frowned. "You shouldn't have torn out her garden. That was an awful thing to do. I really got in trouble having Hector fix it. My mother is barely speaking to me over it. I'm lucky she even allows me out of the house."

"Why were you stupid enough to ask Hector to do it?"

"I wanted to help her out."

"Pam tore out her own garden, Robbie. I'm telling you, she's crazy."

"Oh, c'mon," Robbie said.

"It's the truth," Mindy said. "She wanted you to

think it was me. She had Boyd do it." Mindy walked closer to Robbie and stared into her puzzled expression. "He did it right before you showed up at her house that day. Ask him yourself. She told him it was a joke she was going to play on you."

"That makes no sense, it wasn't my garden she tore up."

"Pam has no sense, nothing she does has to make sense." Mindy went to the couch and sat.

"You're talking to Boyd now?"

"Yeah, we're friends. He's furious at Pam. Seems like she's tired of his company."

"She was always tired of his company."

Mindy laughed. "Pam screwed him, but that's not surprising, she screws everyone. Most of all you." Mindy leaned forward and stared into Robbie's eyes. "That's the game she plays, Robbie, 'who can I screw next?'"

"You're friends with Boyd Baxter?"

"He asked me to marry him." She grinned.

Robbie started laughing. "What? You've got to be kidding. He's a rapist."

"He's gay, Robbie." Mindy's stare was all but lethal, but Robbie held her eyes anyway. "He doesn't rape women."

Robbie stared at her. "What?"

Mindy nodded. "Yeah, he said it would appease his parents for him to marry. He's so totally in the closet. They never leave him alone about finding some nice girl to go out with … that's the only reason he hangs with Pam."

"You're kidding, right?"

"Grow up, Robbie. He just loves that she's

beautiful. Christ, Robbie, they're more likely to go shopping together than have sex. You know that whole rape story back in high school? They made it up, Pam did. They thought it would take any suspicion away from Boyd being gay, because it was starting to get around that he was. Then when the police accused him of trying to force himself on Pam, the rumor died. Boyd said his father gave him this whole lecture about not forcing himself on women, but Boyd could tell his dad was so relieved he liked girls and proud to give him an alibi, too. He became big man on campus for attempting to rape a girl. Sick, huh?"

Robbie leaned back in the comfortable club chair and stared at the ceiling. "Why wouldn't Pam have told me that Boyd was gay? I mean, I was so jealous of him."

Mindy smiled maliciously. "She probably enjoyed your pain. I mean, why should she do the right thing? She's convoluted. Anyway, he swore her to secrecy about him being gay."

Robbie sprung to her feet. "Do you know where Pam is? I haven't been able to reach her. I'm worried."

"Pity."

Robbie had butterflies in her stomach, as if something bad was about to happen, or perhaps, had happened.

"C'mon, Mindy. Please tell me where she is."

Mindy's anger was palpable. "I can't believe you still have a thing for that lying bitch."

"You didn't kill her, did you?"

"Very funny." Mindy smirked at her.

"I haven't been able to reach her for five days,

Mindy. Do you know where she is or not?"

"I'm sure she's just not answering her phone, too busy. Perhaps she just tired of you, you're too easy." Mindy gave her an odd smile and got to her feet. She stood before Robbie.

"You're a liar." Robbie had said it softly, as if she didn't really believe it.

"She's got a lot of admirers, Robbie. She's probably entertaining one of them as we speak."

"Do you know something that I don't?" The two stared, full of hate for each other.

"She's seeing lots of people, male, female. She never discriminates. I hear she has a thing for Jeremiah Lennox. He lets her eat for free at that five-star restaurant of his."

"Gross," Robbie said. "He's over fifty."

"And that matters to Pam because?"

Robbie was ready to throw up. "Shut up."

"Don't look so upset. You didn't really think you were the only one? I saw her with that high school teacher she's so crazy about. Sean? He was leaving her house at three in the afternoon the other day. I stopped my car and just stared at them. He was holding her hand, or at least trying to."

"You're a fucking liar, Mindy."

Mindy walked closer to Robbie and slapped her hard across the face. "Don't you dare call me a liar. You don't get to call me anything, you son of a bitch."

Robbie was stunned and put her hand to her cheek. "Wow, what's wrong with you?"

"What's wrong with you? Something has to be."

"You just hate Pam. You can't stand to see me happy with her," Robbie screamed at her.

"Happy with Pam? Oh, please." Mindy got up and picked Robbie's gift up off the floor. "This will look better on you, I'm sure. Now take it and get the hell out of here." She shoved the gift into Robbie's hands. "That girl is going to wipe the floor with you, you idiot."

"I'm sorry, Mindy, really I am." Robbie took the gift and looked around, looking for a place to leave it.

"I'm vindicated. You got what you deserved. Pam left you high and dry. That little bitch doesn't mean a word she says to anyone. She let it out that Boyd was gay, told his sister, who went back and let it slip to his parents. Thank God his parents still think gay means happy-go-lucky and didn't know what the hell she was talking about, but the rest of Pickens knows what it means."

"Why would Pam do that, for God's sake?"

"She got tired of Boyd hanging around her all the time when she wanted to see her handsome teacher or that other old man from The River House. Boyd was starting to annoy her."

"That doesn't make any sense."

"I think she only told his sister because the ugly little duckling became hot and sexy, and we know how Pam likes hot and sexy girls." Mindy winked at her. "Probably even more than she likes old men."

"I don't believe it."

"You should see her."

"I mean about Boyd."

"He's furious at her. It's all over town now that Boyd is a flamer, thanks to Pam."

Robbie turned to the door. Her cheek still stung from Mindy's slap, and she was sick to her stomach.

She turned back to look at Mindy.

"I guess this is the end of our friendship." Robbie stared at her. "I don't even like you anymore, Mindy."

"Get lost, Robbie. Were we ever friends?" She shoved Robbie toward the door. "You messed up any possibility for us to ever be friends. You cheated on me when you didn't have to. You could have told me the truth. I have no respect for your stupidity, and I hate liars."

Mindy opened the door and shoved Robbie out. "Don't ever contact me again," she shouted.

Robbie heard something hit on the other side of the door as she closed it behind her. "Creep," she heard Mindy holler.

Robbie put Mindy's gift on the passenger seat and drove by Pam's house. Anxious and sad, she wasn't even sure whether she was angry. She hated to lose Mindy's friendship, but Mindy was being unreasonable. They had never spoken about being faithful to one another. Maybe Mindy just expected it, but Robbie hadn't wanted an exclusive relationship. She was going away to college for God's sake, how could she be exclusive? Well, she'd write her from New York and try to make up.

She was happy to see Pam's Kawasaki in the drive. Finally, she'd come back from wherever she'd been. Problem was, there was a strange car in the driveway as well, one she didn't recognize. She noticed a rental car sticker on the plate.

She waited, just to see if anyone came out of the door.

It was nearly 6:00 p.m. when a guy left Pam's house. She was shocked to see it was Sean Dowd. He stood at the door with Pam, and she watched as Pam shoved him back. He reached out and tried to grab her. They both looked angry. Robbie watched as the man grabbed her again, screaming at her. She shoved him back and slammed the door in his face. After a moment, Robbie got out of her car.

"Excuse me," Robbie said as she brusquely walked up to Sean. "What are you doing here?"

He stared at her for a moment as if trying to place her. "What business is it of yours?"

"You were her teacher, isn't that a little strange?"

"Robbie Darling, right?"

She nodded. "Yeah, I had you in tenth grade."

"I saw you at your brother's wedding."

"Yeah, right."

"Look, I'm trying to make amends with Pam." He stared at her, and she saw the blush rise to his cheek. "We've got an issue between us that we need to resolve."

"An issue?" Robbie laughed. "I'll bet you do."

"Get your mind out of the gutter, Robbie."

"I just saw you roughing her up."

He stared at her. His eyes were small and angry. "You're hallucinating," he said.

"You still after her, huh, Mr. Dowd?"

Sean had a sick expression on his face. "I was never after her. She's still telling people that I am, though. Hopefully, no one believes her. She's a habitual liar."

"Well, at least you got that right. But I just saw you shaking her."

"Look, Pam hallucinates, and it seems you do too. She threw herself at me inside her house, I pushed her away. I don't care what you think you saw."

Robbie stared at him wide-eyed. "You really are full of shit."

"You got it all wrong."

"Sure," Robbie said. "You seemed pretty angry with her. It was a little scary to me."

"What do you think, Robbie, that I'm going to kill her?"

Robbie froze at those words. Even in jest, they sounded so threatening. "I hope you're kidding, Mr. Dowd, 'cause you look angry enough to do just that." His expression frightened her, but she didn't look away.

"Yeah, you really better think I am kidding," he said.

She watched as Sean got into his car and drove off. Robbie stared after him until he was out of sight. He probably rented a car so no one would notice his vehicle in her driveway. Who could miss it, he had an old Volkswagen bug? She went around the back, into the garden and began to pull up the flowers. She pulled until almost every flower lay on the grass. After a few minutes, Pam came running out.

"Stop, stop, what are you doing?" she called. "Robbie, stop."

"There now," Robbie said as she wiped her hands together. "We're even."

"What have you done? God, Robbie, I've missed you so much and you do this? What about our plans to go to New York? Why have you done this?"

"You're having an affair with Sean Dowd."

"Who told you that?"

"Mindy."

"That little bitch is spreading lies."

"I don't think she's lying. I just saw it for myself. You just had a lover's quarrel."

"What, don't be ridiculous. Sean stopped by to try and get me to stop telling people he came on to me. He told me what I said to Leighton about it, and he's furious I told his girlfriend what a creep he is."

"He said you threw yourself at him."

"What? No, Robbie. He tried to have sex with me."

"I've been trying to reach you for five days."

"I was in Columbia visiting my mother. I was trying to make up with her. I just got back, and Sean came by."

"I called you a thousand times."

"Oh God, I left my cellphone home."

"You're such a liar."

"I'm not lying," Pam yelled out.

"Enjoy yourself in New York but not with me."

"How will I fix this?" she screamed, looking frantically around.

"Use your father's inheritance." Robbie smiled. "Don't ever call me again, you psychopath."

With tears streaming down her face, Robbie drove home. She would pack for her trip, spend time with her brother and Prissy, have her dad take her on one of his nature walks and never think of Pam Tilly again. Yet she had an odd feeling in her stomach, a foreboding. She couldn't get that heated argument she'd just witnessed out of her mind.

Chapter Twenty-Six

Jeremiah walked to the window and lowered the blinds. He turned back to the girl.

"I told you never to come here during the day. People will talk."

"What am I going to do? I have to get to New York."

"New York? Why the hell do you have to get to New York?"

Pam threw herself back on his couch. "I need to get out of this town, Jeremiah."

As though making it a point not to go near her, he remained standing at the window. "Why? I like it here? It's a fine town."

"I mean, my mother doesn't even live here anymore."

"Way you talk about your mother, that should make you happy."

"You don't understand."

"What don't I understand?"

"I'm pregnant," she screamed at him.

The blood drained from his face, and as if about to faint, he reached out for the chair opposite her and slowly sat. "Well, it's not mine, is it?" he asked.

She gave him an ambiguous smile that quickly turned aggressive. "What do you think? Why the hell do I need to get out of town, Jeremiah? If you don't give me money for an abortion, you think no one will know who the father is once I give birth to a Black baby?"

If he'd remained standing, he would have fallen over. "How do I know it's mine?"

"If you don't know it now, you'll certainly know it in eight months when I give birth to it. And so will everyone else in this town. If I can't afford an abortion, that's what will happen." She screamed at him, her eyes narrowing to slits, "Give me the money to get to New York and get an abortion, Jeremiah. I need to get out of here. You do that, and I'll never bother you again."

"Of all the places in the world, you want to go to New York. Do you know how expensive New York is?"

"Give me enough money to afford it then. I know you have it, that restaurant of yours is making money hand over foot."

"I have two partners in that restaurant, Pam. I can't just go and take money from it."

"Give me two thousand dollars, that should cover it. I won't tell anyone we had an affair if you give me the money."

"We did not have an affair. We had a one-night stand." He glared at her. "And not one I initiated."

"You could have kept it in your pants, you know?"

"I guess you don't remember that night like I do." Jeremiah lit a cigarette and blew the smoke toward her.

Pam looked lost for a moment and then she threw her head into a pillow and started to cry. "She thinks I don't love her. I need to go to her and prove I love her. I don't want anyone else."

"Who you talking about?"

"Robbie Darling."

Jeremiah shook his head for several seconds. "You better watch who you fuck girl. Deborah Darling finds out about you and her daughter she's likely to kill you and your unborn baby. I wouldn't mess with Deborah."

"Robbie loves me. But I can't go to her pregnant. No one will ever know, Jeremiah, if you just give me the money to get rid of it."

"You going to tell that girl we slept together?"

"If I do, I'll tell her it was before I knew her, and it really was before I knew her. Remember, I told you she came back in my life, and I couldn't see you anymore?"

Jeremiah nodded. "I wasn't planning on seeing you anymore anyway. Fooling with a twenty-year-old girl is not my idea of using the sense God gave me."

"I'll never come back here. I promise. You'll never see me again."

Jeremiah stared at her, as if peering through her brain. "Your baby isn't mine, is it, Pam? We slept together once, just once."

"Once is all it takes," she said.

"Who else you sleeping with?"

"Robbie."

He gave her a stern look. "What other man, Pam?"

"No other man," she said quietly.

Jeremiah sat still and looked at the floor as if he'd find answers there. "Didn't you tell me you had an inheritance?"

"I can't get my hands on it, not till I'm twenty-one."

"That's coming soon enough."

She glared at him. "What do I do now, have this baby because I can't afford to get rid of it? I can't expect Robbie to raise a child with me. That's the last thing she wants, she's just starting college."

"You could say I raped you. Isn't that what you do, accuse men of raping you?"

"I did that only once. Boyd asked me to do it."

Jeremiah stood to his feet and walked toward her. "You going to show up on your lesbian lover's doorstep and expect Deborah Darling's daughter to welcome you with open arms, especially if she finds out it's my baby you're trying to get rid of? Girl, you don't look as dumb as you are."

"If you don't give me the money, Jeremiah, I'll ask Deborah for it. I'm sure she'd want it hushed up that Barnaby and Robbie Darling are going to get a bastard sibling if she doesn't give me the money to abort it. She'll pay me off."

Jeremiah looked furious; he clearly didn't like being blackmailed by a twenty-year-old girl.

"If you go to Deborah Darling with that bullshit, you just might find yourself six feet under."

"I wouldn't. I was just talking." She turned away.

"Get out of here," he said. "I don't want anything

to do with you or your bastard. Here me, girl? Now, go. I ain't the only Black man in this town you can pin this on."

"We had a nice night, didn't we? We could have been lovers." She walked toward him, but he put his hands up and stepped back. His wallet was on the end table. She stood in front of the table and reached behind her and slipped the wallet deep in her back pocket.

"I like guys sometimes, especially if they're older and look like you. I didn't know I was going to meet up with Robbie again. But I liked you so much, Jeremiah. If I hadn't met Robbie again, I would have continued to see you. We could have been a proper couple. I'd only sleep with girls now and then. I'd be true to you mostly."

"Aside from that bullshit, the age difference between us would never make us a proper couple."

"Shit, Jeremiah. That wouldn't matter. You look younger and I look older."

"You sure Robbie even wants you?" he said with a grin. "You're trouble, like some other woman in that family I know. It runs in their blood."

"Well, she's mad at me, but she'll get over it."

"You best get your shit together, girl. You got too many lit fires. You destroying lives, you know that? You ain't going to destroy mine."

Pam walked closer to him and confronted him eye to eye. "You best help me, or I'll cry rape."

"I'll take my chances with a paternity test. This ain't the sixties, Pam. No one is going to pin a rape on me just on your word, especially not on *your* word. We got DNA now."

"Fuck you," Pam said.

Jeremiah got up and held the back door open for her. He watched as she walked away and then turned back, gave him the finger, and stood with her middle finger up in the air until he slammed the door behind him. He went to his liquor cabinet and fixed himself a drink. "Shit," he said. "What a crazy little bitch she is."

Chapter Twenty-Seven

Leighton looked across the room at Sean. Her ambivalence bubbled up inside her like a slow boil. Although sorry for him, he'd been through so much — his wife's murder, Pam's accusations — she had to keep him at arm's length. She didn't want a comingling of intimacies with Sean Dowd. She wasn't ready to become his significant other.

"I love you," he said out of nowhere and the words just hung there like heavy weights.

She brought her head up sharply. "What?"

He met her eyes. "I love you. I don't want you to think I'm a shit, Leighton, that'd I'd ever come on to a teenage girl. I went to see her, to ask her to stop lying about me. It's got to stop. I know what she told you about me."

"What, recently you went to see her?"

He nodded.

"You should not have done that, Sean. You need

to stay away from her. If you're seen with her, people will assume the rumor is true. That's just how people think. It's logical."

"I'm a teacher, for God's sake. I can't have those kinds of rumors going around about me. I begged her to just stop it. I'm entitled to do that, to protect myself, aren't I?"

Leighton felt her mouth hang open. "Sean, please let it go. If you let it go, it will die out. She'll find somebody else to focus on. There is absolutely no proof that you came on to her or any other minor. It's really just her word against yours right now."

He shook his head. "Right now? You don't believe what she's saying, do you?"

"No, I don't. I don't believe it."

"She's not a child." He laughed. "She's not a child, Leighton. She's a devious fully grown little bitch is what she is."

"Have any of your students ever accused you of being inappropriate with them?" she asked casually.

"No, of course not. I'm sure you would have heard about it if they had."

"I suppose so," she said.

Leighton wanted to scream. Everything she'd been feeling for him rose to the surface, all the ambiguity, but also the attraction. She wanted to take him in her arms and comfort him, poor, poor Sean. But she felt it too invincibly, the desire not to trust him, to protect herself. She didn't really know what the truth about Sean Dowd was and until she did, there'd be a problem.

"She came on to *you* then?" she asked as casually as she could.

"She sure did." He looked at her pathetically. "I told you that. I would never have made any moves on her."

"She told me she was a lesbian. It seems strange that she would come on to you."

Sean laughed. "She's whatever turns her on at the moment. I think she's hung up on seduction, proving her sexuality. She's into men, women. She enjoys seducing people." Sean hit the arm of a chair with a hard slap. "Having some kind of power over them, I guess."

"I imagine sexual power is pretty potent, but there is certainly no excuse to come on to her mother's boyfriend," Leighton said.

"She hates her mother."

"Do you know why?"

"It's a teenage thing, nothing specific as far as I know."

"She said you stood before her naked and tried to molest her."

She watched his face turn red. "I came out of the shower, I didn't know she was in the house, so yeah, I was naked, and I was standing in front of her."

"You winked at her."

"I didn't."

"She's a beautiful girl. Was she difficult to resist?"

He stared at her as if she had three heads. "No, she wasn't difficult to resist. She was my student. She was my girlfriend's daughter. I didn't like her that way. I'm not interested in young girls, Leighton. She kept trying to seduce me, I swear she did. I teach these kids ... do you think I would try to seduce a child, even if the child is Lolita?" he sneered.

Leighton felt he'd been in quite a sensitive position, especially if he were telling the truth about the girl. It must have been hell living in Marlene's house with her daughter throwing herself at him at every opportunity ... if he was telling the truth.

"Why didn't you have a towel around you?" she asked.

He looked at her as if he didn't have an answer but then he said, "Marlene forgot to put the fresh towels in the bathroom." He reached for her hand. "Listen, I don't want that nasty rumor to get between us." He stared at her, and she noticed how stern his expression was.

"I don't believe what she's saying, Sean."

He paused for a moment. "She told me she was pregnant." He stared at her, and she saw the fear in his eyes.

"What?"

"Yeah, can you believe it?"

"Well, it's not yours," she said slowly. "Is it?"

He looked away. "Of course not."

"You went to see her?"

"Yes, to ask her to stop telling you that I am some frigging degenerate."

"God, it's not your baby, is it?"

"Shit, no, Leighton. I just told you it wasn't. She wanted money. Said she had to get an abortion and then go to New York."

"New York? Why?"

He shrugged his shoulders. "I need to get rid of that girl. I'm not who she says I am. I am not that person she's making me out to be," he shouted.

She looked at him and tried to smile. "I've been to

see Dorothy Sanders," she said quite suddenly, mostly to get him off the subject of Pam and to give herself something to say.

He looked surprised. "What did you want with that bitch?"

Leighton was astonished he referred to Dorothy that way. "To see if your wife really did have a restraining order against you," she said carefully.

"She didn't, but you could have asked me."

"She told me that Pam used to sit in front of your house."

He put his face in his hands. "You see? It's true. Dorothy knows it's true. I don't know why Pam is doing this to me. I never did anything to her. She's pregnant with another man's baby, not mine. I swear it."

"Were you violent with your wife, Sean?"

"No," he said. "I loved my wife. I just told you that."

"Why didn't you tell me your wife was murdered?"

Shocked for a moment, he quickly recovered. "I couldn't. I don't like to think about it, and I didn't want us talking about it."

"I understand why you're so interested in my case now. Your wife's murder is likely related to two other bodies we found on the Swamp Rabbit Trail. Human remains, actually. They'd been dead a while." She looked at him and noticed the startled look on his face.

"Really?"

Leighton nodded. "This man has murdered three times and nearly four. But he was only able to get away with rape this time, not murder. His victim is recovering nicely." She bore her eyes into his and he turned away.

"You said there were two other bodies," Sean said with his back to her.

"We think your wife was the first victim of this serial killer."

"Shit." Sean put his hands over his face. "Shit," he repeated.

"I'm sorry, Sean."

He picked his head up sharply. "You've been to see her, the girl who lived?" He turned back to her.

She nodded. "Yeah."

Sean walked to her refrigerator and got himself a beer. He looked at her as he snapped off the cap. "My wife's murder was four years ago. Your husband died two years ago. I think we both need to move on. We can help each other forget."

"I think we need to take it slow," she said. "We're both still in mourning, and if it has a chance of working for us, we need not to rush anything. I'd like to recommend a therapist for you, Sean."

His head came up sharply. "What? A therapist? No."

"It might help."

"My wife has been dead four years, Leighton … I need to move on. I don't need a goddamn therapist. I need you."

Leighton sighed. "We'll get where we need to be." She sat next to him on the couch. She took his hand and held it. The subtle hint of evening peeked in as they sat in the stillness, their thoughts blended in the silence.

"We need to be a couple, Leighton," he said finally.

She didn't respond to that. She sent him home after he finished his beer. Their kiss at the door was brief. She would not sleep with a man she didn't trust and her trust for Sean was dwindling. Her emotions, disturbing and gnawing at her, lacked the clarity she needed. It's not that she didn't believe him, but it wasn't that she did, either. The misty pale-eyed dawn crept in on quiet feet as she stared into the darkness, aware of some disturbing, instinctual truth that was too far back in her mind to reach.

Chapter Twenty-Eight

Pam put the twenty-dollar bill she'd taken out of Jeremiah's wallet on the counter. It had bought her a burger, fries, and a milkshake. She put the change back in the wallet and put the wallet in her back pocket. She was broke, except for the seven dollars in change in Jeremiah's wallet.

"Great day," the waiter said as he grinned at her.

She grinned back and winked, and the boy blushed so red he might have had a bad sunburn. She hopped on her motorcycle and tried to figure out how she would get the money for her abortion, as well as getting to New York, where she just had to be. Robbie had left without even saying goodbye, but she knew how to get past Robbie's anger. She supposed she could get a job and stay in Pickens for a while, save up some money. She was sure the Pickens Diner would love to have her waiting tables and then that pimply waiter could drool all over her. Pam laughed; nothing worse than being drooled over by a pimply boy.

She did have a couple of other options. She could blackmail Boyd, threaten to broadcast his sexuality. She could threaten Mindy's life, scare her into coming up with the two grand, use that gun she'd taken from her father's room before he'd died. She'd been holding on to that gun for years. Her mother didn't even know she had it. Best bet was to blackmail the little bitch, Mindy, say she'd keep quiet about her affair with Robbie Darling. Little sexy girlie girl, Mindy, wouldn't want the town knowing about that. And if that didn't work, she could blackmail Deborah Darling into keeping quiet about her daughter's sexual preference. She could give the drag queen another try. Maybe Dickie Darling was ready to give her the money to keep her mouth shut about him being a drag queen. She felt good flying down the street on her Kawasaki: she had options.

She was surprised to see Boyd's car in Mindy's driveway. So, the little creep ditched me for that repugnant Mindy Peach and her bottle-blonde hair and her weird Bette Davis eyes. Ha, she thought as she knocked on the door.

The expression on Mindy's face was priceless, at least to Pam. She looked like she'd just seen a creature from the Black Lagoon.

"Get lost," Mindy cried out indignantly and tried to slam the door in Pam's face, but Pam was too quick. She put her foot up and kicked the door open. Boyd sprang up as she entered.

"Hanging out with Mindy now, huh? Fickle boy."

"What do you want, Pam?" he asked.

"Two thousand dollars," she said. "I need to get to

New York."

Mindy and Boyd looked at her like she was crazy.

"You've got to be kidding," Mindy finally said. She eyed Boyd. He eyed back, as stupefied as she was.

"I'm calling the police if you don't leave my house." Mindy stared at her with a leer.

"I think the whole very backwards town of Pickens needs to know the next two homosexuals to lynch." Pam flung herself on Mindy's couch and put her feet up on the coffee table.

Boyd laughed. "No homosexuals lynched in this town, Pam."

She grinned. "To your knowledge."

"Get out of here, Pam, or I'll pick you up and throw you out," Boyd said.

Pam reached behind her and took the small Ruger out of her pocket. Mindy and Boyd froze where they stood. She got to her feet and pointed the gun at them.

"You got a bank card?" she asked Mindy.

Mindy nodded. "This is crazy, you can't get away with this."

"You got a bank card?" she asked Boyd.

He nodded. "What the hell are you doing, Pam?"

"Put the fucking gun down, you crazy bitch," Mindy shouted.

Pam walked behind Mindy and slammed the butt of the gun across her back. Mindy stumbled forward and fell to the floor.

"My God," Mindy cried. "You fucking hit me."

"Now, I want your bank cards and your passwords, and if they don't work, I'll come back here and shoot you both."

"You threatening to kill us?" Mindy said.

Pam laughed. "Who said anything about killing you? I'll cripple you, that's worse."

"We'll call the police." Mindy snarled.

"I'll be long gone. Sorry I just planned this over lunch, but it will work." She quickly turned to Mindy. "Where is your rope, twine, whatever."

"In the kitchen," Mindy said.

Pam turned to Boyd. "Get it. Then come back in here and tie her up. You got that?"

Boyd nodded. "There is no need to do this, Pam."

"Nobody wants to give me any money, guys. I have to do something." She followed Boyd into the kitchen. "Try the drawer on the left, it's probably in there."

Mindy spied the small vase on the end table. She got to her feet, but couldn't grab the vase fast enough.

"Bank cards, please," Pam demanded as she walked back into the room.

Boyd reached for his wallet and Mindy went to her purse. They each handed Pam the cards.

"Passwords?"

"Boyz11Men," Boyd said.

"Mariah," said Mindy.

"How cute," Pam said, "as in Carey?"

Pam aimed the gun at Mindy and pulled the trigger. "Click. It's not loaded, you fools," she said and laughed hysterically. "But don't act up, I've got the bullets for it."

Enraged, Mindy saw red dots in front of her eyes. She grabbed the vase and swung.

Chapter Twenty-Nine

Leighton's feelings toward Sean were tainted by the questions she didn't have answers to. Oh, she had *his* answers to her questions, but she did not necessarily have the truth. The more she saw of Sean the less she knew him and the more ambivalent she was. Of course, he wouldn't admit to anyone if he had been inappropriate with his students. She wondered if she should question his students. But at this point, she had no reason to delve that deeply into Sean's life; he wasn't being officially accused of anything illegal. She had to separate what she wanted to know on a personal level, and what was necessary to solve a crime.

On the surface, Sean didn't appear convoluted, and yet he was. He refused to talk about his wife, told her it was best left in the past. He asked her never to bring up Pam Tilly again. So, she didn't. She was afraid she'd sound too official, as though interrogating him. But then she had no other choice but to question him: Marlene Tilly hadn't seen or heard from her daughter in two weeks, and had filed a missing person report.

"Pam Tilly is missing," she said over dinner, nonchalantly. They were at some small popular Italian restaurant in the center of town. She hadn't seen him in a while, and she didn't want him to think she mistrusted him or that she was avoiding him, even though she supposed she was. He was definitely still a person of interest, but unfortunately, more as a suspect than a lover.

He raised his eyes to hers. "Really?"

"Her mother filed a missing person report last night. No one has seen the girl for about two weeks. They're putting up fliers and forming a search party."

Sean continued to eat his food. "Food is out of this world. My compliments to the chef," he said to a passing waiter.

"My late husband taught them," Leighton said. "The chefs worked for Beau at one time."

Sean nodded. "What do the police think?"

"You mean about Pam?"

He nodded again and stared at her, his face devoid of expression.

"It's odd that she hasn't been in touch with her mother, or anyone else for that matter," she said. "Though it's not unusual for Pam to disappear, still, it's a bit of a long time."

Sean laughed. "I didn't kill her," he said.

She brought her head up sharply. "No one said she was dead."

"They're going to question me, aren't they?"

"When was the last time you saw her? They'll ask you that."

"About two weeks ago," he said.

"She's been missing for two weeks, Sean."

He put his hands through his hair and put his head down. "Are they going to arrest me?"

"They'll question you. They have no evidence at all to arrest you."

"Maybe she told someone it was my baby? That would make me look bad."

Leighton brought her eyes to his. "There's proof on whose baby it is, Sean. We can prove it isn't yours once we find her."

"What? How?"

"DNA," she said. "We'll do a paternity test, prove who the father is."

"First they've got to find her, though." He smiled. "Slippery little bitch could be anywhere."

She gave him an odd look. "I suppose so," she said.

Chapter Thirty

Lottie reached out and took her friend's hand. "She'll show up, Marlene. You know how kids are."

They were sitting in the porch rocking chairs with a pitcher of tea between them. Marlene turned to her.

"It's been two weeks."

"Well, you got to spend some time with her. That was nice, wasn't it?"

Disappointment written all over her face, Marlene stared at Lottie. "The only reason my daughter came here to visit me was to try to talk me into giving her the money her father left her. I told her she couldn't touch it until she was twenty -one. After that, we did nothing but argue the whole time she was here."

"She wants to move to New York?"

"She says Robbie is expecting her. She's in a relationship with that girl."

"Didn't you tell me she was seeing someone else, a man?"

"That was before she took up with Robbie again. My daughter has no sexual boundaries. Men. Women. How can people do that?" Marlene put her face in her hands. "That's why she threw herself at Sean, no sexual boundaries."

Lottie sat up straighter in her chair and stared at her. "Threw herself?"

Marlene nodded. "Well, yeah, I knew something was going on, but I was humiliated by it. She's my daughter and she'll sleep with anything with two legs, including the man her mother was in love with."

Lottie sighed. "Did he succumb to it?"

"You mean did he screw her?" Marlene laughed. "He more than screwed her, he had an affair with her."

"Affair?" Lottie gasped.

"It was an affair. It became one anyway."

Lottie noticed that Marlene looked about to cry. "You hated us for believing Sean and not believing your daughter, now you're saying he did come on to her? He was lying to us?"

"You really think I could not have taken my daughter's side? Anyway, what difference does it make who came on to who? They were sleeping together. Who initiated it isn't important."

"Well, it is important, she was underage."

"When has that mattered to a man?"

"She's a young, beautiful girl." Lottie turned to her. "She should get some therapy."

"He screwed my daughter, Lottie. It's time I told the truth."

"You can't be sure of that, Marlene. You're just assuming he did."

"I am sure." Marlene looked at her sadly. "I am quite sure."

"Look, Sean is a teacher, it's not likely he slept with your daughter."

"I caught them together."

That startled Lottie and she sat up quickly. She stared at Marlene. "The sex was consensual then?"

"I told you, they had an affair. I had to protect my daughter. She was a teenager. I kicked him out, threatened him."

"You could have gone to the police, have rape charges brought against him."

"It wasn't rape. It was consensual. But I took Pam to the police anyway, she was still underage, but at the last minute, she talked me out of pressing charges."

"You were so angry at me for sticking up for Sean, for calling Pam the liar. He was just as responsible, if not more. I mean he was the adult."

"I'd rather blame him than have people think that about my daughter, that she'd do something like that. But you know men, they're capable of seducing a young girl, some of them, anyway."

Lottie reached out and poured herself some tea from the pitcher. She was disgusted with Sean, If she could she'd pay him a visit, she'd give him a piece of her mind.

"I read in the paper about some bodies discovered in Greenville, on the Swamp Rabbit Trail," Lottie said to change the subject.

"Yeah, I read that."

"Oh, shit, I didn't mean to bring that up. I'm not implying that has anything to do with Pam's disappearance."

"It's alright, Lottie. I'll try not to let that into my consciousness that my daughter might be the victim of some sick Rabbit Trail serial killer. Thank you for putting the thought there, though."

"I said that wasn't what I was implying. I truly am sorry. I was just attempting to get your mind off Pam for a while." Lottie reached out for her iced tea and took a sip. "I'm sure that's not the case."

"Let's pray not."

"We're booked right up until Christmas." She squeezed Marlene's hand, happy to change the subject.

"Thanks to our buddy, John. Who knew he was all ensconced with the Human Rights Campaign Fund, and knew all these wealthy gay people. That boy is going to keep us in business, Lottie. We are all over the gay circuit."

"Dear Blessed John," Lottie said. She closed her eyes and let her head fall back. Dickie came to mind as he often did when she closed her eyes. She was sometimes sick with it, the feelings of missing Dickie. He'd be so proud of her success. My God, she even missed Deborah. She'd forgive Deborah if she were standing there. She'd open up her arms to her but, of course, Deborah would never let it slide, her long affair with Dickie. Lottie couldn't blame her, not really, but she'd never stopped caring for Deborah. Dickie didn't like to admit how much he loved his wife, but it was always there. They both loved Deborah, and they both knew that the other one did as well.

"She slept with a Black man," Marlene suddenly said, jarring Lottie out of her thoughts, her deep regrets.

"What's that, Marlene?"

"Pam told me when she was here. She said she'd always had a crush on him, he was just so handsome, 'movie star handsome.'" Marlene put her fingers into air quotes. "She told me he had invited her to his house to teach her how to play chess but when she got there he had other plans and she didn't resist. She said he was dreamy. Her exact words."

"Who was dreamy?"

"Jeremiah Lennox."

"My God, Marlene, Jeremiah is an ex-con."

"He was proven innocent."

Lottie fell back with a slam. "I don't understand your daughter, Marlene. She's clearly beautiful, she doesn't need to sleep with everything that looks her way. What is she trying to prove? Jeremiah is in his fifties, for God's sake."

"I called Deborah for Robbie's phone number in New York. Robbie may know where Pam is."

Lottie sat forward with a jolt. "My God, you didn't mention me to Deborah, did you?"

"No, I just got the phone number, told her Pam was missing and Robbie might know where she is. What's going on with you and Deborah, anyway, seems like you're hiding from her."

"Was Robbie upset?"

"No, she said Pam disappears on people, but she always comes back. She reassured me, actually."

"You didn't mention me to Robbie, did you?"

Marlene sat back and stared at Lottie. "What's going on, you running from these people?"

"I'll explain some day. I promise. Just don't ever

bring me up with any of the Darlings."

Chapter Thirty-One

Ethan was questioned about the Rabbit Trail murders along with several other men who had been in the bar the night Susan Engel was abducted and left for dead on the trail. As far as Leighton was concerned, they were all suspects, but not necessarily guilty ones. She put aside the disturbing thoughts she had about Sean and concentrated on finding the killer. Ethan had been in the bar the night Susan Engel was attacked because it had been his buddy's birthday and they were celebrating, but other than that, this wasn't a bar he frequented, "Too many college kids," he'd said. He also said he had no idea who Susan Engle was. However, when he wasn't driving Lillian around, Ethan worked at the campus and could have seen Susan there, and then followed her to the bar in Greenville or had followed her enough times to know that's where she hung out. But there was nothing directly tying Ethan to Susan Engel, and he most likely didn't know her.

Leighton and Tom were able to question Susan once her condition was confirmed as improving. She had been severely traumatized, but her knife wounds were not fatal. She had been lucky. Kept in the hospital for her protection, she had facial damage from the encounter, but those wounds would probably heal and only require minimal plastic surgery.

Tom reached out and took the girl's hand, a gesture that did not go unnoticed by Leighton. "We're keeping someone outside your room until you're able to fly home. I don't want you to worry. Nothing will happen to you before we get you on that plane," Tom said.

"Right," she said. "It already has happened to me, though, hasn't it?"

"Nice to see you in recovery," Tom said gently.

Susan smiled at him. She was a pretty girl, and her smile revealed a dimple and sparkly white teeth.

"Thank you," she said softly.

"Can you describe the man who attacked you?" Leighton asked.

Susan sighed and said, "I'm not sure. I'll try."

"Anything you remember will be helpful,"

Leighton said quickly.

"I knew him, well, not actually knew him, but he was very, very familiar, that's why I agreed to give him a lift. Also, he didn't have a sinister face, he had a nice face. I knew him from somewhere, around town maybe, but I'm not really sure exactly where."

Tom had his notepad out and was taking notes. "Where did he ask you to take him?"

"He wanted a lift to the Shell station, said he needed gas. I knew the station and it was only about a mile away, so I didn't see any harm in it. He looked respectable. He looked normal." Susan shook her head several times. "Why did I do that? Why did I agree to let him in my car?"

"You probably felt safe." Tom squeezed the girl's hand for reassurance. "You said you knew him? Knew him from where, Susan? Anything you can recall will be helpful."

"I think I used to see him in Greenville, maybe in Clemson, too. I saw him in Greenville with some woman, his girlfriend maybe. Maybe his wife, who knows? I had a friend in Greenville, so I went there pretty much, and I go to school in Clemson. I'm fairly sure I saw him there as well." Susan looked up at Tom. "I'm an idiot, aren't I?"

"What did his girlfriend look like, can you recall anything about her?" Tom asked.

"She had blonde hair, she was very pretty and well dressed." She looked at Leighton. "She was wearing sunglasses the day I saw him with her, but I could still tell how attractive she was."

"Could you tell how old she was?" Leighton asked.

"Young, I think."

Leighton wrote that down and suddenly thought of the woman she had seen with Ethan. She'd have to find her. She'd had blonde hair, but she certainly wasn't young.

"Was the man that got into your car middle-aged?" Leighton asked. "Or young?"

"Maybe middle-aged but I'm not sure. He had a cap on. He had a cap on the day I saw him in town, too. I didn't pay that much attention to him. His voice was an older voice, though."

"Would you recognize his voice again?" Tom asked.

"Maybe," Susan said. "But he didn't speak much."

"He could have disguised his voice," Leighton said.

"What can you recall about him? Height, build, anything will be helpful." Tom looked at her intently.

"He was wearing a cap that night, like I said, but he had thick hair, dark hair. The cap made him look younger than he was, I think." She looked up at Leighton. "I'm sorry."

"Did the cap have any insignia on it?" Tom asked. "Like Clemson U?"

"No," Susan said. "I don't remember anything on it."

"Did he have a Southern drawl, or did he speak like he was from somewhere else?" Leighton noticed that Tom had kept a reassuring hold on Susan's arm.

"He was definitely a Southerner," she said. "He was pretty tall, when he got in my car his knees were high off the ground."

"And that was the same man who approached you in the parking lot, the man you remember from town, the familiar-looking man?" Leighton asked.

Susan nodded. "I think so. I saw him in the bar. I noticed that he looked at me and I remember hoping he wouldn't approach me. I don't like being bothered by men. There was something in the way he smiled at me that made me think he was noticing me too much. I didn't like that. Men intrude on a woman's space so much of the time." She looked at Leighton sadly. "That should have been enough for me not to let him in my car. I mean, I thought he was going to hit on me."

"Are you gay?" Leighton asked out of the blue.

A blush appeared on Susan's face, but she answered Leighton. "I am," she said. "Does that matter?"

Leighton smiled at her. "It might, it might not."

"Don't blame yourself," Tom said, giving a glance to Leighton and raising an eyebrow. "You were trying to be helpful, he said he needed gas. Did you happen to notice the car he was driving?"

"No." Susan looked at him sadly. "He just came out of nowhere."

"That's okay," Tom said.

Susan turned away. "I didn't see him again inside the bar after my friends showed up, but I wasn't looking for him. My friends took a booth and I joined them. I just didn't care if the man was there or not once my friends came."

"How did he get you out to the Rabbit Trail?" Leighton asked.

"He put his knife up to my neck at the stop sign on Pine and told me to take a left or he'd slit my throat."

Tom looked at Leighton. "The stop sign on Pine is fifteen miles from the trail."

"Pretty deserted at that time of night," Leighton said.

"He kept the knife at your throat?" Tom asked and Susan nodded.

"Can you describe him for us again?" Leighton also had her notebook open, eager to get a handle on what this guy looked like.

"Good looking, I guess, Susan said. "Well built, muscular, like he was an outdoor type. If I were straight, I might have found him attractive. But I'm not." She looked at Leighton. "I don't know the color of his eyes. It was dark, but I felt like they were light."

"That's great," Leighton said. "Anything special you remember about him? Any moles or scars?"

"He had a beard, a short one." Susan looked at both Tom and Leighton. "He was tan, very tan."

"Do you know Lana Shaw or Keri Richardson?" Leighton asked.

"No," Susan said. "Why?"

"They were the names of the other two girls found on the trail." Tom told her.

"They were both gay," Leighton said. "Like you. That's why I asked you earlier if you were, it seems an odd coincidence."

"Oh."

"Did you know Ashley Dowd?"

Susan shook her head. "No, sorry."

"You've been a big help," Tom said. "Thank you, and we'll be back in touch."

"Oh, one other thing ... before he raped me, he used a condom."

Leighton caught Tom's eye. So much for a semen sample, she thought.

Tom looked at her in the car. "Why'd you ask her about the first victim, Ashley Dowd?" he asked. "Ashley Dowd wasn't a student."

"Not sure why I asked her," she said. "But

whoever killed Lana and Keri and nearly killed Susan is the same man that killed Ashley. Quite sure of that. Ashley Dowd was my boyfriend's wife."

Tom gave her an odd look. "You're serious?"

"Dead serious," she said. "The student connection might not be important, but the gay connection might be."

"Didn't know you had a boyfriend." He looked straight ahead and drummed his fingers on the dash. "I guess that means I'm out of luck?" He turned to her and smiled. "Unless, of course, he turns out to be a serial killer."

She smiled back. "Are you messing with me, Tom?"

"You don't suspect your boyfriend of murder, do you?

"Of course not."

"Look, we've still got the rape kit from Susan. We might get something."

"I doubt it. She said he used a condom."

He took a deep breath and changed the subject. "You think it means something that the women were gay?" he asked. "They were also all blonde."

"I found out the sexuality of both girls quite by accident when I questioned Keri and Lana's parents. An odd coincidence, I think. Maybe the guy had some sort of vendetta against gay women."

"Your boyfriend's wife was gay?" he asked, the surprise in his voice apparent.

Leighton shook her head. "I don't know. I have suspicions. I need to question Dorothy Sanders again."

"You suspect Ethan in these rapes and murders?" Tom looked at her. "I can't find any reason to suspect him."

"He works on campus and he's a cocky little bastard, but I don't."

"Good, not enough evidence to suspect him. Cocky is not cause. Anyway, Susan's car was wiped clean except for a hair fiber on the passenger side."

"So the bastard took the time to wipe down Susan's car before he walked back to town?"

"So it seems. We'll get DNA results off the hair fiber in about a week. Maybe we've got a match to the rapist. Why did you suspect Ethan, what would he have against gay women?"

She looked out the window. "Maybe he just doesn't like blondes. Anyway, he lives near the campus, and he works on campus. He could have scouted out any one of those girls, followed them, and murdered them. If he was observing them, he knew a lot about them. Ethan's overly obnoxious with women."

"He would have been quite young at the time of the first murder." Tom waited for her response. "Ashley's murder? He would have been around fifteen."

"I know, but old enough to hold a knife in his hand. But you're right, most likely too young for murder, but fifteen-year-old boys have murdered."

Tom continued to stare at her. "Why do I get the feeling you want Ethan to be guilty? If you're really invested in that, I'd like to know why."

Leighton stared straight ahead. "I just want the murderer to be caught. I'm not invested in anyone yet."

"Well, they're extrapolating DNA from the hair fiber so we'll have our answer soon enough. The hair could also be from a friend of hers."

"A friend that killed her?"

Tom hunched his shoulders up. "Could be."

"So, how did the rapist get back to the bar in Greenville? We know he left Susan's car up on the Rabbit Trail wiped as clean as he could get it."

Tom shook his head. "He might have walked partway and then hitched."

"I doubt if he'd hitch. Someone might have remembered seeing him. I think it's too far to walk," Leighton said. "maybe he called a cab?"

"I don't think he would have been that stupid. A man in good shape can walk fifteen miles." Tom turned to her. "There was a break of about two years between the Ashley Dowd murder and the Lana Shaw murder. The wounds are consistent with a hunting knife. Most likely a Bugout."

Leighton nodded. "The murder weapon was never recovered. You think it's still up there?"

"Not unless he dropped it, but I doubt it. That would have been careless of him. He might still have it, though."

"Well, we could do a search, if we had the evidence to suspect anyone."

"The next victim was found approximately a year later. Is that his pattern, to kill a woman every year or so?" Tom stared at her for a moment. "Any theories on that, Detective?"

"No theories on that yet, but I find it interesting that three of the women were gay." Leighton looked back at him. "Coincidence?"

Tom smiled. "Like I said, three of the women were also blonde," he said. "I don't think it has anything to do with their sexuality. I mean how would you explain Ashley Dowd? She was married, Leighton."

"I'll let you know what I come up with after I question Dorothy."

"I like a cop with instinct," he said and grinned at her, "and yours are very interesting, a bit unorthodox but damn good, so do your thing, Leighton, even though I think you may be off track on this one. Married women aren't usually gay, to my knowledge."

Leighton smiled. "That's not necessarily correct," she said, thinking of her mother, but thank you for your support." His smile warmed her and she had to admit that she found him attractive, likable, very much like Beau. Oh, life can be so confusing, she thought.

Leighton rang Dorothy's doorbell and only waited a moment before she appeared at the door, somewhat rattled to see Leighton. She quickly recovered and graciously held the door open for her.

"Detective McArdle." She stared at Leighton. "Didn't expect to see you again."

"Some things I forgot to ask."

Dorothy stepped back. "Of course. I'm afraid I don't have any cookies today," she said as she led Leighton into her living room. "But I can offer you some coffee."

"No, thank you," Leighton said. "This shouldn't take long."

"Please, please have a seat." Dorothy pointed to the couch and sat opposite in a lavish plump chair. She stared at Leighton and waited for her to speak.

"I'm going to be blunt," Leighton said. "But I have to ask this, were you and Ashley having an affair?"

Clearly startled, Dorothy sat back and didn't speak for several moments.

"Wow," she said. "Whatever gave you that idea?"

"Please, Dorothy, it's important. I need the

truth. It's a hunch, that's all."

Dorothy sighed and she and Leighton stared at each other for almost a minute before Dorothy finally spoke. "It was more than an affair," she said after her pause. "We were terribly in love. We planned to leave our husbands for each other … we were planning to move in together, to live together."

"Sean knew?"

Dorothy nodded. "Yes, she told him a few weeks before she was murdered. He blew up, gave Ashley quite a black eye. I talked her out of the restraining order, said he hit her in the moment out of shock, but she was afraid of him after that. He wasn't a violent man … he was startled by our news, that's all. I told her he would calm down and he did eventually. My husband threw a table across the room. I imagine it was quite a shock for both of them."

Leighton leaned forward. "Sean hit his wife?"

"Well, can you blame him?"

"Dorothy, that makes him a suspect in her murder. You do know that, don't you? He had motive."

"But he had an alibi. He was at the high school that night. He was cleared of any wrongdoing."

"I'm looking into the timeline. The police back then might not have had the correct time of death."

Dorothy put her head down. "I'm so sorry not

to have told you about Ashley and me. Really I am. I didn't think it would matter. I didn't want to make it worse for my husband, you know, if people knew. He did not take the news in his stride, either. I thought he was going to expire, he got so angry. He might have had a heart attack."

"I understand," Leighton said. "This revelation could solve our case. Sean could have killed his wife."

Dorothy looked at her feet. "That's ridiculous," she said.

"Tell me about that night."

"Ashley moved into the motel near The Steak House, the Ramada Inn. She moved out right after he hit her. She brought her kids to her mother's. We had rented an apartment and planned on moving into it the first of the month, picking up her kids then."

"But she was murdered before you could do that?"

"Yes," Dorothy said.

"So, Ashley was living in the motel for a while? So, we really don't know what night Ashley was murdered."

"I suppose not," Dorothy said.

"Her parents took her children?"

"Yes, her parents had them after she moved out. I believe they still do."

"How did Sean take that, that she moved out

and left the children with her mother?"

"I didn't want to go near Sean, so I don't know. He was furious with me. I didn't want him socking me in the face. Ashley said he was still quite angry."

"You told the police you knew what time she had left to pick up dinner the night they assumed she was killed, but that wasn't true. You just knew she was at the motel and would probably have dinner at The Steak House. She could have had dinner at any time on any night. Did Sean know she was at that particular motel?"

"I think he did. She called him from there, so maybe she mentioned it."

"This could look very bad for Sean," Leighton said.

"Personally, I don't care." Dorothy looked right in her eyes. "I loved her. He thought he owned her. He was so possessive it makes me nauseous to think about it. He called us freaks. My husband said he'd pay for my therapy. They both acted like a couple of jackasses."

"Why didn't you tell the police any of this, Dorothy?"

"I thought it was none of anyone's business and I never suspected Sean of hurting her. I had to think of my husband's feelings, I didn't want it all over the papers. It would have embarrassed him. It was our business."

Leighton stood up. "Thank you for seeing me

today. I'll let myself out."

She stopped at the door and turned back to Dorothy. "Is your husband ...?" She broke off her sentence, trying to figure out the best way to phrase it.

"We're divorced. He has an apartment in Clemson near the university. We never had children together, so we have no reason to speak to each other anymore, but we do still speak." She looked at Leighton sadly. "He pretty much thinks I have a malady," she said. "We sometimes meet in town for lunch, to catch up. I think he'd like us to get back together, but for me it's not possible."

"Did your husband ever have a beard?"

"Yes, he still does. He didn't have one when we first met, though. Why?"

"Oh, just curious, that's all."

"He let his beard grow after Sean grew his. They often looked like brothers."

"Were they close?" Leighton asked.

"Ridiculously so, especially after they found out about us."

Leighton felt sick. Confusion wafted over her like some giant wave and at any minute the wave would slam down upon her, and she would be knocked to the hard sand. The answer is right in front of me, she thought. Why would it matter if Sean and Ed resembled each other? Yet she felt it did matter.

Her hands shook as she started her car. Sean had a motive to murder his wife, a cheating spouse, and with another woman no less. He might be working out his revenge on the other two women, hating their sexual orientation because his wife had left him for a woman. She prayed she was wrong. She prayed that the DNA would eliminate him. She wanted anyone other than Sean to be the guilty man. Ethan did not have a short beard, he had worn his beard long before he cut it and Tom was right, he'd been too young to kill Ashley. But it couldn't be Sean. Sean would be exonerated. He had witnesses that placed him at a parent's evening on the night of Ashley's murder but the exact time of death was never determined. As Ashley's husband, he'd been investigated and no charges had ever been brought against him. He was innocent. Yet something gnawed at her. My God, she had considered, however briefly, sleeping with him, even loving him without knowing who he was. She put those thoughts out of her mind and drove home.

Chapter Thirty-Two

Dickie leaned back in the porch chair and stared at Leighton. He could tell she was terribly upset about something, and he couldn't elicit just what that was; she wasn't talking. Maybe she found out he'd been lying about having lunch with his mother the day of the fire. Lillian had called him in a panic a week or so ago, "Tell her we had lunch the day of the fire, in the dining room," she'd insisted. "It was too hot for the lawn. She's going to ask you about it, Dickie, so tell her that."

And so he did.

"I hear Robbie is settled in New York, starting college tomorrow." Leighton looked at him and gave him her dazzling white smile. "You proud?"

He lifted his head up quickly. "Sure am proud, worried though."

"Of course," she said.

"She's all alone up there."

"She'll make friends." Leighton put her head back and felt the sun on her.

Dickie kept thinking about that damn day, the day he'd buried Lottie's body in the swamp. He wondered how his seventy-seven-year-old mother could have gotten Lottie's body into her car. There was no one there to help her. He wondered why he'd never questioned that before. He remembered something about her telling him Lottie was still alive when she'd first gotten to her house, and she was able to walk to the car. But then she died? Didn't make all that much sense to Dickie.

"So, you don't think Sean Dowd came on to Pamela Tilly?" Leighton asked. "I think you could be wrong." Leighton lifted her head and took in his facial expression, one of surprise.

DIckie was startled, for sure. He knew she was dating Sean now. She couldn't possibly believe that Sean would have come on to Pam, could she?

"The girl is a liar," he said.

"We're all liars," she said. "Your wife is lying to me. She set that fire at Lottie's house, and I know it."

He looked at her and held her eyes. "Prove it."

"I can't. I can't prove anything just yet."

"Just yet? Are you implying that it's only a matter of time before you do?"

She closed her eyes against the sun. "Maybe," she said.

He leaned his head back as well, and brought his straw hat lower on his forehead, thinking of his mother and how on earth she could have gotten Lottie's body into her car. He guessed Lottie wasn't altogether dead, and she had somehow stumbled to the car? Well, he supposed that was possible. Dickie sighed. But then, had his mother put a pillow over Lottie's head once she got her back home to ensure her deceased status? No, his mother was not strong enough for that. Even injured, Lottie was younger and much too agile to let someone overtake her.

"Earth to Dickie," he heard Leighton say.

"Just wondering what you're not telling me," he said.

"Did you know Sean's wife was murdered?" she asked.

He opened his eyes quickly. "What?"

"It's true. Her body was left on the Rabbit Trail. Did you know that?"

"God, no, I thought she died of cancer. Did Lottie know that?"

"You tell me."

"She never told me that. Maybe he swore her to secrecy, didn't want it known."

"Maybe she didn't know, either."

"Lottie was family, she had to have known."

Leighton sat up a bit and reached for her iced tea. "Well, you know how families are, the things we keep from each other?"

His thoughts immediately returned to his mother. How had she gotten Lottie into her car? His mother could barely lift an ice bucket. He'd have to ask her that. He grinned at Leighton. "Ain't that the truth," he said.

"We think Sean's wife was the first victim of the Rabbit Trail murderer," Leighton told him.

"Oh, boy," he said, "Rabbit Trail murderer? Need help solving that one? I can clear my schedule.

Nothing like tracking a serial killer."

Leighton laughed. "Where is your charming wife this afternoon, Dickie?"

"At the beauty parlor." He smiled. "She goes every other week."

"She sure keeps up appearances, doesn't she?"

"I don't believe you answered my question. I could be of some help."

"We girls have to look our best," she said. "or the eyes of our lovers may wander."

"Amen." He smiled, thinking of Lottie, her thick brown hair he loved to feel on his hand like some fine, soft yarn. Still overcome with grief, he could not imagine never being able to touch her hair again.

Leighton put her tea back on the wicker table and thought of Sean, the haunted look in his eyes when she mentioned Pam's name.

"If I need you, I'll call you," she said to Dickie, who didn't seem much appeased by that answer.

Leighton had another thought about the killer. Aside from Sean, who else had any emotion attached to Ashley's murder? Would Ed Saunders have motive? His wife was leaving him for a woman; maybe in Ed's mind, it was enough reason to get rid of the competition. But how would that explain the other two murders and Susan Engel's rape?

Leighton dug into Ed Saunders's past. She continued to eliminate Ethan as a suspect. She agreed with Tom, he had been too young at the time of Ashley's murder, and as far as Leighton knew, he didn't know any of the women. The murders would have been random for Ethan and not tied in any way to their sexuality.

She discovered that Ed taught at the college of Business at Clemson and the other two victims, after Ashley, had taken classes with him, but Susan had not. However, it was possible that Ed had been more aware of Susan than she might have known. He might have been aware of her sexuality, followed her around campus without her knowledge. Susan bore a striking resemblance to Ashley Dowd. For a man enraged to learn of his wife's passion for another woman, that might have been a trigger.

Before Leighton approached Ed, she'd question Susan again, before her release from the hospital.

"I'm getting out tomorrow," Susan said and smiled at Leighton. "I can't wait to fly out of here."

Leighton stood at the foot of Susan's bed. "I'm happy for you," she said. We have a passenger list of everyone on that plane. You'll be safe."

"I've tried to remember more, but I can't."

"That's okay. I just want to ask you about a professor at Clemson. Professor Saunders, did you know him?"

Susan thought for a moment. "No," she said. "Should I know him?"

"Well, you might have seen him on campus if you didn't know him directly."

Leighton reached for the folder under her arm. "I'm going to show you a photograph and I want you to tell me if you recognize either of the men in the picture, or both if that's the case."

"Okay." Susan reached out for the photograph as Leighton walked around the bed and handed it to her. Susan studied it for several moments. "This is a really bad photograph," she said and handed it back.

"They're all clean-shaven in the picture and it's not a good copy, but can you visualize one of the men a few years older and with a beard?"

"I'm sorry," she said. "None of them look much older than me in this picture."

"So the man who attacked you wasn't a kid?"

"No, I guess not," she said. "But he didn't look like the men in the photograph either, I don't think."

Witnesses were often confused and bits and pieces of the crime returned over time, but for now, Leighton wouldn't get any more information from her.

"Would you be willing to look at our artist's aged portrait of both men?"

"Of course," Susan said.

Chapter Thirty-Three

Deborah didn't know what she was doing. Why on earth did she keep driving by Jeremiah's house — was she spying on him? It was an impulse she couldn't control, though she'd tried to steer clear of the man. She didn't like seeing that girl walking up to his front door the other day, parking her stupid motorcycle in his driveway. Just up his alley, a beautiful, young White girl with the hots for him.

"Stupid son of a bitch," she whispered, her heart accelerating, nearly driving her to barge on in there and throw that little whore out. She couldn't figure out why it mattered, but she felt an ownership when it came to Jeremiah, just as she had when they were lovers years ago, and even when he went off to jail. Problem was that now he could have all the pretty women he wanted. He was a free man. Her sense of ownership was certainly threatened.

She loved her husband. No one in the world more

suited to her than Dickie but her feelings for Jeremiah were like coals in a fire pit, festering and burning till she was about to scream. She wanted the man in a way that she'd never wanted her husband, her sweet Dickie. Sweetness was anathema to Jeremiah. He was rugged and ruthless, 'bout as sweet as sour candy, more like some seductive chocolate cake tempting and cajoling, and forcing her to struggle against her will, against her fucking desire to do the right thing and walk the hell away from that moist fine chocolate cake.

"Shit," she said as she got out of her car. "Never could walk away from chocolate cake."

"You like my hair, honey?" Deborah stood in Jeremiah's front doorway and showed him the prettiest smile.

Jeremiah stood frightfully still and stared at her. "Go home, Deborah," he finally said, and began to shut the door.

Deborah reached out and pushed his arm out of the way. "You know you're happy to see me."

Jeremiah stepped back and watched her walk to the center of his living room.

"Been years since I've been here. Looks better now." She smiled as if she were there to sell him something.

"What the hell do you want?"

"I said you had to return the favor, didn't I?"

"What the hell you talking about, Deborah, what favor?"

"That day out at Sutter's? Remember? I made you a happy man right there in the passenger seat of my

Cadillac."

She walked up close to him and put her hands on his waist. He stepped back quickly. "Get out of here, Deborah. I want nothing to do with you."

"But you're quite in love with me. We both know that. Love just doesn't go away, Jeremiah, remember our youth?"

He glared at her. "You're delusional."

She laughed and went to his big brown overstuffed chair and sat. "Shame you don't mean what you promise."

"I never promised you anything. Now, please leave."

"How many women you have to throw out of your bed, Jeremiah?"

His glare, one of naked contempt, made it clear he was figuring out what the hell she wanted. "You won't be one of them," he said. "'Cause you will never be in my bed."

"Not what you used to say, sweetie."

"I have no recollection of anything I used to say."

"Saw Pam Tilly coming to your house in the middle of the day." She looked at him coyly.

"You spying on me?"

"Don't have to spy. The girl was rather brazen about it, and I was passing."

"Just happened to be passing?" He raised his eyebrow at her.

"Seems I was."

"Go home, Deborah."

"You robbing the cradle again?"

"None of your business."

"I want you to keep it in your pants. You are my

son's biological father. You hear me?" Deborah stood to her feet and walked close. "You hear?"

"What the hell does Barnaby care who I sleep with? For that matter, you shouldn't give a damn, either."

"I don't care, but Barnaby thinks you're distasteful. That was the word he used, 'distasteful'. You embarrass him. I told him what a woman chaser you are."

"Do I embarrass him, or make you jealous?"

She laughed one of those loud lyrical laughs. "Oh, please," she said.

He walked up closer to her and took her in his arms. She barely moved. He kissed her, one of those long soulful kisses. She finally pushed him off.

"Why, what was that kiss about, appeasing my so-called jealousy?"

He winked at her. "Old times," he said. "That's all."

"Still think I want you, Jeremiah? Well, I don't. I am married to the man of my choice, and I don't want anyone else, especially not you."

Jeremiah laughed. "The man of your choice? More like the lady of your choice. Dickie Darling wears dresses, Deborah, or haven't you heard? Looks damn good in them too, I hear."

"You are crude. You are a liar. I will see you burn in hell with your vicious remarks."

Jeremiah picked her purse up off the chair and handed it to her. "Best be going, Mrs. Darling. Shouldn't be trying to seduce another man when you're married to such a rich upstanding one."

Deborah took her bag. "Stay away from all those

girls ... underage girls going to get you lynched, Jeremiah."

"Anyone going to get me lynched, Deborah Darling, it's you."

She put her hands up around his shoulders. "Don't mess with me," she said. "You hear, don't mess with me." She pressed herself into him and moved her hips around, lifted up her dress and moaned deeply.

"Can't promise that," he whispered breathlessly, as he picked her up in his arms and carried her to his bedroom. "you're just too good at rousing me."

Chapter Thirty-Four

Turned out there were surveillance cameras across the street from the restaurant where Sean had roughed up Ethan that night. The images were very grainy but there was a good shot of the woman who had shown up in the parking lot and defended Ethan. Leighton blew the photo up and had a good still shot of an attractive older woman with blonde hair. She went back to the restaurant and questioned everyone at the bar and the entire staff about the woman's identity. She was from Clemson and had been to the restaurant several times with Ethan, who, according to the gossip, was her young paramour.

"Good police work," Tom said to her. "Have you questioned her yet? I'd like to eliminate the kid for good this time."

She looked up at him and nodded. "Yeah, she lives in Clemson with her husband but she's obviously fooling around with Ethan. Told me he's a nice kid.

She gives him money. She calls it an allowance. She said he's completely nonviolent and has absolutely nothing against gay women as far as she knows. Oh, and she met up with him later that night, the night of Susan's attack."

"Her husband know about her little arrangement?"

"Didn't ask. I didn't think it was important to the case. He didn't do it."

"We'll have DNA results by the end of the week. We might find something."

"And we might not," Leighton said.

"Don't believe in DNA?"

"We both know he didn't do it, Tom. But I had to question it. Turns out he had an alibi anyway. He couldn't have raped Susan and then met up with his lady friend."

"I'm counting on the DNA to tell us who did this."

"I want to question Marlene Tilly," Leighton said suddenly.

"What's that going to prove?" Tom asked.

"I want more insight into Sean Dowd."

Tom did a bit of a double-take. "Your boyfriend, Sean Dowd?"

Leighton nodded her head. "Yeah, I need to look more deeply into this. He might have had motive for the killings. Pam Tilly could be in danger. She's gay and she's blonde."

Tom nodded his head and looked at her.

"His wife was leaving him for another woman," Leighton added quickly.

"Whoa, Leighton, you've got to have more for me than that. You think that's cause for murder?"

"Of course it's cause for murder," she snapped. "What happened to 'do your thing, Leighton'? She was a cheating spouse, Tom."

He smiled at her. "Okay, give me what you got."

"Fine. Just listen. Victim number one, his wife. He was enraged to find out she was leaving him for another woman and he kills her. Two years after his wife's murder, he moves in with Marlene Tilly, but develops a thing for her young, pretty daughter, who rebuffs his advances because she's gay, to name just one reason. Anyway, his earlier rage toward his wife resurfaces, and he rapes and kills a gay woman ... out of his psychosis ... his rage."

"Why didn't he kill Pam Tilly?"

"Too close to home."

Tom nodded. "Okay. Go on."

"Marlene Tilly throws him out because he eventually acts on his desire for her daughter, and he goes off the deep end again and kills another gay woman, but it's really Pam Tilly he's angry with, she's got too many female lovers. Pam starts rejecting his advances because she's in love with a female. That sets him off again. Boom, our attempted murder. I think he fell in love with Pam. He was enraged by her sexual preference."

Tom stared at her skeptically. "You really believe all that?" he finally said.

Anger stirred in Leighton for what she assumed was his doubt. "You don't think there's motive there?"

"I'll have the DNA from the hair fiber soon enough. Let's wait. Let's see if we get a match."

"You're too hung up on the DNA, Tom. I want to question Marlene. If he did commit these murders, we're introducing strong motive, especially if we can prove an affair with Pam, her sexuality, his wife's sexuality, are too similar, the sexuality of the victims. It ties together. He was most likely in love with both his wife and Pam Tilly. For all we know, he might have been rejected by those two girls and *wham*, he flies into a rage and murders them."

"Whoa, slow down. It sounds like you're assuming murder here. Anyway, DNA is stronger evidence than who sleeps with whom."

"And it might not exonerate him. We may not be able to match it. That's all we have right now, some DNA that might belong to anyone who sat in that car, not necessarily the killer."

Tom sighed. "Keep me posted, Leighton."

"It's not just Sean. Ed Saunders is also a suspect."

"The husband of the woman Ashley left Sean for?"

"Yep," Leighton said. "I'm on to something, Tom."

He smiled and shrugged his shoulders. "Do your thing, Leighton."

Chapter Thirty-Five

Leighton had always loved Columbia and would not have minded meeting Marlene there but when she'd called, Marlene said she was going to check on her house and would be in Pickens for a few days. When Leighton rang the bell, she found a very confused and despondent Marlene.

"Come on in," Marlene said as she held open the door. She led Leighton into her sun porch, which faced her gardens.

"Whoa," Leighton said as she stared outside.

"Just had the gardens repaired too."

"So sorry," Leighton said, "what happened?"

Marlene hunched her shoulders up. "I have no idea."

"Why would anyone rip up a garden?"

Marlene shook her head. "I don't know. I'm going to have to get the debris removed but I can't afford to replace what I had." Marlene looked about to cry.

"I know this is going to be a touchy subject, Marlene, but I have to ask you a few questions about Sean Dowd."

Marlene was startled. "I thought you were here to discuss my daughter's disappearance."

"Your daughter's disappearance is being handled by the Pickens County Sheriff's Department at this time. I work cold cases."

"Can you tell me if there's any updates on my daughter? I don't wish to discuss Sean Dowd."

"There is no new information on Pam, no."

"Well, I see her picture is all over town, at least."

"We've had search parties out too, Marlene. We'll do everything we can to find her."

Marlene put her head down. "Why are there also missing person fliers of Lottie Lacock all over town?"

Leighton stared at her. "I thought you must have heard … Lottie has been missing for over a year now. Her house was burned to the ground and after that, she disappeared."

"I see. No, I didn't know."

Leighton saw the confused expression on her face. "You haven't seen her, have you?"

Marlene shook her head but not before Leighton was certain Marlene knew something about Lottie.

"There have been some bodies found on the Swamp Rabbit Trail," Leighton began.

"And this is important because?"

"Because Sean is a suspect. Not officially, but there is motive. His wife was the serial killer's first victim. Sean's wife was leaving him for a woman."

Marlene's head sprang up quickly. "He told me his wife died of cancer."

"No, she was murdered," Leighton said.

"I had no idea. I don't remember hearing about that."

"Two other women were murdered up there, we think by the same man. Their bodies were found recently."

"His wife was gay?" Marlene was dumbfounded when she asked.

Leighton nodded her head. "Did he have an affair with your gay daughter, Marlene?"

The tears came to Marlene's eyes quickly. "Yes, he did," she said softly. "It might not have been consensual at first. I don't know for sure."

"Was he in love with your daughter, or was it just sexual?"

"He couldn't take his eyes off my daughter."

"Who made the first move?"

"Doesn't matter a damn who seduced whom, does it?"

"I'm sorry," Leighton said.

"That's when I kicked him out and why."

"So, your daughter's sexuality is pretty adventurous?"

"Guess so," Marlene said. "But why does that make Sean guilty of murder?"

"Well, it doesn't, but he might have had a vendetta against gay women in particular. Pam tried to stop seeing him when she met a girl. He might not have liked that. What he's not saying is that he might have been pretty hung up on her."

Marlene's eyes suddenly opened very wide, "Are you hinting that he's responsible for my daughter's disappearance?"

"I think it's a fair assumption, yes."

When Leighton got to her car, she called Tom. He picked up right away.

"Leighton?"

"Yeah, listen, Sean had an affair with Pam Tilly. For all we know, he's responsible for her disappearance. Pam could be another Rabbit Trail victim."

"Maybe," Tom said.

"I think he really had a thing for her, Tom. His rage makes him our best suspect for the Rabbit Trail murders. He had motive."

"The DNA results are in from the hair fibers found in Susan's car," he said.

"Sean's?" she asked.

"Nope, no match to Sean. He's clear, but you were on to something."

"What do you mean?"

"They're a match to Ed Sanders' DNA ."

"Ed Sanders?"

"There would be no reason for Ed's DNA to be found in Susan's car … she said she didn't know him."

"How did you get Ed's DNA for a match?"

"Mart questioned Dorothy Sanders and she gave us a hairbrush of his."

"Well, I'll be a son of a bitch," Leighton said.

Chapter Thirty-Six

Marlene turned to look at Lottie. They were in the backyard, sunning on their lounge chairs ahead of a busy weekend. "Thirty years?" she asked in disbelief.

"Thanks for not giving me up," Lottie said. "I appreciate your discretion."

"Were you in love with him all that time?" Marlene asked.

"I'm still in love with him, Marlene."

Marlene looked shocked; an expression that hadn't left her face since Lottie had just relayed the last year of her life.

"I can't believe what that old woman did to you."

"Well, I let her do it to me. I went along with it."

"Any chance you'll go back to Pickens? I mean, you can't let Lillian Darling run your life."

Lottie shook her head. She'd contemplated it, obviously, but the consequences would be dire. She'd have to deal with too much anger. She was sure Lillian would find a way to destroy her. She was happy in Columbia, she loved running Cottonwoods, meeting new people all the time. She didn't think she could ever adjust to Pickens again. Most people knew she'd had an affair with Dickie and their sympathies were with Deborah. Deborah was downright dangerous. Lottie was sure she'd meant to kill her that day she'd started the fire.

"I can't believe Deborah did that, set your house on fire." Marlene looked at Lottie with that same shocked expression.

"You must have been reading my mind. I was just thinking about her."

"God, whatever for?"

"She was my best friend, Marlene."

"Remind me never to get a best friend."

"I miss her terribly."

"I can't imagine why."

"I miss Dickie terribly."

Marlene turned to her. "Why don't you get in touch with him, let him know you're all right."

"He thinks I'm dead, Marlene."

"You're not dead, Lottie. That poor man must be suffering. He loved you."

Lottie lay her head back and closed her eyes. "The damage has been done," she whispered. "I can never go back."

Lottie wondered if Dickie ever traveled to Columbia, but even if he did, she wasn't likely to know about it. She dismissed her thoughts of Dickie and brought them to what was on the agenda for the weekend, a cross-dressing retreat, of all things. She smiled, doubting Dickie would ever come out of the closet and walk around town in a dress the way Ginger did. He'd certainly never show up at a cross-dressing retreat, that was for sure.

"You ready for the cross-dressers this weekend?" she asked Marlene.

"Oh, please, Lottie. It's bad enough I have to deal with lesbians and drag queens. What the hell is a cross-dresser?"

"I thought you'd come to terms with this wonderful array of delightful ladies." She turned to grin at Marlene. "Straight men who like to wear women's clothes, that's all."

Marlene made an odd sound and turned her head away. "Weird. You hear me, Lottie? Downright weird." She turned back with a grimace, as if she'd bitten into a lemon.

Of course, Lottie hadn't mentioned that Dickie liked to cross-dress, that was pretty much the secret about Dickie that few people knew.

"It's quite an elegant event, I hear," Lottie added. "They've ordered Champagne for Saturday night and rib-eye steaks."

"How will I keep a straight face?" Marlene said sarcastically.

"Oh, loosen up, Marlene, these men will remind you of your ladies' canasta group. You'll feel right at home."

Once the forensics artist added twenty years to Ed's age, Susan recognized him as her attacker and Ed Sanders was arrested for Susan Engel's rape. Ed pleaded not guilty, said he had no idea who Susan

Engle was, and to his recollection, he'd never been in her car, but a jury found him guilty. Tying him to the murders of the two other girls was more difficult, but the case against him for those murders was active. His trial for the murder of Ashley was set for the following year.

The team was celebrating at The River House. A rowdy crowd that night, they were ecstatic that they had their suspect in jail. Fortunately for the rest of the diners, the group was given a private room.

Mart held out his glass and made a toast to Leighton. "You had it nearly right, Leighton, but you should have kept your money on Ed Sanders, not Sean Dowd. But God, you were close."

"Thank you, Mart," she said. "But I prefer condemning the right man, and for the record, I would have. I was getting there."

"Well, now you can marry Sean, he's clean." Tom looked at her and grinned.

"Who says I want to marry anybody?" Leighton looked around the table. She noticed she'd gotten a toast from two female detectives.

Tom ignored her comment and continued to eat, drink, and make small talk. Leighton was very aware of him. She was almost directly across the table from him, and their eyes kept meeting. She was excited to see him again, even if it were only to walk by him in the office. She didn't have any guards up and she didn't feel ambivalent about it either. It was an odd sensation, like the way Beau had comforted and titillated her at the same time. Maybe she was even relaxed enough to ask him out on a date. She had broken it off with Sean and promised to remain friends, but doubted they would see each other much. He had been a bit perplexed by her sudden decision, but he didn't try to talk her out of it. He kissed her on the cheek and walked away, saying he'd call, but so far, she hadn't heard from him since he'd congratulated her on Ed's conviction.

She ran into him in town once and took note of the cap he wore, his deep tan with a sudden jab. Susan's attacker had been very tan and had worn a cap, but it was Ed who had murdered Ashley and raped Susan, not Sean. Still, Sean was the avid hiker, not Ed. It would have been easy for Sean to walk fifteen miles. She dismissed her niggling perceptions and walked on. They did not have the wrong man. They had their killer.

Pam Tilly was still a missing person, but Ed swore he had no idea who she was aside from some teenager his buddy had a thing for. Sean was questioned, but he could not be tied to Pam's disappearance. There was absolutely no evidence against him.

Later that evening, after the party was breaking up, Leighton found herself leaving with Tom.

"I'll escort you to your car," he said.

The evening air felt warm on her skin, a sweet breath across her cheek. The sky was filled with stars, there seemed to be too many of them, but each star had its own designated space from which to shine and blink. Voices came from the distance, even music from someone's car radio – an old song her mother used to sing to her. She wanted to remember the moment because she knew it was moving her toward something, a new beginning perhaps.

"Love this song," she said. "It's one of my mother's

favorites."

"You like New York in June?" he asked.

"Never been there."

"A Gershwin tune?"

"Sure do."

"Moonlight, motor trips?"

"Check."

"A fireside when a storm is due?"

"Check again," she said with a smile.

"Potato chips?"

"You betcha," she said.

"I like the song too," he said. "My mother used to sing it to me. She had a voice like Karen Carpenter."

"Karen Carpenter, huh?"

"Loved seventies music, my mother did. Me too."

"And Frank Sinatra?"

"Oh, yeah, definitely Frank Sinatra."

"Really? We have a lot in common." She smiled at him and noticed his serious expression.

"I wanted to do this the first time I ever laid eyes on your face," Tom said, turning her toward him.

"What's that?" Leighton asked.

He took her in his arms and kissed her, and the new beginning trembled in her hands. The words to the old song lingered, and her knees might have given way, and the stars might have fallen from their designated place in the sky, fallen and glistened in her hair.

Chapter Thirty-Seven

1998
Five Years Later
Three days after the Halloween Party

"You should have seen their faces," Dickie said and laughed. "I've never seen anything like it, they were stunned."

It was the first time he'd seen Malcolm since Halloween night and hadn't really had the chance to gloat over his grand entrance, his 'coming out' party as Miss DeeDee. "Oh, I wish you could have been there."

Malcolm snapped at him. "I offered to come, but you would have nothing to do with me in front of your fancy friends."

"Nonsense," Dickie said. "I just didn't want them to associate me with drag, that's all."

"Heaven forbid," Malcolm snorted. "When a man

puts on a dress, it's drag, Dickie." He made a face. "Anyway, you looked marvelous, darlin'. Of course, they were stunned. Were they accepting, you think?"

"I think they were," Dickie said as he sipped on his wine spritzer and smiled. "My God, even Deborah was enthralled." He winked at Malcolm, "but not enthralled enough to let me walk around town in women's dresses ... not that I want to, mind you."

Malcolm laughed. "Your Deborah is full of surprises. Who knows what she'll come to accept as her beauty fades? She just might do your makeup and push you out of the door to dazzle the world. DeeDee will become Deborah's new next interest." He smiled broadly at Dickie. "Age increases our tolerance level, I hear. And she's what now, over sixty?"

"Perhaps age softens us." Dickie grimaced. "Well, my dear Malcolm, if my wife's beauty fades, then mine will be fading as well. She'll love having someone to share old age with, our wrinkles, our pasty memories." He sighed. "Now that Lottie is gone, I'll at least have Deborah."

"Oh, for God's sake, Dickie. Lottie has been gone for years now. She's not coming back. I wish you'd get over it. You talk about Lottie as if she just disappeared yesterday."

They were in the cottage lounging in front of the fans. Dickie had not yet put in central air and on ridiculously hot days, the cottage seemed to sweat. Despite the heat, the fans helped, not to mention the cold wine spritzers. Malcolm was not in drag; he was wearing very loose white pants and a pale blue open shirt that revealed a chest he had not yet waxed.

It was just days after the Halloween party, days

after Dickie's amazing entrance as DeeDee. People were still talking about it. But they were not talking about it with any kind of malice or sarcasm, as far as he knew. No, they just thought Dickie was a wonderfully amusing man, full of hilarious pranks.

"What gets me through life now, Malcolm, is how well I lie to myself." Dickie got up and went to the window. "I still speak to her, you know, to Lottie. Practically every day, I speak to her. It keeps her near."

"We all lie to ourselves. We all speak to ghosts and tell ourselves that they hear us."

"Thought I heard a car," Dickie said

"Who is it?" Malcolm asked as he joined Dickie at the window, wiping his brow with a handkerchief taken from his pocket and peering past the inviting creek, its clear, cool waters, an invitation to wade knee deep.

"My other daughter, the famous Leighton McArdle Hart, purveyor of crime." Dickie stood at the ready. "Perhaps she needs my help in solving a mystery." He grinned.

"She hasn't yet, Dickie," Malcolm said.

Leighton walked into the cottage and acknowledged her father with a kiss on the cheek and a wave to Malcolm.

"You two should be in bathing suits. It's almost Christmas and I'm baking out there. Do you believe this heat?" Leighton walked over to a chair and sat.

"Oh, darlin', my legs are a mess, hairy as a man's." Malcolm giggled. "I won't be in a bathing suit until next spring. At least," he said. "If ever," he added, patting his gut.

Leighton stretched out her legs and Dickie sat on the couch. "Must be hard being pregnant in this God-awful heat," he said and looked at her sympathetically.

"Well, it will pass. It's unnatural weather, a fluke. Got a cold bottle of water, Dickie?" she asked.

"I'll get it," Malcolm volunteered.

"To what do I owe the pleasure of your company?" Dickie grinned but instinctively knew she was about to dump little Lesley on him, a favor he'd performed many times in the past. Deborah barely tolerated the little toddler, preferring her 'blood' grandchildren or as she described them, her 'real' grandchildren, but Dickie, on the other hand, thought Lesley was a little kindred soul, a little crime buff in the rough.

"I have an unfortunate task to perform, and Tom is in Savannah," she said.

"You want me to watch Lesley?"

Leighton grinned. "I do."

Dickie smiled; he was already thinking about the fun he would have with his granddaughter. The little girl loved to watch him fish at the river and exhaust himself in the backyard with tent building and Lesley's little doll house. The little girl loved her tea parties with her tiny little plastic people. But most of all, she loved to watch *Forensic Files* with her granddaddy. Neither Dickie nor little Lesley could get enough of *Forensic Files*. It was their evening weakness.

"I'd be delighted." Dickie said and thought of the last lesson he'd given the little girl on the Wren and how to spot them. "There are a few new species of birds I'd like to teach her. She isn't yet familiar with the Rose-breasted Grosbeak."

"I'll only be gone a day and leaving her with my

mother isn't worth it, not for this short a visit." She looked at him appreciatively. "Oh, and don't let her watch *Forensic Files*, Dickie."

"Certainly," he said. "What's the unfortunate task?"

Leighton sighed. "We found a body out at Sutter's. Well, teenagers found it, unfortunately."

Dickie jumped to his feet. "You found Lottie?" he screamed out.

Leighton was startled. "No, not Lottie. Turns out the body was Pam Tilly. Remember, she hasn't been seen since 1993?"

"Oh, no," Dickie sat back down. "Did you find anything else out there?"

"Oh, that poor young girl," Malcolm said as he handed the water to Leighton. "I remember her. What happened to her?"

"We don't know yet." Leighton turned back to Dickie. "Anyway, I have to inform Marlene and I wanted to do it in person. I didn't want her to get the news over the phone from a stranger."

"Oh, that poor woman," Malcolm said.

"What else were we supposed to find out there, Dickie?" Leighton asked.

"Lottie," he said softly. "I thought you might have found her body."

Leighton shook her head. "Only other thing we found was an old trunk."

Dickie knew his face had turned beet red. "A trunk? Oh, no, what was in it?" He shuddered to think of what Lottie looked like now.

"Old books," she said.

"How odd," Malcolm said.

"Old books?" Dickie stared at her, addled and perplexed. "That's all?"

"What else were you expecting, Dickie, another body?"

Furious, Dickie drove to his mother's house at top speed. What the hell had he buried five years ago? Maybe it was a different trunk, not his mother's trunk, but how many people buried trunks in a swamp?

He stopped in front of the cottage with a screech and despite the heat, ran up the porch stairs. He found his mother in the library reading her latest historical romance novel. Winded, he stood in front of her and fixed his eyes on her startled expression, fire flaring from his mouth and smoke from his nose.

"What the hell did we bury in that trunk five years ago?" He walked closer and bent down to her eye level. "Mother, what the hell did we bury in that trunk?"

She seemed confused as she stared at him. "Whatever are you talking about, Dickie?"

"Where's Lottie's body?"

"Well, surely, I don't know."

He looked at her in utter bewilderment. "But we buried her in that trunk, took her out to Sutter's and buried that trunk in the swamp."

"Yes?"

"Well, it isn't there. No sign of Lottie. The police found the trunk and there was nothing in it but old books."

"Shame to just cast away books," she said. "Just because they're old."

"Mother, what did you do with Lottie?"

"Why, she's in Columbia, son. Been there five years or so."

"What?" Dickie reached out for the chair. He needed to hold on to something, in danger of falling.

"What's got you so riled up? She's fine, having the time of her life, I hear. Now go on home to Deborah and stop all these histrionics."

Dickie curled his hands into fists and held his breath. He wanted to hit her. He wanted to pick her up and knock her to the ground.

"I will never speak to you again, you devious old woman. You had no business meddling in my life."

"Why are you so angry, Dickie?" Lillian's face was a mask of confusion.

"You knew she was alive? All this time, you knew she was alive?"

"Of course, Lottie is alive." Lillian shook her head, as if he had suddenly lost his mind.

"Where? Where is she in Columbia?"

"Well, surely, I don't know that."

"I don't believe it. I hate you," he yelled and slammed the door on his exit.

Lillian stared after him. She wondered why he was so angry. She hadn't done anything to him. Damn shame her last thoughts of him would be this — this angry confrontation. She slipped to the floor and lay there so still, the memory of her son held in the shadows, that murky place that fades so fast and dissipates in an instant.

Chapter Thirty-Eight

Deborah reached up and took the pin out of her small, dark hat sitting on top of her head like a little spaceship. Lillian's funeral had exhausted her. So many people crowded into Grace Methodist, crying into their hankies as if they didn't resent Lillian for her hold on the town, her wealth. Deborah wasn't sure how she felt, Lillian's death had been so sudden, she hadn't had time to process it. For sure, she thought the old woman would live forever. It had all been so dramatic, half the people talking about Lillian at her funeral like she was a saint and the other half pretending they didn't know the witch that woman was, stuttering over their praises, holding back an urge to regurgitate.

Deborah stared at herself in the mirror. She looked haggard and drawn. She'd have to rush into town tomorrow for a facial, perk herself up. Dickie had been inconsolable since he'd gotten the news of his mother's death. He hadn't stopped crying. She used to think that the ease with which tears came to Dickie's eyes was endearing, now she thought it was irritating, the most annoying trait for a man. She didn't want to deal with his tears, she wanted him to deal with hers.

Of course, she shed no tears for Lillian; the woman had never wanted Dickie to marry her in the first place, called her superficial and vain. But at least she wasn't a control freak, hiding information about poor Lottie that would have alleviated everyone's grief and fear. Lottie was in Columbia, according to Dickie. He said his mother told him that right before she had the heart attack that killed her. Carla had found Lillian on the floor right after Dickie left that day. She'd been dead only minutes. Carla knew that because she had just left the room to give Lillian privacy with her son. She heard Dickie yelling and almost ran in to rescue Lillian from his angry shouts, but then it became quiet. She heard Dickie slam the door. And after that, the only thing she heard was the baleful silence of the dead.

Dickie put a private detective on Lottie's whereabouts before Lillian was even cold. They were waiting to hear if he'd found anything out about her in Columbia, most specifically her address. Dickie was beside himself, grieving over his mother and unable to hide his excitement over Lottie.

Deborah tried to muster up some tears in the church with Lillian's body lying in the coffin. The old woman looked like chiffon pie with her pasty skin and her white hair. She looked confused. Well, she probably was. Over the last couple of years, the poor woman couldn't remember the names of her great-grandchildren. Dickie took such good care of her, going over there to check on her comfort and adhere to her demands, of which there were many. Her admitting that Lottie was in Columbia was quite a shock for all of them. If Lillian hated anyone more than her daughter-in-law, it was her son's mistress. Considering Lillian's distaste for scandal, she would have paid Lottie handsomely to leave town and play dead, but why on earth Lottie agreed to it was hard to guess.

She didn't want Dickie to find her dry-eyed, so she sat and thought about Jeremiah's wedding to that schoolteacher, a pretty Black schoolteacher two years older than he was. That was reason enough to weep. The man was in love? Deborah found that hard to believe. The woman wasn't rich and no more attractive than your average fifty-nine-year-old Black woman. She came with a quaint yellow house near the public school, a fox terrier, and a yard full of grandchildren. She heard Jeremiah was walking on air. The woman must have a hidden dowry, was Deborah's conclusion.

She thought about the last few years, all the wild sex they'd had. Her jumping in the shower to scrub his scent off her so Dickie wouldn't know, wouldn't sense the euphoric cloud she'd just come off of because she stank disgustingly of sex. Of course, she thought Jeremiah was in love with her, but apparently he wasn't, he just liked the thrill of sneaking a White woman into his home and making her feel like a sex machine, obscenely horny, something Dickie couldn't make her feel, and maybe never had. She was an old habit for Jeremiah, but he broke himself free of it. She had been just a nasty drug, keeping him hooked with some kind of sexual pull, like a stick of dynamite one shouldn't be holding on to but can't let go of because it's such a pretty thing.

The tears came then, and she knew Lillian was turning over in her grave. Deborah was sure that the dead could hear the thoughts of the living. "You think your son really cared?" she whispered. "He gave me a perfunctory fuck over the course of our marriage and then turned over to remember how Lottie made him feel. He shut me out, Lillian."

The tears came harder and faster then. She'd just admitted to herself that Jeremiah was not in love with her, and that her husband performed his sexual duties with the passion of a man in a coma. She felt numb when it came to Lottie. She'd missed her, but would she welcome her back to Pickens with open arms? Probably not. The woman had still betrayed her. Besides, it was unlikely that Lottie would return to Pickens after five years of having the time of her life somewhere else. She probably met a man. Maybe she was married by now and poor Dickie was out of luck.

Deborah turned to see her husband at the door. He walked to her with his quick gait and held out his arms.

"My poor dear," he said. "I know we all miss her." He rubbed some tears off her cheek. "Mother loved you."

Deborah nodded her head and choked back the urge to laugh. "So sorry, Dickie," she said. "How are you holding up?"

"I'm reconciled. Mother was over eighty. It was time and she had a good life. We all have to go." He sniffled and wiped his nose with a handkerchief he removed from his jacket. "But there is good news." He looked at her.

"What news?"

"My man has found Lottie in Columbia."

Deborah fell back into a chair. "What?"

"Yes, he found her under an assumed name, Lottie Cottonwood. I told him to just give me her address and not contact her, that I would."

"Cottonwood? Does that mean she's married?"

"Probably not."

"Don't you mean 'hopefully not'? What does this mean then, Dickie, that you're taking up with Lottie where you left off?"

"Of course not. I just want to assure myself that she's okay and find out why she left Pickens."

"Your mother probably blackmailed her, Dickie."

"We don't know that."

"Maybe she met a man from Columbia, and she married him … a somebody Cottonwood. Why can't you accept that?"

"Maybe," he said slowly.

"We should let sleeping dogs lie," she said as she thought about Lottie telling the police the truth about the fire. She shuddered. "Yes, we should let sleeping dogs lie," she repeated.

"I think not, Deborah, we need to know what happened to her."

"Then I'm coming with you to Columbia, Dickie. She left me too, not just you."

Dickie slowly nodded. "I don't think that's a good idea," he said.

"Why not?"

"Well, for one, you tried to kill her. You think she's going to forget that? You and I both know that you set that fire."

"Well, I didn't kill her, did I?" She looked at him indignantly.

Dickie took himself a long sigh and walked to the bar for a scotch.

Chapter Thirty-Nine

Leighton left for Columbia right after Lillian's funeral. Over the years, she had gotten to know Lillian, had been invited for several luncheons, many dinner parties, lawn parties and of course, holidays. Her mother and Rhonda were always included in the big Christmas dinners where Deborah waltzed around the room giving sideway snide glances at Leah and her 'lesbian' lover. Deborah also gave Tom a few flirtatious flutters, which never went unnoticed by Lillian, who quickly diverted Tom, as if Tom might fall prey to Deborah's fading charms.

Tom, on the other hand, found Deborah a bit of an egotist but he found Lillian absolutely charming. "Captivating," he had said. His words, actually. Leighton smiled. Lillian had still beguiled men and unnerved women despite her age. Leighton had come to appreciate her, though she didn't always agree with her. Lillian was of the generation that insisted upon outdated manners, the privilege of class, and the sanctity of marriage, a marriage that once entered into was sealed for life and could never be unsealed. In Lillian's mind, unfaithfulness should be ignored, boredom tolerated, and weaknesses of the spirit, such as drunkenness, avoided in public. The husband was always right, of course, so wives should always turn the other cheek and defend their man.

What a newfound family Leighton had discovered. Her biological father spent most of his time with Malcolm, a drag queen, better known as Ginger Tea. That amused Leighton. Her father was clearly not a drag queen, but he was fascinated with cross-dressing. She wondered if Deborah knew he secretly made up his eyes and his favorite lipstick color was fire engine red. She was sure that Lottie had understood him, probably part of the attraction. After five years, Lottie was still a missing person and the case had gone cold. Leighton did not spend time on it. In her mind, this strange cast of characters were all guilty of something, and she really didn't want to discover what it was. For better or worse, they were family, and the skeletons in their closets needed to remain out of sight, out of mind.

She got into Columbia late in the afternoon and checked in to a Hyatt. She told Tom she'd stay the night, would probably be too tired to drive back. He had wanted to accompany her, but their schedules conflicted.

"For God's sake, you're pregnant," he'd said.

"Only three months." She threw a kiss into the phone. "Thank you for taking such good care of me," she told him. "But I promise to drive like an old lady.

Did you get my kiss?"

"Yeah, I got it," he said with a smile in his voice.

Every time Leighton thought about Tom, she was fervently sweetened, like a sugar cube dissolving. He was nectarous, as Beau had been. Of course, she didn't wish to compare them, but she couldn't help herself. She somehow knew that Beau approved, and that approval was important to her. If she had married Sean Dowd, she was sure Beau would have turned over in his grave and scowled.

She had the address of a real estate office for Marlene in Columbia and got there about five, only to be told that Marlene was at some Bed & Breakfast, where she also worked, that she was the chef. A woman in the office gave her directions to Cottonwoods.

"You're going to love it," the woman said. "It's elegant."

Leighton was perplexed. "Does Marlene own it?" she asked.

"Oh, no, it's owned by some other woman. Marlene just cooks for her."

"Oh," Leighton said as she headed in the direction of Cottonwoods. "That's interesting."

Leighton was certainly impressed by the large and elegantly inviting house. But she had butterflies in her stomach: she wasn't looking forward to telling Marlene that her daughter's body had been found in a swamp. The teenagers had come upon the body a week ago, but the identification had come in right before Lillian's funeral. At first, Leighton had done everything she could to find Pam, but then the case had gone cold, even though Leighton still considered it an active case. The Rabbit Trail had been thoroughly searched and all leads had been exhausted. It was assumed that Pam had met with disaster because she had never claimed her inheritance, something she surely would have done had she been alive. Leighton assumed she was dead and had questioned everyone that knew Pam but none of the leads panned out.

Of course, she'd questioned Sean Dowd. Pam had said she was pregnant and that made Sean a suspect; the baby could have been his. Sean denied it and without Pam's body, there was no way to prove otherwise. But now that they had the body, Leighton was curious what it would reveal.

Those were her thoughts as she rang the doorbell of The Cottonwood Bed & Breakfast. She wasn't prepared for the woman who opened the door before her. Leighton stared in amazement at the elegantly dressed familiar face with perfectly applied makeup and a welcoming smile.

"Lottie?" Leighton uttered. "Oh, my God."

The welcoming smile faded fast as Lottie stared into Leighton's perplexity.

Lottie stood back and held the door open as Leighton walked inside, almost tripping over her own feet, the shocking revelation numbing her.

"Come into my parlor," Lottie said politely and led the way into a stylishly comfortable room. Lottie sat in a chair and stared at Leighton. "I see you found me," she said.

"I wasn't looking for you," Leighton said. "But it's good to finally find you, anyway." She smiled.

"Why are you here?" Lottie asked. "I can't imagine anyone is still looking for me."

"I was told I'd find Marlene Tilly here."

"What do you want with Marlene?"

"A body was discovered at Sutter's. Turned out to be Pam."

Lottie brought her hand to her heart quickly. "Oh, my God. Pam is dead?"

Leighton nodded. "Murdered, we believe."

Lottie let out a long sigh and put her face in her hands.

"Is she here?" Leighton asked.

"In the kitchen," Lottie said. "She's preparing for tomorrow night's meal. Can I be there when you tell her?"

"Of course."

In the parlor after dinner, after Marlene had been given a sedative and put into a spare room, Lottie and Leighton sat in the parlor and talked.

"I'm going to let her stay here so she won't be alone," Lottie said. "Pam was her only child. I think she's been expecting this news, but when you finally get it, it becomes a terrible and painful reality. It becomes so much more devastating with the truth. You know, what you don't know can't hurt you."

"Thanks for dinner," Leighton said.

"Marlene's leftovers."

"Quite tasty."

"Look, Leighton, do the Darlings know where I am?"

"As far as I know, they don't. Why did you leave

the way you did? People thought you were dead."

"I haven't committed a crime, have I?"

"Only to the people who love you."

Lottie looked lost for words.

"Lillian Daring died a few days ago, a heart attack … have you heard?" Leighton asked.

Lottie's entire body stiffened, and she stared at Leighton without saying a word. Leighton's instinct told her that Lillian was responsible for her disappearance.

"Thanks for telling me. I didn't know," she said after the silence.

"Did Lillian blackmail you out of town to keep you away from Dickie?" Leighton asked.

Lottie ran her tongue over her lips. "Something like that."

"Who burned your house down, Lottie?"

Lottie looked away and said nothing. Leighton waited patiently before she asked. "I know it was Deborah, wasn't it?"

"Don't be ridiculous," she said softly.

Chapter Forty

Lillian had left her son and her grandson, Barnaby, her entire fortune and had included trusts for her great-grandchildren. She made Leighton her executor, which would give her a hefty twenty percent of Lillian's fortune. She'd left Carla one hundred thousand dollars and Ethan was bequeathed her Mercedes. She left several thousand dollars to charity; the largest donations went to the Animal Shelter of Pickens and the Children's Cancer Fund. Several other charities received generous amounts as well. Interestingly enough, she left her granddaughter, Robbie, her cottage and several thousand dollars for her 'business expenses', as well as her interest in The River House.

"What do you think this means?" Robbie asked, staring at her father.

Dickie shrugged his shoulders. "I think it means she wants you to stay in Pickens, live in the cottage ..."

he turned to Gillian, "and run The River House."

Gillian looked back at Robbie, her eyes widening in her apparent confused expression.

"But we live in New York," Gillian said.

The immediate family had just returned from the lawyer's office and the reading of the will. Robbie had been in a state of confusion ever since she'd heard what Lillian had bequeathed her. "She wants me to have the cottage?" she said to no one in particular.

Barnaby smiled at her. "It seems she wanted you to make your home here."

Robbie looked pathetically at her father. "She knew how much I love living in New York."

"Oh, who could love living in New York?" Deborah looked at her daughter and raised her eyes.

Robbie looked at Gillian and let out a long slow sigh as she turned her eyes back to Dickie. "Daddy?"

"Well, I think she thought she was doing something good. I think good intentions were always the source of her deeds and actions. No matter what they were," he added.

"She meddled," Deborah said loudly.

Dickie ignored his wife's comment. He looked around the room until his eyes landed on Gillian's. "She knows you're a master chef, Gillian. I think she wanted to give you an opportunity to own your own restaurant. She knew whatever she left Robbie would be yours as well."

"But Jeremiah and Deasia also own River House," Barnaby said.

"Together, they own thirty percent, the larger share is now Gillian's and Robbie's." Dickie looked at his daughter and smiled. "She left it to you, but she wanted Gillian to have it, to run it."

"She hardly knew me," Gillian said.

"Well, she tasted your food," Prissy said and smiled.

"Look, Robinette," Dickie said. "You can paint anywhere, and if you need to be in New York, you certainly have the means to get there. Your grandmother wanted to give you the incentive to remain here."

"Pickens is a nice place to live," Deborah said. "A nice place to raise children." She frowned. "That wouldn't pertain to you, naturally, but it is."

Robbie got up and sat on the arm of Gillian's chair. "The cottage is beautiful," she said. "I'll show it to you soon."

Gillian stared at her in disbelief. "What about New York, Robbie?"

"Oh, what about it?" Deborah said. "Build up your reputation as a chef here in Pickens and then open a restaurant in New York, if that's really where you want to be. You'll have a reputation for Southern cuisine by the time you do that. The city of Manhattan will flock to your doors." She smiled, as if it were settled.

Dickie smiled as well. "She has a point, Gillian. Go look at the cottage. I think you're going to fall in love with it."

Gillian put her hand over Robbie's. "I'll give it a look." She said sadly. "But I'm not promising anything."

Chapter Forty-One

Forensics found an indenture in Pam's skull, an indication she might have been hit with something heavy before she died, but forensics determined that the blow to her head was not what killed her. She had been stabbed just once in the heart and it had been fatal.

"Was she raped?" Leighton asked.

"Not as far as we can tell," Mart said.

"Any similarity at all to the Rabbit Trail killings?" Leighton asked.

"The knife used could have been a Bugout." Mart looked at her and raised his eyebrows.

"How popular a knife is a Bugout?"

"Well, I have one."

Leighton leaned on the edge of her desk and looked at him intently. "So the knife that killed Pam could be consistent with the one the killer used in the Rabbit Trail murders, is that what you're saying?"

"That's correct. I think we have to ask ourselves if the Rabbit Trail killer is still out there," Mart said.

"A long shot," Leighton said. "We're pretty sure Pam was killed prior to Ed's arrest, but why would Ed kill Pam?"

"But not impossible that he didn't kill her." Mart looked at her with a puzzled expression, as if the certainty he'd felt was faltering.

"If there's another killer, that could be why he buried Pam at Sutter's and not out on the trail. He doesn't want to raise suspicion. He wants us to believe we have the right man for the Rabbit Trail murders behind bars. I'm not so sure we do."

"We do have the right man," Mart said. "The girl identified him."

Leighton rubbed her forehead with her hand. "Yeah. This is weird, she said."

It was weird and getting weirder. The day before she'd had a visit from Boyd Baxter. He told her that Pam threatened him and Mindy with a gun and Mindy took a vase and knocked Pam on the back of the head with it. It hadn't yet been printed in the paper that Pam had died of the stab wound, and Boyd thought Mindy had killed her in self-defense.

"For the time being, I'm eliminating Boyd Baxter and Mindy Peach," she said to Mart, who appeared to be deep in thought.

"Boyd doesn't know about the stab wound?"

"No, he thinks she died later of the head wound. He told me she was still alive when they threw her out of the house."

"Where's the gun she supposedly pulled on them?"

"Well, according to Boyd, it's at the bottom of the river."

"Never fired?"

"There were no bullets in it, according to Boyd."

"Why did Boyd come forward with this, he didn't have to?"

"He thinks Mindy killed Pam, and he wants to make sure we know it was self-defense. Either that or he wants to make sure Mindy doesn't accuse him of hitting Pam over the head."

"Yeah," he said. "What are friends for? Look, go question your suspect. I'll be next door."

Leighton walked into the interrogation room and sat opposite Jeremiah Lennox. She gave Prissy a look, an acknowledgement.

"You're representing Jeremiah?" she asked and Prissy nodded.

"Well, you are within your right to have an attorney present, Jeremiah. Any statements you make today can be used by the prosecution to convict you of a crime."

"That's why I'm here," Prissy said and touched Jeremiah's arm for reassurance.

"I just want to ask him a few questions." Leighton smiled. She and Prissy were not only sisters-in-laws, but they were also good friends. It wasn't the first time their work had brought them together. "This shouldn't take long," she assured Prissy, as well as Jeremiah.

"Just know I will stop you if anything you ask might incriminate him," Prissy said.

Leighton nodded and then turned her attention to Jeremiah. She started the tape recorder.

"Jeremiah, your wallet was found with Pam Tilly's body. Do you have any idea why she had your wallet on her when she was murdered?" Leighton stared into his eyes.

Jeremiah shook his head. "She came to see me in my home, and she might have stolen it while she was there."

"So, she had opportunity in your home to steal it?" Leighton asked.

"She did," Jeremiah said.

"What was she doing in your home?" Leighton asked.

"You don't have to answer that," Prissy said.

"No, it's okay. She wanted money from me for an abortion. I didn't give her any money, so she must have stolen my wallet."

Leighton looked at Prissy. "Why didn't you report your wallet stolen?" she asked as she turned back to Jeremiah.

"I just thought I lost it." Jeremiah looked confused. "I didn't realize Pam took it until you told me it was found on her body. It was only then I figured she stole it that day."

"Did you argue with Pam that day?" Leighton asked, even though she didn't think that Jeremiah killed Pam; he would not have been stupid enough to leave his wallet on her body. "The day she came to your house, did you argue?"

"We argued, but she didn't stay long. I told her I wouldn't give her money, and she left. I never saw her again after that." Jeremiah looked at Prissy. "I swear it."

"Was it your baby she was carrying?" Leighton asked.

"You don't have to answer that," Prissy said.

"It wasn't my baby. I had sex with her once, just once." He looked again at Prissy. "It wasn't my baby," he repeated.

"Ever been out to Sutter's?" Leighton asked and noticed he averted his eyes.

"Again, Jeremiah, you don't need to answer that." Prissy looked at Leighton. "Please keep your questioning focused specifically on the evidence."

"Okay, Jeremiah, let's get back to the wallet."

Jeremiah nodded his head.

"Did you give her the wallet?" Leighton asked, almost nonchalantly.

"No."

"Did you sleep with her?" Leighton asked quickly.

"You don't have to answer that," Prissy said. "It's really irrelevant at this point."

"Just once, like I told you," he said and looked at Leighton. "She came to my house to learn how to play chess and I was a bit drunk. It never happened again. I swear."

"Well, we can't substantiate that." Leighton looked at Prissy. "We only have his word."

"That's correct," Prissy said. "Please keep your questions in line with what he's told you. You have no evidence to the contrary, and he is allowed a personal life."

"Okay, so you had a one-night stand with the victim and your wallet was found on her dead body, but you have no idea how it got there, unless she stole it."

Leighton was about to continue her line of questioning, but Mart stuck his head in the door and asked her to step out.

"I don't think he did it," she said to Mart as she leaned against the wall. "He would have known the wallet was on her and gotten rid of it."

"He might not have known she had the wallet." Mart looked at her earnestly. "If it was in her pocket, he might not have seen it. He might not have bothered to check her pockets."

Leighton shook her head. "You have a point."

"I think he could have been distracted the day she came to his house, rattled by her pregnancy. He probably wasn't thinking about the wallet."

Leighton pursed her lips together. "I suppose not."

"And the baby? He wanted no part of it."

"There's no proof yet on whose baby she was carrying."

"We'll know soon enough. Well, anyway, do you remember Susan Engel?" Mart asked.

"Sure."

"She's outside asking for you. I'll finish up with Jeremiah."

Leighton was surprised. Susan Engel was the last person she expected to hear from. She thought Susan was still in Florida and had finished her education at Gainesville.

"Susan," she said as she walked to the young woman and gave her a hug. "It's good to see you,"

Leighton said. "Been five years."

"Yeah, it has."

"Is everything alright?"

"No," Susan said. "Can we go somewhere to talk?"

Leighton led her back to her office and Susan took the chair opposite Leighton's desk.

"I never expected to see you here in South Carolina." Leighton gave her a wide smile.

"I've seen him," she said.

Leighton saw the fear on her face. "Seen who?"

"The man who attempted to murder me, the man who raped me and left me for dead."

Leighton was confused. "That man is in jail, Susan. He can't get out of jail."

"I'm telling you that I saw him ... in Greenville. I live there now. I got a great job there and I'm in a relationship. My whole life is here now, and I've been very happy. I've been in Greenville over a year. I thought I'd be safe ... thought I could put it behind me, but I think the wrong man is in prison. I saw the man who raped me on the street. He was next to me on the street. Close."

Susan's eyes were huge when she looked at Leighton, the lines in her forehead deep.

"You identified the photograph, Susan, after we aged it for you, you identified Ed Sanders as the man who hurt you."

"It was the other man," she said.

Leighton was speechless. She means Sean?

"But DNA identified the hair fibers in your car as belonging to Ed Sanders. He had motive, Susan."

"Motive?"

"Jealousy, revenge. I think you saw someone who

looked like the man who hurt you, that's all. That happens all the time to victims of violent crimes."

"I don't think so." She looked Leighton right in the eyes, her expression intense. "I remembered something later on. I saw no reason to tell you five years ago because I didn't think it was important. But I remembered that I had lent my car to Jeremy Johnson, another student, around the time I was attacked. He might have given Professor Sanders a lift that day. You should question him. I think I was too confused right after the crime to identify anyone, or to remember Jeremy might have had my car."

Leighton nodded. "I will question him, Susan. Don't worry. You'll be safe, though. I want you to know that. We'll put a man on you."

Chapter Forty-Two

Dickie and Deborah pulled up in front of The Cottonwood bed-and-breakfast. Deborah brought the car to a full stop.

"What the hell is this?"

"Looks like a bed-and-breakfast," Dickie said. "It's beautiful."

Deborah gave him an odd look. "What's she doing in a bed-and-breakfast ... she live here?"

"I would assume so," Dickie said.

They got out of the car and walked to the front door of the gracious house. Dickie looked admiringly around. "This street is lovely," he said.

Deborah gave him an odd look. "It's not as pretty here as in Pickens," she said indignantly. "Wouldn't you say?"

Dickie was about to tell her it was 'just different' when he noticed that someone had opened the front door and was staring at them.

"Is that Lottie?" he asked softly

"I think so," Deborah said.

No one uttered a word as Deborah and Dickie got closer. Lottie was stunned into silence but she stood stoically and stared at them. "Hello," she finally said.

"Hello," they said in unison, still uncomfortably silent after their greeting.

"Would you like to come in?" Lottie asked.

Deborah gave Dickie a brief nod and followed Lottie into the house.

"I call it my drawing room," Lottie said as she offered them seats in a large, beautifully decorated room with oval windows that faced on to another charming street, houses adorned with vibrant flower bushes and picket fences.

"This is lovely," Dickie said.

"Thank you. I can give you a tour if you'd like."

"I'd like that," Dickie said and smiled politely.

"No," Deborah said. "I don't want a tour. I want an explanation."

They sat in silence and stared at each other for a bit. Finally, Lottie spoke, "Would you like some coffee?"

Deborah and Dickie shook their heads. They continued to stare at one another.

"Go first, Lottie," Deborah said. "Explanation?"

"I'm not sorry," Lottie screamed the words out. "Is that what you're waiting for Deborah, my apology? Well, you won't get it. You burned down my house."

"I have waited five years for your apology and that's what I want." Deborah glared at her.

"And I just told you that you won't get it. I loved that house."

"You slept with my husband. Why?" Deborah continued to glare at her. "You were my friend."

"It just happened," Lottie said uncomfortably. "Life just happens …"

"I'm sorry about your house," Deborah said loudly, bursting into tears. "I didn't mean to burn it. I just wasn't in my right mind, Lottie. I was furious. God, I'm sorry, Lottie. I know you loved it."

Lottie got up from her chair and Deborah from hers; the two women met in the middle of the room and embraced, still crying, still apologizing over and over again, a dozen apologies as they wept. "Oh, I'm sorry too, Deborah," Lottie said, hugging Deborah tightly. "I wish I could take it back, take back any pain I've caused you."

Dickie looked on in amazement. I really don't understand women, he thought.

Lottie insisted on giving them a room for the weekend, there had been a cancellation and she insisted they take advantage of the opening. The King Louis suite was Lottie's favorite guest room, and she knew Dickie would love it. Deborah was eager to take advantage of the offer, but Dickie remained quiet and followed Deborah's lead. Deborah's approval of the King Louis suite was graciously complimentary, and Lottie knew that Deborah might not say it, but Cottonwoods impressed her.

Dickie had said little since their arrival, perplexed and completely dissociated from his feelings. He stared in front of him like a man on some potent hallucinatory drug.

After unpacking, he had fallen deliciously asleep on the plush king-sized bed. When he woke, Deborah had not yet returned from wherever she had gone. He went to the window and looked out. Sitting together in the most gracious garden was his lover and his wife, laughing like schoolgirls. Dickie wondered if Lottie was still his lover; it had been five years. He stared at them from the window, admiring their gaiety and desiring their consonance.

"I have missed you, Lottie," Deborah said. "I am so sorry about the fire."

"I don't think about it. As you can see, I've made out alright." Lottie smiled at her. "I forgive you, Deborah."

"Lillian forced you out of Pickens, didn't she?"

Lottie nodded. "Yes, but I think I only took her up on it because I felt like shit."

"About Dickie?"

"And about you. I couldn't stay in Pickens after that. I couldn't have a life there while you were still its favorite citizen. You were my best friend." She turned to Deborah. "You still are." She reached out and took Deborah's hand. "Strange as it sounds."

"I haven't replaced you either, Lottie. I never will."

"I have missed our bickering. I have missed our friendship."

"I haven't told the children yet, but they will be so happy. My children love you to death, Lottie. I love you to death. Honestly. Barnaby could barely get through his wedding without you."

"And I love them. And you. How was Barney's wedding?"

"I have photographs to show you. He and Priss have two beautiful boys and a precious little girl."

Lottie clasped Deborah's hand tighter. "Oh, my God," she said. "How wonderful."

"Did you tell Leighton I started the fire?"

"Our secret, Deborah. I'll never tell anyone."

Deborah smiled. "Leighton married a police chief. He's handsome, she's got a child on the way and a little girl, a sweet precious little thing."

"I'm so happy to see you," Lottie said, and the tears ran down her cheeks like open faucets.

"I've missed you so damn much," Deborah said and brought Lottie's hand to her lips. "Do you still love my husband?" she asked.

"Probably," Lottie said.

"Well, he is a gracious son of a bitch."

From the window over the garden, Dickie still looked on. "My God, they're holding hands."

Chapter Forty-Three

Leighton questioned Jeremy Johnson, who now had a job in admissions at Clemson University. He said he didn't remember the exact date he'd borrowed Susan's car, but it was most likely a Wednesday or a Friday.

"How can you be so sure it was a Wednesday or a Friday?" she asked. Susan was attacked on a Friday night.

"Because she parked on Jersey Lane on Wednesdays and Fridays, and I had to get over to Bowman field on those days. I'd leave Susan's car at the Visitors' Center, and she'd pick it up there. It just worked out for us."

"And do you remember giving Professor Sanders a lift?"

"I do. I gave him a lift often, because we both finished a class at the same time over near Brooks Center. Susan liked to be able to pick her car up from the Visitors' Center, it was close to her dorm, and it would have meant a real sprint across campus for the professor and me. It just worked out for everybody."

"Didn't you or Professor Sanders have your own cars?" she asked.

Jeremy shook his head. "No. His wife used to drop him off in the morning and pick him up in the evening, and my parents didn't get me a car until my sophomore year."

Leighton turned to leave, but then she turned back to Jeremy. "Oh, one more question, Jeremy."

"Yes, Detective?"

"Did Professor Sanders know whose car he was in?"

Jeremy thought for a moment. "No, I don't think so, the car was pretty non-descript, a green Toyota. I don't believe I ever mentioned it was Susan's. He didn't know Susan."

Leighton thanked Jeremy and drove toward Edgefield. Ed Sanders was serving time in a Federal Prison there and she needed to speak with him. The inmate the guards brought to her was a bit of a surprise. Thinner than he had been, he looked as if he was on some trendy diet and about to have cocktails on the terrace of The River House, despite his prison uniform.

"I remember you," he said, "the detective who insisted I murdered three women and raped another. Did you find another body, detective, that you'd like to pin on me?"

"As a matter of fact, we did. A young woman by the name of Pam Tilly, stabbed through the heart."

"Pam Tilly, huh? I didn't do it, just as I didn't

commit the other murders I was accused of committing." He smiled at Leighton, but it was not a genuine smile, too many of his teeth showed.

"I'm going to show you a photograph, Ed. I want you to tell me if you recognize anything in it, specifically the stuff on the ground."

Leighton handed the photograph to him from *The Greenville Gazette.* She watched as Ed scrutinized it.

"It's a picture of my wife and I on a camping trip, at least twenty years ago." He gave her a puzzled look. "What the hell is this?"

"Can you identify any of the items in front of you?" She handed him a blowup of the items."

"No. I mean it looks like a canteen, a knife, a backpack, I think."

"Who did the items belong to, do you remember?"

"They weren't mine. My wife and I didn't go camping. Sean and Ashley talked us into it."

"Here's a blowup of the knife, does it look familiar?"

Ed shook his head. "No. Why? What's this all about?"

"Well, I think you're innocent of murder, Ed. I'm just trying to find out who the real murderer is."

"Any chance you'll succeed?"

"How well did you know Sean Dowd?"

"You trying to pin this on him now?"

"How well did you know him, Ed?"

"Pretty well."

"What can you tell me about his affair with Pamela Tilly?"

Ed sat back and stared at her. If he'd had on a tie

she was sure he would have straightened it.

"What do I get for telling you anything I know about Sean and Pam Tilly?"

Leighton smiled. Her gut told her that Ed Sanders would have a problem killing a spider. But five years ago, she had thought of him as a cold-blooded psychopath.

"I think we were quick to judgement. You help us, and I'll guarantee you a retrial based on new evidence," she said.

Ed sat forward. "He was obsessed with the girl. A couple of years after his wife died, he fixated on her. He used to talk about her to me, how gorgeous she was, how seductive … things like that."

"Did he have an affair with her?"

"Why didn't you ask me these questions during my trial? If you felt I wasn't guilty, why didn't you say so?"

"Pam Tilly was murdered five years ago … her body was dumped in a swamp. You were being interrogated for Ashley's murder, so I know you didn't kill Pam."

"I didn't kill the other women either." He glared at her.

"No, I don't think you did. And you haven't been tried for their murders. But there's new evidence, Ed, it's going to get you out of here."

He studied her intently. "What evidence?"

"You were shown photographs of Susan Engel's car at trial. Couldn't you have identified being driven around campus in that car?

"No, I never paid attention to the car."

"So you didn't remember that there was this kid who used to drive you around on campus in Susan

Engel's car?"

Ed rubbed his forehead. "No, I didn't connect the dots. I didn't remember the car and at the time, I had no idea whose car it was."

Leighton nodded, unfortunately if he had remembered, it might have gotten him off for raping Susan. She stared at him. "Did Sean have an affair with Pam Tilly?"

Ed laughed. "He raped her the first time, that's my guess. He didn't admit it, but I think he did. Anyway, they just started doing it together. The kid was seventeen. I told him he could get in trouble."

"Did it ever become an affair?"

"Yeah, they had an affair. Then she met someone else and broke it off. I've never seen anyone so angry. The girl was a dike, like his wife."

Leighton felt cold in the pit of her stomach. Ed had no reason to lie about Sean and Pam Tilly. "Do you know what kind of knife is in the photograph, Ed?"

"What? No. I don't know anything about knives. That was Sean's knife."

"Did Sean have any reason to kill Pam? Was she going to leave him?"

"Yeah, she told him she was in love with some girl. He was quite beside himself."

"I see. Anything else?"

"She was blackmailing him because he made her pregnant. He wanted me to loan him two thousand dollars to buy her off for an abortion."

"He didn't have the money?"

"No, he taught high school and he spent money like it was water."

"So did you lend him the money?"

"I did. I wanted to help him."

"Did you give him cash or a check?"

"A check, but it was never cashed."

"What's the date on the check, Ed?"

"Sometime in September, early September 1993. I don't remember the exact date. Ask my ex-wife, she keeps everything, bank statements and things like that."

"Dorothy knew what the two thousand was for?"

"She never asked. We often gave money to charity, to the democratic party, even the zoo, so she didn't question it. I made it out to cash, I believe."

"Thank you, Ed," she said. "I'm going to recommend a defense attorney and she'll file a motion for a retrial."

"Are you saying Sean killed his wife?" he asked

"I'm not saying anything just yet, Ed."

"Are you saying he killed those other two women?"

"Like I said, I'm not saying anything yet."

He seemed skeptical as he said goodbye; skeptical, but hopeful.

"Are you serious about this?" he asked.

"Dead serious, Ed," she said.

We need a search warrant for Sean's house," Leighton said as she walked in through their back door. Aspen was old now, but he managed to get up and wag his tail as she entered.

"What are we hoping to find?" Tom asked.

"Possibly the knife. Possibly the check." Leighton looked at Tom and relayed her visit with Ed Sanders.

"What check?"

"Ed gave Sean a check for Pam's abortion. It was never cashed. I mean, why pay back what he never needed? Anyway, he told me Sean was obsessed with Pam."

"You're taking this on the word of a convicted killer?" Tom looked at her skeptically as Lesley sat on his lap and gave her mother a goofy look.

"I never asked Ed about Sean and Pam Tilly in '93. We were focused on the Rabbit Trail killer, and Pam was still very much alive."

"Yeah?" Tom stared at her.

"I'm saving the best for last," she said as she scooped Lesley up in her arms. "Sleepy time, sweetie." Leighton took the child into her bedroom, all decorated with teddy bears and little dolls. The room next door was decorated for Jeffrey, the new baby whose sex was officially unknown at the moment, but Leighton was sure he had a boy's kick. They held off on the football wallpaper, but the room was blue, and baby toys with blue ribbons sat on the dresser. Leighton told Tom that if it turned out to be a girl, the little Teddies would all have their ribbons replaced with pink bows.

"You've left me here in suspense, Leighton, what new evidence?"

Leighton smiled at him as she poured herself a glass of wine. "You should have listened to me five years ago." She tilted her head and winked. "He didn't walk fifteen miles from the Rabbit Trail. He took a cab."

"You're right, I should have listened to you. Proof?"

"I spoke to the cab driver who took our suspect from a mile or so off the Rabbit Trail to the bar in Greenville the night of Susan's attack."

"You're kidding? He remembered the guy enough to ID him after five years?"

"The guy told him that the blood on his clothes came from a car accident, that he'd hit a tree. The cabbie remembered that."

"Still, it was five years ago. How can he remember the guy?"

"We don't need his ID, Tom."

"Why? Does he have a credit card receipt from that night?"

"He sure does, his fare was paid with a Visa credit card in the name of Sean Dowd."

"Why the hell didn't we know this five years ago?"

"We were stupid enough to think he wouldn't be that stupid."

"You've got your search warrant, sweetheart." Tom smiled and grabbed her around the waist. "I married a genius," he said.

"We need DNA on Pam's baby, pronto. If we find the knife and the check, we've really got him."

Chapter Forty-Four

Marlene couldn't believe her eyes. She came down to the dining room for breakfast and right there in front of her, Deborah Darling was buttering her toast, and Dickie Darling was sipping hot coffee. She rushed into the kitchen and found Lottie at the stove scrambling some eggs.

Marlene had a dumbfounded expression on her face as she shook her head and stared wide-eyed at Lottie.

"No, you are not seeing things. The Darlings are at the breakfast table waiting on their eggs and bacon." Lottie met Marlene's expression with her own.

"What the hell are they doing here?"

Lottie smiled. "They found me, I guess." She heard a tremendous sigh come out of Marlene. "Are you alright?"

"The question is, are you alright?" Marlene took the spatula away from Lottie. "You're beating those eggs to death. Let me make my bacon and cheese omelet." She got a fresh bowl from the cupboard and started from scratch, cracking the eggs, and laying the bacon out to fry.

Lottie put her hand on Marlene's shoulder. "How are you, Marlene? You know you don't have to cook today, or this weekend at all."

"Are you crazy? You want our cross-dressers to come back each quarter like they've been doing? Part of the reason they come back, Lottie, is my cooking."

"I want you to do what you need to do, that's all." She gave Marlene a hug.

"You okay with the Darlings being here?"

Lottie nodded. "It's good to see them, actually."

"Go back in there and let me finish breakfast. I'll serve it soon as it's done."

Lottie walked back into the dining room, where the sun was streaming in through the windows. She loved to see the sun in the morning. The light made an attractive glow on Deborah's hair, showing up her reddish highlights. They both smiled at her as she took the chair opposite Dickie, and they made small talk. Lottie told them she had a group that would be showing up for the weekend, but they were welcome to stay, that she would like them to.

Deborah eagerly agreed and mentioned going into Five Points for some shopping. Dickie offered to help around the inn. He was happy to spend more time with Lottie, but he was still tongue-tied and barely spoke to her.

"Thank you, Dickie, I just might put you to work." Lottie looked in his eyes, eyes he quickly averted.

Both Dickie and Deborah were shocked to see

Marlene walk out from the kitchen and serve their food. Dickie put his hand out and touched her wrist.

"So sorry about Pam," he said.

"Thank you, Dickie."

"Yes, so tragic," Deborah said.

Marlene nodded her head, about all she could do for Deborah. She didn't want the woman's sympathy; she couldn't stand what she had done to Lottie, and Deborah was as phony as plastic flowers.

"What are you doing here?" Deborah asked.

Marlene smiled at Lottie. "I am the chef for Cottonwoods, been here since Lottie opened the place."

"Excellent omelet," Dickie said, grinning at Lottie. She lowered her eyes and looked off.

"Wait till you taste her lobster tails with chive butter," Lottie said, turning to Deborah. "That's tonight. We have a group ..." she looked at Marlene, "our cross-dressing group, they come every quarter and they requested it for tonight."

She purposely avoided Dickie's eyes, but then she heard him laugh.

"Cross-dressing group? What the hell is that?" Deborah asked. "Like Ginger Tea? Drag Queens?" She giggled.

"Sort of like a girl wearing a tie or a man wearing a, ah, a wig," Dickie said. "Not drag queens."

"How weird," Deborah said. "I didn't bring a tie, can I still come to dinner?" She winked at Lottie.

"That's perfectly alright, Deborah, come any way you want, you will be welcome." Lottie took in her grin, the old playful Deborah. She felt happy that it was over, the distance.

Deborah had returned from her shopping spree in Five Points with several boxes but "No tie," she told Dickie. He had questioned Lottie on her clientèle, but she had been too busy to speak with him. She needed to check the rooms, and the guests started arriving at two. Dickie sat out on the back patio, treating himself to a pink daiquiri and wondering how much things had changed between him and Lottie. He felt numb, and he wanted to feel even more numb as he asked for another daiquiri.

He got up and took his second daiquiri into the front parlor and watched with enormous curiosity as the men arrived. They had not yet changed into women's clothes, and he noticed that none of the men were effeminate. Lottie told him they were all married, all except for 'Greta,' who had lost his wife a few years ago to a long bout with cancer.

Dickie took a nap and dressed casually for dinner, but he yearned to be like the men he heard down the hall, all of whom seemed to be friends with one another. He wanted to be a part of them. He felt like ripping open one of Deborah's packages and showing himself off as DeeDee in what he was sure would be an elegant new dress. His wife had such magnificent taste, and he knew he could pick any box, whatever he found inside would be stunning.

However, he wouldn't embarrass his wife, it wasn't Halloween, and he was sure she'd be livid with him, and humiliated. Even though it was explained to her, Dickie still didn't think she grasped what cross-dressing meant. For Deborah, it a was common thing, like an earring in a man's ear or slacks on a woman.

Dickie watched as his wife engaged in a lively conversation with the cross-dresser named Greta. He wondered if she understood that she was actually speaking to a man, but she didn't seem to. Greta was one of the pretty ones. A few of the other men looked strange to Dickie, not pretty, not like he and Malcolm when they made up.

He leaned over to Lottie and cupped his hand over his mouth.

"How did you get mixed up in this?" he asked.

She looked at him coyly. "Actually, it was a mistake," she said. "I ran an ad in *Gay Travel* and that's become my clientèle."

"You do know these men aren't gay?"

She avoided his eyes. "I certainly do," she said. "You of all people shouldn't have to ask me that, Dickie."

He looked away and then turned back to her. "Do you think Deborah knows that Greta is actually Gregory?"

"I couldn't begin to tell you what Deborah knows or doesn't know, anymore."

Dickie ran his fingers over Lottie's thighs under the dinner table. It was the first bold move he had made, instigated by alcohol, he was sure.

"I've missed you," he said softly. "But I'm not sure I forgive you."

Lottie took a sip of her wine and laughed at something someone said. He wished he knew what she was feeling.

"This is so much like coming to someone's home for a dinner party. Oh, my compliments to the chef." The man that gave the toast was one of the pretty ones. Dickie noticed how young he was, probably no more than twenty-five. He noticed that the oldest one was probably in his sixties.

They all raised their glasses to Marlene, who was a bit tipsy, but she managed to stay focused as she said, "Thank you."

On the drive home the next day, Deborah never shut up about her new friend, Greta.

"So she's really a man?" Deborah asked and Dickie almost drove off the road.

"Yes," he uttered. "He was cross-dressing."

"Well, whatever he is, he's going to join me on all those damn committees I inherited from Lillian. She or he, whatever the hell, told me he'd love to volunteer. He or she," she turned to Dickie and smiled, "lives in Pickens, Dickie, isn't that wonderful? And she's retired, or he's retired." She giggled and turned to look out of the window.

"That's great," he said, stifling an urge to laugh.

"I want to see more of Lottie," she said. "I have missed her so much."

"Me, too," he said sadly.

"But now I have Greta. What a relief." She turned to him again. "Lottie said she'd never come back to Pickens, she loves it in Columbia."

"Pity," he said softly.

"Let's make it a point to visit Columbia monthly, at least."

"I just wonder if you will have the time, you're taking on a lot of responsibility."

"Your mother expected me to take on her duties. God forbid any of her executive duties fell to anyone else but a Darling. Anyway, I have Greta to help me now. Lillian would be pleased. We're meeting for dinner Friday night, at The River House. Will she come as a woman?"

Dickie smiled to himself. "Would you girls like me to join you?" Dickie asked with a snide grin.

"Oh, no, Dickie. We'd bore you to death."

Dickie felt he needed to warn Greta that Deborah would probably have a heart attack if he showed up as a woman, even though she was acting very cavalier about it.

Chapter Forty-Five

The paternity test proved that Sean Dowd was the father of Pam's unborn baby. The search warrant revealed the uncashed check from his personal effects and the Bugout. The knife was sent over to forensics, and a speck of Pam's dried blood was found on the blade. Sean was arrested for Pam's murder as well as the attempted murder and rape of Susan Engle. Ed Sanders, released from prison, was suing for monetary compensation and an official acknowledgement of wrongful conviction.

"I think we can safely expect the wounds on his wife and the two other deceased women will reveal the same knife wounds inflicted on Susan and Pam." Tom sat back in his chair. They were in his office and the phone rang. Leighton answered it.

"Single-edged knife," Tom continued. "All three women's wounds were on the left side, so he was a right-handed killer." He smiled at her. "I think it's a slam dunk." He slapped the edge of the desk. "Four counts of murder."

"He's been offered a plea deal." Leighton put the phone down. "The bastard is going to plead guilty."

"Murder?" Tom asked.

"Three counts of murder, one count of rape."

"I hope he gets life," Tom said.

"I would have preferred he gets the death penalty." Leighton stood up and went to the window. Mart was walking through the parking lot. He waved and she waved back. She turned back to Tom. "I want to hear his confession," she said.

"Show up in court then." Tom looked at her and shrugged. "His plea is confession enough."

"A jury would have given him the death penalty, Tom."

"Go get your confession, Leighton."

"I want to hear it for his wife, for the three girls he didn't even know, for Pam. I want a confession."

Leighton showed up in court with Dorothy Sanders for Sean's sentencing a few weeks later. Susan Engels and the families of the women he had killed were also present. Leighton had been to see Sean the day before after not having laid eyes on him for the last five years. He was heavier and his once handsome face had become jowly. The skin under his eyes sagged and his beard was nearly all grey. He stared at her as if he had trouble remembering who she was.

"Hello, Sean," she said.

He looked away. "I wish I could say it was good to see you."

"We found Lottie in Columbia," she said.

He nodded his head. "That's good," he said. "That's really good."

"She's running a bed-and-breakfast." She smiled. "It's quite successful."

"Interesting," he said.

"Why did you kill Pam?" she asked. "Was it because she wanted to get to New York?"

He looked at her impassively "She said she had proof of our affair and she was going to tell the school board that she'd been underage when it first happened." He turned to her. "She was blackmailing me."

"What was her proof ... her pregnancy?"

"Guess so," he said.

"Why did you lie to me about having had an affair with Pam?"

He turned to her again, sharply, his impassive expression remained. "You're kidding, right?"

"You initiated the affair, and she finally gave into it?"

"I'd say it was a two-way street."

"If you rape a woman, then it's not her choice to sleep with you, so I wouldn't call it a two-way street."

"She wanted me to rape her," he said and smiled. "She liked to play act."

Leighton felt she wanted to throw up. "She called you to pick her up the night she was murdered?"

"Yeah. Her head was bleeding, and she didn't want to drive, said she felt dizzy. She needed me to take her home."

"But you didn't take her home, did you?"

He shook his head. "No, I took her out to Sutter's.

She thought I was going to give her the two grand. I stabbed her instead. She didn't expect it. She thought I was good with everything, thought I just wanted to talk, give her the money and be on my way. I guess she was a dumb blonde, after all."

"Why Sean?"

"She was going to abort my child and go to New York to be with that girl."

"You were in love with her." Leighton had said it softly, not as an accusation but as a fact.

He didn't answer her. He turned to the wall. "We all have a cross to bear, Leighton."

As the judge announced Sean's life sentence, Leighton squeezed Susan's hand. The families of the victims were crying and hugging each other, coming over to Leighton and thanking her.

"Life with no possibility of parole?" Dorothy said to her. "Not good enough."

Leighton rubbed her arm and smiled. "He won't get out," she said. "He'll never get out, Dorothy. That's good."

"The death penalty would have been better," she said.

Chapter Forty-Six

Dickie pulled up in front of Gregory's impressive ranch-style home. It was on at least fifty acres of land and not far from where Leighton and Tom lived in the Sassafras mountains. He had butterflies in his stomach as he approached the front door.

He should not have been surprised at Gregory's transformation, but he was. Gregory was quite masculine, and his thick grey hair still had streaks of the deep black it had once been, and his eyes were a striking blue, sort of like cobalt.

"Oh, forgive me," Dickie said. "We met at Lottie's B & B this past weekend and, I, ah … well, I wonder if I might speak to you."

Gregory was quite gracious and led Dickie into his house, which was nearly all windows. Dickie took in the breathtaking views and noticed the wonderful horse paraphernalia. There were horse paintings, horse statues, and real live horses grazing in the distance. Dickie laughed, "I see you like horses," he said.

Gregory smiled. "May I offer you something to drink, Dickie?"

"Water if you have it." Dickie took a seat on the long comfortable couch the color of golden champagne. He ran his hand over the material once Gregory had gone for the water. It felt as soft and as plush as a stuffed Teddy Bear.

"Would you like me to add some scotch to the water?" he asked as he walked back into the room.

"That would be just great," Dickie said and watched as Gregory went to a beautifully carved cabinet, which when opened, revealed what appeared to be bottles and bottles of the finest liquors.

"Do you ride?" he asked.

"Oh, no. I do go to the horse races, though," Dickie laughed.

"Those are my horses out there. We have five of them. My wife and I love horses. Well, when my wife was alive, that is. She died a few years ago."

"I'm sorry," Dickie said.

"Thank you." He sat opposite Dickie and waited for him to speak.

"You should ask my wife to ride. She loves it. She and her sisters grew up with horses." Dickie smiled at him.

"I'd be delighted to ask her." Gregory took a sip of his drink and smiled back at Dickie. "Lovely woman, your wife."

Dickie took a sip of his scotch as well. "Gregory, I know you're meeting Deborah, my wife," he said and looked at Gregory to make sure he remembered.

"Anyway, I want to ensure you are not going to keep up the charade of being Greta when you meet up."

Gregory threw back his head and laughed. "Oh, my God, no, I wouldn't do that. I don't ever cross-dress except when I'm with the group and we leave town for that."

"But my wife thinks she's meeting Greta to talk about her charities. However, she knows you're a man, but I think it will embarrass her if you show up as a woman. She's a bit confused."

"Would she have a problem if I showed up as myself?"

"A better choice, I'd say."

"Well, I was telling her the truth. I'm retired and your wife is very charming, very persuasive. I do think I'd like to help out with the fundraising. I'm sure I could introduce her to some important people."

"But you intend to meet her this Friday night as Gregory, not as Greta?"

"Well, yes. I only cross dress with the group. I assumed she just knew I was a man. I mean what was she doing at Cottonwoods if she wasn't aware of our purpose there?"

"Well, Lottie is her best friend. They go way back."

"Then I assume she's like Lottie, sophisticated enough to understand our crossdressing is for play."

Dickie nodded his head. He couldn't tell Gregory what to do and he certainly couldn't predict how Deborah would react.

"I'd like to join your group, Gregory," he said stoically.

Gregory sat back, clearly surprised. "Marvelous, Dickie, we'd love to have you. We'll be going to the

Caribbean this spring. We've hired a crew and a ship of our own. Interested?"

"Very much."

"It's just us on these trips. We don't take our wives or anyone else." He met Dickie's eyes and held out his hand.

Dickie smiled and reached out his hand as well. The two men shook. "Thank you for volunteering to help, Deborah," he said. "I'm sure she'll be delighted to get your expertise on who to talk to."

Chapter Forty-Seven

Robbie hadn't been to the cottage since the day of Barnaby's wedding. For the last few years, the cottage had housed relatives during the holidays, and she had avoided it. As much as she hated to admit it, the cottage held memories. Now, she felt strange walking up to it, remembering that afternoon on the porch with Pam the day of Barney's wedding, recalling what followed, their sexy few nights in London.

She'd heard about Pam's murder, and she felt numb thinking about it; sad, too. She'd never heard from Pam again since that evening she'd ripped out her garden and seen Sean at her house. She figured Pam would contact her at some point, but she hadn't. She assumed she was just being Pam, disappearing and not giving a damn who it hurt. But Pam must have been killed soon after that day. That made Robbie sad and guilty that she'd hated Pam all these years.

A SAFFRON SUN

Robbie had met Gillian during her third semester at NYU. They'd both been to the same LGBTQ meeting on campus and their attraction was pretty instantaneous. Gillian's dark, captivating looks immediately appealed to Robbie and she made it a point to sit next to her. They were different enough to be complementary. Gillian was headstrong and outgoing, while Robbie preferred to shrink into the background and hope no one noticed her. Probably the result of growing up with her mother, who she always feared would recognize her sexuality like some siren going off and lights flashing and banish her to hell, where all sinners resided.

After meeting Gillian, Robbie didn't give a damn what her mother thought and completely and proudly came out of the closet. Her mother treated Gillian like the relative with palsy, but at least she acknowledged her as being somehow attached to her daughter in whatever capacity, probably as an 'unnatural' friend.

She watched carefully as Gillian walked around the cottage, her loud exclamations of approval warning Robbie of the possibility that she just might have to remain in Pickens and be known as Deborah Darling's spinster daughter.

She followed Gillian up the stairs. They had eaten in The River House the night before and Gillian remarked that the food could be just a bit more 'innovative.' However, she'd loved the restaurant and talked all through dinner about teaching Deasia and Jeremiah how to make Tartiflette and Pieds de porc.

Now she stood at the window of the master bedroom, looking like a movie star posing for *Elegant Homes* magazine.

"What do you think?" Robbie asked.

"Well, we live in nine hundred square feet in Manhattan. We look into another building, and we share our floor with six other people and three dogs. Oh, and lest I forget, we pay nearly two grand for it."

"Meaning?"

"This house is beautiful, Robbie."

Robbie stared at her. She had a feeling where this was going. "You want to stay in Pickens?"

"I want to give it a try. This house is beautiful, the town is quaint, and I love the idea of running my own restaurant."

"My grandmother always knew what she was doing," Robbie said. "I found a loft space about a block down from the restaurant. I can use it as a studio. I'm sure she knew I'd find it."

"Is this meant to be?" Gillian asked, her light eyes picking up the sunlight, glowing verdurous, like the color of some rolling meadow.

Robbie sat on the large king-sized bed and reached for Gillian's hand. "There was a girl I used to know. I never told you about her."

Gillian looked at her oddly for a second. "So, you want to tell me about her now, is that it."

"She was murdered."

"Oh, my God," Gillian said and sat beside Robbie.

"We used to meet here in this cottage. We were kids, really young, but I loved her."

"And the cottage reminds you of her, right?"

Robbie nodded.

"You don't want to stay here?"

"No, I do. I just want to admit something to you."

"Okay."

"I knew he was going to kill her." The tears came to Robbie's eyes, but she let them fall. It was the first time she'd confessed that to herself.

"How could you know anything about that, Robbie?" Gillian stared at her.

"He told me he was going to kill her, in so many words.'"

"What did he say?"

"He said he was going to kill her." She looked at Gillian. "Right before I left for New York, I went to Pam's house, and he was there. I watched while they had this angry confrontation. Then I got out of my car and challenged him. I wanted to ask him to stay away from her, that whatever it was between them had to stop. I told him I'd help Pam get to New York if he didn't leave her alone. I could tell, seeing them together, that it wasn't right."

"Did you tell the police that?"

"I didn't tell anyone. But he said he'd kill her if she left Pickens. Maybe he just intimated it, but there was something in the way he said it. I believed him. Then no one heard from her, and I thought of what he said. I thought he must have meant it."

"You had nothing to do with her murder, Robbie."

"He was jealous of me. I felt it."

"You didn't kill her, Robbie."

Robbie looked out over the expanse of sky, the beautiful Southern twilight. Pam came to mind briefly and faded.

There are moments in life that are so still, so perfect, that even when it starts out wrong or badly, it twists suddenly, turns and makes itself right. But in this case, the turn led back.

"I guess not," she said softly. "But could I have saved her?"

Chapter Forty-Eight

Deborah sat at a table facing the river, the light on the water romantic and serene. It was early for dinner and light murmurs carried over the room, titillating intimacies, words both captured and unheard. Some secrets, perhaps. Secrets not meant to be shared. She waved to a few people she knew, and they gave her a welcoming and friendly acknowledgement. She'd ordered a glass of wine and sat waiting for Gregory to arrive, though she only knew him as Greta, would she recognize him? She noticed a tall good-looking man speaking to the maître d' and then, confused for a moment, saw he was being led to her table, as if he were expected. The man was smiling at her with familiar good nature. Oh, I like him better this way, she thought.

He took the chair opposite her. "Deborah, so good to see you again." He reached for her hand and kissed it.

"Do I know you?" she asked with a coy smile.

"Yes, of course, we met last weekend."

"We did?"

"At Cottonwoods? I sat next to you at dinner."

She searched her memory. "But I sat next to Greta. That's who I was expecting to meet tonight. Greta. Not that I mind you showing up. How similar you are to her."

He investigated her bewitching grin. "Forgive me, but I am Greta, or that is to say, I was Greta last Friday night. This Friday night, I am Gregory and you are toying with me." He grinned.

"Hello, Gregory," she said."

"I like to cross-dress, Deborah, like your husband."

"So you are unusual, like my husband?"

"I guess I am."

"I know nothing about my husband's interest in women's clothes," she said quietly. "Let my husband have his secrets."

"I am here to help you fundraise for your charities, to volunteer. I can think of nothing better I'd like to do in retirement. Would you prefer I leave? Do I make you uncomfortable?"

"Leave where?"

"Well, if you don't want me to help you, I won't."

"No. Of course I do. I would welcome your help."

"Wonderful," he said and sat back. "Have you ordered?"

Deborah slowly shook her head.

Gregory raised his hand for the waiter's attention and studied her. She studied him. She noticed how graciously he was dressed. She took in his handsome face, his tall, well toned frame, his gorgeous blue eyes.

How unusual, she thought. "So, you like to dress as a woman?" she asked.

"Yes, but I promise not to do it in public, certainly not at our meetings." He laughed.

"You're so cavalier about it."

He shrugged. "What are your secrets, Deborah?"

"Well, surely I have none I couldn't mention to anyone."

"There are many things, or perhaps just one thing in particular that we do in private that we wouldn't share with the world."

"I have no secrets," she said. "Well, maybe a few," she smiled sweetly.

He smiled back at her. "I won't ask you to share them."

She wondered why she found him attractive: he was a freak, wasn't he?

Dickie pulled up in front of Cottonwood's and turned off his engine. It was Friday night and he had left Deborah a note. He told her he was meeting a client in Savannah and would stay the night.

Marlene opened the door and stared at him.

"How are you, Marlene?" Dickie asked.

"Well, fine," she said.

Her addled expression unnerved him for a moment. "That's good." He wondered why she wasn't stepping aside to let him in.

"Where's Deborah?" she asked, looking over his shoulder.

"Where is Lottie?" he asked almost simultaneously.

"Oh, up in her room." Marlene stepped aside.

"Which room is her room?"

"Last one on your left," she said as Dickie moved swiftly past her.

Marlene turned to watch as Dickie took to the stairs. She went back into the kitchen when she lost sight of him, wondering what the hell he was doing there but then telling herself she knew exactly what he was doing there.

When Dickie got to the landing, he walked to the left and knocked on Lottie's door.

"Come on in," she called.

Dickie opened the door and closed it behind him. She was in the bathroom. He heard her brushing her teeth. She thought it was Marlene and started to talk to her about one of the guests who had an allergy to dairy. She walked out of the bathroom and stared at Dickie, somewhat startled. Then after a moment, she smiled.

He walked to her and took her in his arms. "My darlin'," he said. "My dear sweet one."

She kissed him. Murmurings in the hall rose and fell, undetectable words caught in laughter as people walked down the stairs. But for Dickie, there wasn't tomorrow, only the quiet evening. And that's how he made love to her, as if it were a quiet evening and there was no tomorrow.

Deborah got home around 10:00 p.m. She'd had an enjoyable dinner with Gregory and found him quite appealing. She didn't question him about his 'hobby', his fetish for women's clothes. She assumed it was a fetish. Many people have them, she told herself.

She picked up the note Dickie had left her on the foyer table, the place they always left notes for each other. *Had to see a client in Savannah*, it read. *Will stay the night.*

She laughed before she picked up the phone and called Gregory to thank him for a lovely dinner, even though she had thanked him several times as he walked her to her car.

"Gregory?" she said sweetly.

"Deborah," he said. "Is everything alright?"

"My husband has gone to Columbia to see his mistress."

"Oh, I'm sorry."

"Don't be," she said. There was a long pause. "Gregory," she said. "Can you get here in thirty minutes? I'd like to thank you for dinner."

There was only a slight pause. "Certainly," he said.

"Oh, and please leave Greta at home. I'd prefer it."

Deborah gently put down the phone and smiled. "And the end of something brings the beginning of something else." She dialed Lottie's cellphone.

"Hello," Lottie said as she picked up.

"Enjoy him," she said quietly.

Lottie heard the click and turned back to Dickie. "Who was that?" he asked.

Lottie smiled. "Your wife," she said. "I believe she has just wished us well."

Chapter Forty-Nine

1999

The afternoon was provocative; the sun, beguiling; a breeze swept the air with congenial warmth. Leighton saw them all as she stepped from her car — friends, family, people she barely knew. She took the hands of her children, Lesley, and Jeffrey. Lesley's hand felt sticky in hers. She'd likely stuffed her pockets with butterscotch candy. Tom scooped up Jeffrey in his arms as they walked toward the barbeque; The sizzle of steaks made her hungry and her stomach made a low growl. Her husband walked beside her, his brown hair streaked gold with sunlight. He reached over and took her hand. The warmth from it made her feel lucky, unassailable.

Robbie and Gillian's cottage stood in the distance like some enchanted illusion, a shimmering glitter of welcome, almost ethereal under the saffron sun.

Leighton still couldn't get over why anyone would call it a cottage; it was graciously and charmingly present, sizable as a castle.

The barbecue was a celebration for Robbie and Gillian, their fifth year together. The opening of a second River House in Savannah was a month away. There certainly was a lot to be grateful for. Leighton heard the subtle sound of music. Laughter floated in the breeze as Tom put his son on the ground and he and his sister ran to their grandmother and flopped in her lap.

"Good to see you, Mother." Leighton gave Leah a kiss and leaned over to grab Rhonda's hand. "Will you watch the children?" she asked. "My husband needs to make the rounds." She winked at them with a bright blue eye, her golden hair falling over her shoulder.

"Oh, we love taking care of the wee little ones," Rhonda laughed as she scooped up Jeffrey, who giggled uproariously. Tom kissed the cheeks of his in-laws and they continued on their journey across the lawn.

People swarmed to Tom now that he was Lieutenant Governor. He shook their hands with a propitious smile, the quintessential politician, Leighton thought. The buzz from the crowd was appealing, conversations she couldn't altogether hear, laughter that sounded like melodies. Male and Female voices blending together in gaiety and in foolishness. Screams of joy pierced the air, fading away like the last notes of a song.

She smiled as she noticed Jeremiah. "Congratulations, Jeremiah," she said as she extended her hand to him. "You're going to be running the

Savannah restaurant?"

"Sure am. You have to come to Savannah, Leighton, the second River House has a view all the way to the harbor. Beautiful place." Jeremiah grinned; his excitement tangible.

"Still serving French cuisine?" Tom asked and Leighton secretly smiled. Tom was a steak and potato guy and shied away from the pigs' feet and calves' liver – 'Too French' for him, he'd said.

"We'll have the best rib-eye steaks you ever tasted, sir." Jeremiah winked at Tom and the two shook hands. "As well as the best bottle of wine. You just let me know when you're coming."

Tom clasped his hand again and Leighton reveled in the strength of it, the friendship between them.

As she and Tom continued their stroll, Deasia and Jackson were watching all three of their grandchildren while Barnaby and Prissy sat with Dickie and talked about internet stocks. Leighton overheard them as she approached and stopped to reprimand Dickie for talking shop on such a lovely social afternoon.

"Perfect place to talk shop," Dickie said as he offered Tom a handshake. "Do you own any Xcelera.com?"

Tom smiled and shook his head, just as Lottie approached with a tray of canapes. "Stole this from the kitchen," she said and kissed Leighton on the cheek.

She and Tom each took a few mushroom tartlets and ate as they walked. Leighton stopped for a moment to survey the crowd and fix the strap on her sandal. Tom continued to hold her hand. Gregory and Deborah were laughing unselfconsciously with Ginger Tea over his new Barbara Streisand routine. He sang

'Cry Me a River' dramatically holding his heart.

"Jilted again?" Leighton asked, approaching them. "Or do you just like to sing?"

"I do the jilting, darlin'. Anyway, performing it at The Red Lady in two weeks. You two ought to come." Ginger swished around in his caftan and laughed.

"Well, I can't promise that," Tom said, "but I will promise not to raid the place."

Ginger Tea gave him an odd look. "I hope you're kidding, sir."

Leighton laughed and put her arm around Tom's waist.

"I, for one, will be there," Gregory said, "with my charming wife."

"No, sans your charming wife," Deborah said and winked at Leighton. "No offense, Malcolm, but I'd rather be home knitting my granddaughter a sweater."

"Then I will be there for the two of us." Gregory kissed his wife on the cheek. "In your honor, sweetheart," he said to Ginger, who laughed loudly.

"I shall certainly miss your presence, darlin'," Ginger said to Deborah and kissed her hand.

Leighton turned toward the giggles she heard and noticed that Prissy and Barnaby had joined Deasia and Jackson and were now playing ball with their children. The children's giggles were caught in the breeze like bubbles. She watched as Jeremiah appeared and his grandchildren chased him mercilessly. One of the dogs nipped at his pant leg, and they all laughed. Leighton smiled.

Well, there was a lot to celebrate that day. Deborah and her new husband, Gregory, had just returned from a honeymoon in Europe, and Dickie had moved to Columbia to help Lottie with her bed-and-breakfast. Dickie sold the house in Pickens and was buying an old farmhouse in Columbia not far from Cottonwoods. He and Lottie were engaged to be married right after the busy season. Dickie had promised to book a vacation and take Lottie anywhere in the world she wanted to honeymoon, secretly hoping it wouldn't involve going anywhere one couldn't drive to.

Robbie was making a name for herself in the art world, and she and Gillian didn't have any plans to leave Pickens. They were both becoming celebrities with constant write-ups in the paper, Gillian for her trendy and popular restaurant, and Robbie for her enormous gift with conceptual art. The River House was renowned for its elegant and authentic cuisine, though incredible Southern breakfasts were still offered on weekends which Deasia presided over, paying homage to Beau's spicy scrambled eggs and his Spanish omelet. Leighton stopped to congratulate Robbie and Gillian on the opening of the second restaurant in Savannah.

"Thank you," Robbie said as she gave Leighton a kiss on the cheek. "Great party, huh?"

Leighton nodded as she stared at the puppy who kept jumping into Gillian's arms. "New pup?" she asked.

"Yeah, we're putting down roots," Gillian said. "Meet Molly. She's a labradoodle."

Leighton went over to the bar to say hello to Marlene and her little dog Roxie, pulling Tom along with her. She had heard that Marlene had met the most wonderful man through some dating service, and she wanted to meet him. She'd heard that Marlene was quite happy, still at Cottonwoods making her famous and delightful cuisine. She and her new man, Gerald, spent nearly every weekend with Lottie and Dickie and often went out together on Gerald's boat.

"Good to see you, Marlene," Leighton said and hugged her.

Marlene introduced Gerald, and they exchanged handshakes while Roxie barked at the mushroom tartlet Leighton had not finished.

"May I?" She looked at Marlene, who nodded.

"Go on, you little mutt," she said. "Make a glutton of yourself." Marlene frowned at the dog.

Leighton gave Roxie the last of her tartlet only to be thanked by Roxie's aggressive growl.

"I guess she wants another one," Marlene said.

"I hear you're now Lieutenant Governor of the state, Tom." Gerald smiled at Tom, who nodded.

"Oh, yes, I'm very proud of him," replied Leighton, "and I love being the Lieutenant Governor's wife. We'll be able to spend a lot of time in Columbia so Tom can be near the State House." Leighton took his hand.

"Then it will be good to see more of you." Marlene smiled.

They hugged again and then she and Tom walked on toward Mart and his new family, two little twin boys and a wife who loved to fish and camp, sleep outdoors under the stars, and pretty much hike the trails, of which there were many in South Carolina. They, too, had been invited to this gala event and they were swinging on the hammock together as their babies crawled around in front of them. Mart gave Leighton a kiss on the cheek, while Tom gave Fiona, his wife, a hug.

While they were catching up, Boyd Baxter walked over to Tom and shook his hand. He had come out of the closet and was now president of the Pickens Gay Alliance. Tom knew Boyd quite well, and he was at Robbie and Gillian's celebration, with his lover, a young man by the name of Randy Townsend. As far as Leighton knew, Boyd's father had pretty much disowned his son when he made his sexuality public. Leighton walked to Boyd and said hello. Mindy ran up to them and hugged Boyd from behind. It occurred to Leighton that Mindy had never known he'd tried to incriminate her in Pam's murder, and if she did, she was certainly over it now. Well, she'd finally found happiness with a woman who owned the Pet Store on Main. The two of them lived in town and were often seen sharing a meal with Boyd and Randy. Whatever differences there'd been between Robbie and Mindy had been buried behind their newfound happiness with other people, as well. Leighton looked on as Mindy kissed Boyd on the cheek and then ran up to Robbie, and they laughed at something Mindy said.

Leighton thought about friendship as she looked over at Lottie and Deborah, who were now sitting together back by the swings. She thought about how resilient friendship can be. She watched as they spoke to each other in low confidential tones, like teenagers discussing their crushes. It made her smile to watch them. Perhaps they were discussing Dickie and Gregory, perhaps their latest plans to get together. Leighton wished she knew. She had given up on trying to prove that Deborah had started the fire that had nearly burned Lottie's house down; it had become obviously unimportant in the larger scheme of things.

There were so many old friends and family on the lawn that day as Leighton and Tom walked around, saying hello to people they barely knew and people they were pleased to see and hadn't seen in a while. So many children playing together and dogs that chased them playfully. It was quite a party. Several conversations going on at once, rising and falling and starting up again.

Leighton was thinking how strange life is as she sat on the grass and Tom sat beside her. As she looked up at the lazy blue sky, she turned to her husband. "If Beau hadn't died, I wouldn't have the children I gave birth to, would I?"

Tom stroked her arm. "Well, I can't say I'd be happy if Beau hadn't died but, If he'd lived, I'm quite sure we would have had an affair." He grinned at her.

"I would not have married you," she said. "I probably would not have had an affair with you, either."

"Well, if Lottie had not been blackmailed out of town, Deborah would still be married to Dickie, and Lottie would have remained an adulteress. Things just have a way of working out. It's the wheel of life, that's all, a lot of 'what ifs'."

"Yes, and if there had been no blackmail from Lillian, there would have been no Cottonwoods and Gregory would not have become Deborah's husband, because they would never have met."

"That would have been catastrophic," Tom said and smiled. "Consider this, If Lillian hadn't died when she did, Robbie would still be in New York."

"And consider this," she whispered, there would not have been a Barnaby Darling, such as he is, if his mother had not succumbed to Jeremiah's advances and her own sexual desires."

"Why the little harlot," he laughed.

"The victims of the Rabbit Trail murders would still be alive if Ashley and Dorothy had not fallen in love."

"Well, If Pam had not called Sean to pick her up the night she was murdered, she might have made it to New York." Tom looked at her sadly.

"And maybe, just maybe, if Pam had made it to New York, Robbie would not even have noticed Gillian."

"True enough, except it isn't."

"Perhaps." Leighton sighed as she took her husband's hand. "Do you believe in fate?" she whispered in his ear.

Tom kissed her. "I believe in circumstance," he said.

And as he leaned back to smile at her, the soft South Carolina breeze embraced this family. There was something so warm, so appeasing in the caress of the wind. Sometimes perfection reigns. All of their kisses had been sweetened with wine; their secrets buried deep in the wells of their minds. Their shadows fading into the light of a saffron sun. This was their day ... and it was suffused in anticipation, a plethora of promise.

The End

Also By Vera Jane Cook

The Darlings
The Fourniers: When Hannah Played Ragtime
The Fourniers: Glamor Girl
The Fourniers: The Memory of Music
Pleasant Day
Lies a River Deep
Marybeth, Hollister & Jane
Where the Wildflowers Grow
The Story of Sassy Sweetwater
Dancing Backward in Paradise

Under the pen name Olivia Hardy Ray

Annabel Horton, Lost Witch of Salem
Annabel Horton and the Black Witch of Pau
Fox Hollow
Nobody's Road

To join my mailing list please request at:
jane@verajanecook.com